"Glyn and Val had...
had a relationship!"

Rhia could hardly force the words out.

Jared sighed audibly. "Rhia, I know that. It's not an insurmountable problem. You can still pose as Val. I've seen you kiss him, and you don't exactly object—"

"You...swine!" cried Rhia fiercely. "I—I don't like it! I don't want him to kiss me! But I have no choice."

"You're not frigid, are you?" he asked, his voice harsh and insulting, and Rhia caught her breath.

"I don't know whether I'm frigid or not," she declared proudly. "I haven't felt the need to find out. I'm not in the habit of indulging in promiscuous relations—"

"Then let's find out, shall we?" Jared muttered, jerking her toward him. Before she had a chance to protest, his searching lips had captured hers....

ANNE MATHER
is also the author of these

Harlequin Presents

and these

Harlequin Romances

Many of these titles are available at your local bookseller.

For a free catalogue listing all available Harlequin Romances
and Harlequin Presents, send your name and address to:

HARLEQUIN READER SERVICE
1440 South Priest Drive, Tempe, AZ 85281
Canadian address: Stratford, Ontario N5A 6W2

ANNE MATHER

impetuous masquerade

Harlequin Books

TORONTO • LONDON • LOS ANGELES • AMSTERDAM
SYDNEY • HAMBURG • PARIS • STOCKHOLM • ATHENS • TOKYO

Harlequin Presents first edition September 1982
ISBN 0-373-10530-4

Original hardcover edition published in 1982
by Mills & Boon Limited

CHAPTER ONE

'RHIA, I've got to see you!'

Her sister's voice was taut with anxiety, and Rhia
sighed resignedly at the prospect of yet another awkward
situation Valentina wanted her help to escape from.

'Not tonight, Val,' she said firmly, hooking the phone
between her ear and one slim shoulder as she endeavoured
to go on separating the sheets of carbon from the report
she had just finished typing. 'I've got to stay back to take
the minutes of the board meeting, and Simon's picking
me up about seven-thirty.'

'Simon!' Valentina's young voice was scathing. 'You can
put him off. You know you can see him any old time!'

Rhia controlled the impulse to make some equally
scathing retort, and continued pleasantly: 'Nevertheless,
the arrangement has been made, and I'd prefer it to
stand.'

'But you don't understand!' Valentina's voice rose in
her frustration. 'Rhia, something awful's happened.
And—and I don't know what I'm going to do!'

Rhia put down the carefully typed sheets and took hold
of the receiver. 'Look here, Val, you're not a child, you
know. You're eighteen, quite old enough to handle your
own problems. Just because I'm older than you are——'

'But I rely on you, Rhia!'

Valentina's tone broke on what sounded suspiciously
like a sob, and Rhia felt the unwilling sense of responsibility her young sister invariably aroused in her. It
was no use railing that it wasn't fair; that there were only
three years between her and Valentina, and that at eighteen she had had to shoulder the responsibilities of a
family. Old habits die hard, and ever since their mother
had been killed during an uprising in the Central African
state where their father had been working, Rhia had taken
her place—in Valentina's eyes, at least. The two girls had
been at boarding school at the time, and Valentina had
taken the news badly. At fifteen, she had felt the bottom

had dropped out of her world, and Rhia had naturally staunched her own grief to comfort her sister.

Their father had flown home to be with his daughters, but it soon became apparent that he was irked by family affairs. When Rhia agreed to abandon her hopes of going to university and found herself an office job while she took secretarial training at night school, Mr Mallory accepted another appointment in South Africa, and left Rhia in charge of the small flat he had rented in Hammersmith.

Valentina, of course, was expected to continue with her schooling, but at sixteen she had begged Rhia to let her come home, and because her father offered no objections, Rhia had had to agree.

That had been the biggest mistake she had ever made, Rhia acknowledged now. Valentina had proved impossible to control, and ignoring pleas from her sister to find regular employment had skipped from one casual job to another. She had worked in cafés and betting shops, in disco joints and wine bars, and spent a good portion of her time hanging about with a group of teenagers, whose main claim to fame seemed to be their outrageous clothes and hair-styles. Rhia had lost count of the number of times she had been called upon to mediate when some irate employer had called demanding to know her sister's whereabouts, and she had eventually been forced to write to their father and ask him to take Valentina in hand.

The upshot of this had been that Valentina had agreed to try her hand at nursing, and six months ago she had enrolled as a student nurse at one of the local teaching hospitals. She seemed to like it, and Rhia had breathed a sigh of relief, praying that Val would learn to be more responsible. After all, she was eighteen, old enough to be regarded as an adult. She had even found herself a boy-friend, and although Rhia had never met him, she was reassured to learn that he was a student at the London School of Economics. Apparently, his name was Glyn Frazer and he was a Canadian, and although Rhia had her doubts as to how long such a relationship could last, she was glad that Valentina seemed to be settling down at last.

Yet now here she was, phoning her sister at nine-thirty in the morning, evidently in some distress over some new disaster. Rhia used the word 'disaster' advisedly; all Valentina's problems seemed to assume such unnatural proportions.

'So why do you want to see me, Val?' she enquired now. 'If it's so important, tell me now. I'll see what I can do.'

'I can't—that is, I can't talk over the phone,' insisted Valentina desperately. 'Rhia, you've got to make time. I'm on duty again at eight o'clock.'

Rhia expelled her breath resignedly. So at least Val hadn't lost her job, she reflected thankfully. Whatever it was, it was outside the hospital, and surely anything else could not be so important.

'Val——'

'Rhia, please——'

'Oh, very well.' Rhia gave in, as she generally did, she conceded to herself ruefully, and drew her dark brows together. 'How about lunch? I could manage to get over to St Mary's for about one o'clock, if that's any use to you.'

'Oh, yes. Yes!' Valentina was fervent.

'But don't you have to rest?' Even now, Rhia was still mildly suspicious. 'I mean—if you're on nights——'

'Last night was my night off,' explained Valentina hastily. 'See you soon,' and she rang off before Rhia could think of any more questions.

Nevertheless, that didn't prevent her sister from spending the rest of the morning brooding over why Valentina should want to see her, and why there was such urgency about it. She couldn't think of any reason why the younger girl should be so distressed, and as with all such probings, Rhia's sense of foreboding grew. She couldn't help but remember how irresponsible Valentina had been prior to taking the job at St Mary's, and how often she had been called upon to lend her money or pay her bills or simply bail her out of some particularly difficult situation. Something had gone wrong, that much was obvious. Rhia only hoped it was nothing more than another unpaid debt.

The company for whom Rhia worked had their offices in Kensington, which meant she was within walking distance of the apartment. It was an added bonus to a job she had grown to like, and since she had become secretary to one of the company's directors, the increase in salary had enabled her to cope with the increase in its rent. Valentina's contribution to the apartment's upkeep had ceased entirely, since she spent most of the week in her accommodation at the nurses' home, and since St Mary's was south of the Thames, there was no question of her commuting.

When Rhia left the office at lunchtime it was raining, and the seasonable downpour had filled all the buses. Deciding she might as well use the tube, she squelched her way along the High Street, and squashed on to the train that would take her to the Embankment.

It was late when she arrived at Balham, and she still had a ten-minute walk to the hospital. She guessed Valentina would be awaiting her at the gates, where they had met on the few occasions Rhia had visited the hospital, and she saw her sister's dejected figure as soon as she turned into Morton Street.

The rain had eased a little, but it was still drizzling, and Rhia's showerproof jacket was soaked. As, too, was her hair, she realised impatiently, wondering for the umpteenth time why she didn't simply have it cut. It was far too long and cumbersome for a girl in her position, and it spent its days either plaited into braids, or, as today, coiled in a damp chignon at her nape.

'Rhia!'

Valentina had seen her and came hurrying down the street towards her, a pathetic figure in her jeans and yellow anorak. Considering the difference in their ages, they were remarkably alike, thought Rhia, as the other girl approached. Both tall and fair-haired, though it was true that Valentina was the slimmer and her hair was short.

'Thanks for coming,' the younger girl said now, tucking her arm through Rhia's, her pale face eloquent of the fact that this was not something Rhia could iron out in the space of a few minutes. 'Let's go to the pub. We can get a meat pie or a sandwich there.'

Rhia's hesitation was scarcely noticeable, and she fell into step beside her sister without a word. She would have preferred that they had a cup of tea and a sandwich in Val's room at the nurses' home, where surely they could have had a more private conversation.

'What a day!' Valentina commented as they walked the few yards to the Crown and Anchor. 'I was afraid you wouldn't come. God, what a mess I've got myself into!' and her voice broke again.

Rhia was concerned, but a group of people emerging from the door of the public house prevented any rejoinder, and not until they had been served with a cheese roll each and a dry Martini with soda did she get the chance to make any comment.

They managed to find a quiet corner, away from the noisy atmosphere of the bar, and although there was nowhere to sit down, Rhia insisted that it would do. 'Come on,' she said. 'Whatever's happened? You look as if you haven't slept for a week.'

Valentina drew a steady breath and took a gulp of her Martini and soda. 'I feel like I haven't,' she confessed fervently. 'Oh, Rhia, it's just awful! Glyn's been badly hurt!'

For a moment, an uncharitable feeling of relief swept over Rhia. So it was Glyn who was in trouble, not Val, she thought, with weak reassurance. No matter how bad it was, Val was not involved, and for that Rhia was grateful.

'What happened?' she asked now, able to give her sister her full sympathy now that she knew, or could guess, how Valentina was feeling. 'How did it happen? How badly hurt is he?'

Valentina caught her breath. 'He—he's still unconscious. He hasn't come round.'

Rhia frowned. 'You mean there was an accident? Val darling, I know you're very upset, but you've got to try and be a little more coherent.'

Valentina swallowed. 'There—there was a crash, yes.'

'A car crash?'

Valentina nodded, and Rhia's tongue emerged to circle

her dry lips. It would be futile to admit that she had worried on more than one occasion about her sister, since Val had told her Glyn had acquired a fast sports car. It had seemed such a fragile defence against any other vehicle, and she had had to steel her emotions when Val spoke of its speed and acceleration. But at least Val had not been hurt.

'Where is he?' she asked, and Valentina blinked.

'Where is he?' she echoed. 'Why, in—in the hospital, of course. Where else would he be?'

'But what hospital?' persisted Rhia patiently. 'Not St Mary's, I'm sure.'

'Oh, no.' Valentina put an abstracted hand to her temple. 'He—he's in Jude's. They took him there, after the accident.' She shook her head. 'He looked terrible. I—I thought at first that—that he was dead.'

Rhia put out a hand and squeezed her sister's arm affectionately. 'Poor Val, no wonder you're in such a state. But how is he? I mean—do the doctors expect him to recover?'

'He's got to recover,' exclaimed Valentina fiercely. 'He's just got to. I—I don't know what I'll do if he doesn't!'

'Hey . . .' Rhia had never seen her sister so agitated, 'don't get so upset. He'll recover, I'm sure he will. They can do such marvellous things these days.'

'Yes.' But Valentina didn't sound very convinced, and Rhia sought about for something else to say.

'When did it happen?' she asked. 'The accident, I mean. Why didn't you ring me, as soon as you heard?'

'Heard?' Valentina looked blank.

'Heard about the accident,' Rhia prompted gently. 'When did you get to know? Last night, I suppose. Have Glyn's family been informed? I expect they must have——'

Valentina interrupted her, her eyes wild and anxious, her words falling over themselves as she struggled to get them out. 'Oh, you don't understand, Rhia. I know I'm explaining myself badly, but surely you've realised: I didn't *hear* about the accident. I was *there*! I was with him! I was part of it. It—it was all *my* fault!'

Later, Rhia acknowledged that perhaps she had been a little dense in not realising that Valentina's grief stemmed from more than the mild infatuation she had had for Glyn Frazer. She should have known that her sister's sympathies were unlikely to be strained to this extent by anyone other than herself. It was a harsh analysis perhaps, but the truth was that Valentina had seldom shown consideration for anyone, and latterly Rhia had sensed a cooling of the relationship between her sister and her boy-friend.

Now, however, she could only stare at Valentina, scarcely comprehending the import of what she was saying, and the younger girl's face convulsed as she struggled with her frustration.

'Don't you understand, Rhia?' she cried, glancing behind her to ensure her impassioned outburst was not overheard. 'The accident happened last night—my night off. And—and *I* was driving!'

'You!' Rhia gasped. 'But, Val, you don't hold a driving licence!'

Valentina cast her eyes briefly towards the ceiling. 'Isn't that what I'm trying to tell you? Oh, Rhia, what am I going to do? Glyn—Glyn may die, and—and I'll be to blame!'

Rhia wished she was sitting down now. Her legs felt decidedly unsteady, and she thrust the remains of her half-eaten roll into a nearby ashtray as nausea swept up her throat.

'Well?' Valentina's eyes were tear-filled and intent. 'Can't you say anything? Can't you at least tell me you understand? Dear God, Rhia, if you don't help me, no one will, and—and I'm so—I'm so scared!'

Rhia put down her glass and rubbed her unsteady hands together. Then, shaking her head, she said weakly: 'You've got to give me time, Val. I haven't taken this in yet. Right now—right now, I just don't know what to say.'

Valentina's lips twisted. 'How do you think I feel? I haven't slept, I haven't even been to bed!' She sniffed. 'I walked the streets for hours. I was exhausted, but I didn't want to go back.'

'Wait a minute.' Rhia halted her. 'What do you mean, you walked the streets for hours? I thought you said Glyn was taken to hospital, after the accident.'

'He was. I rang for the ambulance myself.'

Rhia could feel a throbbing beginning somewhere behind her temple. 'And they didn't ask you to accompany them? The police—I assume there were police involved—they didn't ask for a statement?'

Valentina bent her head. 'I—it wasn't like that. When we had the crash, there was no one else around. Oh, I don't know how it happened. One minute I was driving happily along this side street, and the next this cat ran across the road in front of us. Glyn said: 'Brake', but somehow my foot hit the accelerator, and the tyres squealed and we—we hit a lamp-post.'

'Oh, Valentina!'

'I know. It was awful. Glyn's head must have hit the windscreen. He—he was covered in blood. I—I just panicked.' Her voice broke, and then, controlling herself again, she went on: 'I knew I had to get out of there. If—if anyone saw me, if anyone identified me——'

'Wait a minute.' Rhia stared at her. 'You said you phoned for the ambulance yourself.'

'Yes. Yes, I did. There was a phone box quite nearby. I made the call—then I ran away.'

'*Val!*' Rhia was horrified.

'I know, I know.' Valentina threaded shaking fingers through her damp curls. 'But what could I have done? I've told you, Glyn looked so awful! I couldn't stick around and risk the chance of being arrested!'

Rhia swallowed the rest of her Martini, trying hard to think sensibly. Then, putting the glass aside, she tried to speak calmly. 'Val, the police are going to know someone else was driving that car——' And as Valentina began to shake her head vigorously, she went on: 'And, let's face it, you are the most likely suspect. You were Glyn's girlfriend. He had probably told his friends that he was meeting you——'

'No, no!' Valentina interrupted her frantically. 'It was late. We were on our way back to the hospital. We'd taken this roundabout route so I could drive. Glyn could have dropped me; he could have been on his way back to his flat.'

'But he hadn't!' exclaimed Rhia forcefully. 'Val, face facts——'

'No one knows that.'

Rhia shook her head. 'You're not being realistic. Glyn wasn't even in the driving seat!'

Valentina bent her head. 'They wouldn't know that.'

'What do you mean?' Rhia felt sick.

'I've told you, Glyn hit the windscreen. It—it was shattered. I managed to pull his legs across——'

'Oh, God!' Rhia gazed at her sister in growing contempt. 'I thought you said you panicked.'

'I did. I did.' Valentina's chest was heaving. 'Rhia, you don't know what I felt like, sitting there, in the dark, knowing Glyn could be dead!'

Rhia expelled her breath weakly. 'You realise you could be guilty of manslaughter, don't you?' she cried. 'Oh, Val, how could you? How could you?'

Valentina thrust her hands into the pockets of her anorak, and looked about her a little sullenly now. 'It's all right for you to talk,' she muttered. 'You don't ever have these kind of problems. Your life is so—so dull! My God, Rhia, there are times when I wonder if you've ever even made it with anyone! Not Simon, I'm sure. Supercilious prig!'

'Val!' Rhia's hand on her arm silenced her sister, but she still looked mutinous. 'You're not going to gain my sympathy by insulting Simon Travis. He's been a good friend to me, and—and I'm very fond of him. I'm just wondering how he'd react to all this.'

'You won't tell him?' For a moment, Valentina's face was anxious, but then, recognising the impatience in her sister's eyes, she relaxed again. 'Fond,' she muttered, as if by speaking about Rhia's relationships, she could eliminate her own. 'What a god-awful word to use about the man in your life!'

Rhia ignored this, concentrating on what Valentina had just told her. At least her sister had not been joking. This was more serious than any scrape Val had got herself into before. And the awful thing was, Rhia didn't honestly know how to advise her. Oh, it was a simple enough choice between what was right and what was wrong; but as the minutes passed and logic took the place of emotion, Rhia acknowledged her own uncertainty in the face of subsequent events. What good would it do to make Val confess? Would it help Glyn's recovery? The answer was evidently, no, and while allowing her sister to escape the justice of her culpability was wrong, if Glyn recovered, her conviction could injure both of them.

Rhia knew she was acting as devil's advocate, that nothing could alter the fact that Val had driven Glyn's car both illegally and carelessly; and that, if he died, she was responsible. But if he didn't die, if he lived, what possible good could be gained from exposing her sister to the process of law? Valentina was irresponsible and reckless, but surely the experience alone would serve as sufficient punishment, and teach her never to do such a crazy thing again.

'Do you want another drink?'

Valentina was watching her from beneath lowered lids, and Rhia shook her head. 'No, thanks,' she said, steadying herself for what she had to say. 'I've got to be leaving soon.'

Valentina nodded, then she clutched her sister's sleeve. 'Rhia?'

'How do you know Glyn's still unconscious? Did you phone the hospital?'

'No.' Valentina gave a negative reply. 'They phoned me.'

'They phoned you?' Rhia's brows arched. 'But——'

Valentina hunched her shoulders. 'It was my handbag. I—I left my handbag in the car.'

'*Val!*'

Valentina sniffed. 'That's why I had to see you, don't you see? I—I want you to tell them that I spent the night at the flat.'

Rhia gulped. 'But—why?' She looked blank. 'What good will that do?'

'Glyn's flat isn't far from the hospital. Like I said before, he could have dropped me and been on his way back to his flat.'

'Dropped you—at the flat?'

'Yes.'

'Why? Why not at the hospital?'

Valentina sighed impatiently. 'Rhia, I've got to have an alibi, don't you see? I told you what happened. I—I walked the streets for hours. I didn't go back to the hostel until this morning. That's when I discovered they'd been—trying to find me.'

Now Rhia understood everything. Valentina hadn't wanted to confide in her. On the contrary, had she not made the mistake of leaving her handbag in the car, she, Rhia, might never have learned of Val's part in the affair. But now she was cornered and, as usual, she expected Rhia to provide a solution.

'So what did you say?' Rhia asked now, her voice cooler than before.

'I told them I'd been with you,' cried Valentina fiercely. 'What else could I say?'

Rhia was angry. 'So all this is just academic. You're not really asking for my help, you're telling me I've got to give it.'

'Rhia, it's not like that.'

'Then what is it like?'

'Rhia, you have no idea how I felt. I had to think of something, some reason why I hadn't spent the night at the nurses' home. I couldn't tell them the truth, could I?'

Rhia was appalled. 'There are times, Val——'

'I know, I know.' Valentina was sulky. 'For heaven's sake, it's only a little thing.'

'A little thing?' Rhia clenched her fists. 'If Glyn dies, you'll have made me an accessory to manslaughter!'

'He won't die——'

'I hope not.' Rhia took a deep breath. 'Because if he does, Val, I have no intention of standing by and letting you get away scot-free!'

Back at her desk that afternoon, Rhia found it incredibly difficult to concentrate. Her mind buzzed with the things Valentina had told her. She could hardly believe her sister could have got herself into such a mess, and the implications were all bad. At times like this, she wondered how she and Val could have the same parents and yet be so

different. It made her doubt her own assessment of her
sister, and she realised that since Val left school, a gulf
had opened between them that she could never bridge.

Her immediate boss, George Wyatt, was not particularly sympathetic to his secretary's loss of concentra-
tion. He was a man in late middle age, with all the
accompanying afflictions of the successful business-man: a
short temper, an expanding girth, and an ulcer.
Generally, he and Rhia worked together very well, she
competent and independent, well able to handle clients
alone, if necessary, and adept at anticipating her employer's every whim. She attended to his engagements,
pacified his wife on occasion, and handed him his tablets
when his ulcer was playing up; but this afternoon she was
self-absorbed and absentminded, and Mr Wyatt lost no
time in giving her the edge of his impatience.

'Rhia, are you deliberately trying to annoy me?' he
demanded, pointing to the tray on his desk. 'I've asked
you twice to hand me the Macdonald file, and you've
simple ignored me!'

'I'm sorry, Mr Wyatt.' Rhia was flushed and apologetic. 'I'm afraid—I—er—I've got a bit of a headache,
that's all.'

'I wish that was all I had,' retorted George Wyatt
shortly. 'This pain in my gut is tearing me to pieces, but
do I complain?'

Frequently, Rhia was tempted to reply, but she merely
gave a conciliatory shake of her head and tried to apply
herself to his dictation. But it wasn't easy, and later in the
afternoon, checking the results of her shorthand, she
hoped Mr Wyatt would not remember word for word
exactly what he had said.

The board meeting was blessedly brief, and Rhia
breathed a sigh of relief when she emerged from the
building to find Simon's car waiting in the staff parking
area. The rain had ceased, and it was a mild April evening, the slowly illuminating lights of the city adding a
sparkle to the darkening streets.

'You're early,' Simon greeted her, as she slid into the
seat beside him, and deposited an affectionate kiss at the
corner of her mouth.

'So are you,' she agreed, returning his salutation warmly. 'Thank goodness it's Friday. I'm exhausted!'

'You do look a little pale,' Simon nodded, studying her features, despite the shadows of the car. 'What's wrong? Has Wyatt been rather tetchy again? I heard that his son was arrested for drunken driving the other evening.'

'Did you?' Rhia turned her face away, and moved her shoulders offhandedly. 'Let's go, shall we? I'm—starving!'

In truth, food was the last thing she needed, but Simon's innocent remark had been too close for comfort. For the first time, she wondered if Valentina and Glyn had been drinking, and whether this was the reason Valentina had chosen to keep out of reach until morning.

'By the way,' Simon had noticed nothing amiss, 'I've got tickets for the Bartok concert on Sunday. I know you said you weren't terribly keen, but you'll enjoy it, I know you will.'

'Will I?' Rhia gave him a swift appraising look. Right now, the idea of Bartok was like the idea of food— nauseating!

'What's the matter?' At last Simon had detected some change in her attitude. 'You seem—tense. Is anything wrong?'

'No.' Rhia forced a light laugh. 'You know how it is. The weekend comes and you just feel like doing nothing.'

Simon frowned. 'You're not annoyed about Wednesday, are you? I just couldn't get away. Those tiles in the kitchen have been impossible to match, and what with the rehearsals for the school play——'

'Oh, no, honestly,' Rhia hastened to reassure him. Simon took his work as a teacher very seriously, and it wasn't his fault that his mother demanded so much of his free time. She was old, after all, and widowed, and Rhia sometimes wondered what she would do if Simon ever decided to move out. Perhaps she expected, if he got married, his wife would be prepared to move *in*, but Rhia knew she could never share a house with Simon's mother. Mrs Travis was too set in her ways, too demanding, and certainly too attached to her son to allow any other woman to usurp her place in his affections.

'You know what Mother's like,' Simon went on now, starting the car. 'She hates the place to be in a mess, and the kitchen has taken longer than I expected.'

'You have had to go to work as well,' Rhia pointed out reasonably, glad to deflect him from her problems. 'I think your mother forgets that.'

'I know.' Simon pulled out into the stream of traffic with a rueful grimace. 'But it's done now, and in future, we'll be able to spend our free evenings together.'

'Yes.'

But Rhia did not feel enthusiastic, and she had to make a determined effort to hide her misgivings as Simon rattled on about his day, and the play, and where they were going to eat that evening.

Chinese food was normally Rhia's favourite, but this evening she only picked at her meal, pushing the chow mein round her plate in an effort to make it look less. Even so, she knew Simon had noticed, and when they were driving back to her flat, he cast her a doubtful glance.

'You're sure it's not something I've done, Rhia?' he ventured, taking one hand from the steering wheel to cover hers where they lay in her lap. 'I mean, if it is, say so. I don't like to think you're keeping anything from me. We're usually so close—very close.' He squeezed her hands significantly. 'In fact, I think it's time we started thinking about the future—*our* future.'

Rhia extricated herself rather awkwardly and patted his hand. 'Not tonight, Simon, mmm?' she murmured, hoping he'd take the hint. 'I really am very tired. I think I'll stay in bed until lunchtime tomorrow.'

Simon took his dismissal with his usual good humour. 'Okay,' he said, bringing the car to a halt at the entrance to the apartment building. 'I won't press you now. But don't expect the same privilege tomorrow.'

Rhia managed a faint smile. 'Thanks, Simon.'

'You're not going to invite me in?'

'Not tonight, no.'

Simon nodded, and after a moment's hesitation, leant across and kissed her. 'Come on, then. I'll see you to your door,' he murmured, his lips brushing her cheek as he drew away, and Rhia touched his face tenderly before sliding out of the car.

'There's no need for you to come up with me, really,' she exclaimed, as he locked the car. 'It's only half past ten. There are always people about.'

'Nevertheless, I'd rather assure myself that you were safely home,' Simon insisted, slipping his hand into hers. 'Brr! It's turning chilly. Let's get inside.'

The block of flats was not new, and graffiti covered the walls of the entrance hall, and adorned the sides of the iron lifts that clanked their way to the upper floors. They were not attractive surroundings, Rhia had to admit, but the flats themselves were not too bad. The one Rhia's father had leased had two bedrooms and a living area, as well as kitchen and bathroom, and the usual offices. When her father was at home, Rhia and her sister shared a bedroom, but while he was away Valentina had moved the things she kept at the apartment into his bedroom.

'Here we are.' The lift had deposited them at the sixth floor, and Rhia indicated her door only a few yards away along the uncarpeted corridor. 'Don't bother getting out, Simon, there's no need. I'll see you tomorrow.'

'Okay.' Simon sounded a little disappointed, as if he had half expected her to change her mind and invite him in for coffee, but Rhia needed to be alone. 'See you tomorrow,' he agreed, tightening his grip on her fingers before letting them go. 'I love you.'

Rhia was glad the lift doors closed before she could make any response. Aside from her anxieties about Valentina, she was not sure enough of her feelings for Simon to commit herself so completely. She liked him, she liked him very much, but love—love was something she had learned to live without.

She had loved her parents deeply, but they had found their children more of an encumbrance than anything, and boarding school had robbed her of their secure, if indifferent, presence. Then, when her mother died and she had thought her father might need her, he had proved otherwise, going off to South Africa with hardly a second thought for either her or Valentina. And now, Valentina was proving that Rhia didn't know her either, and the

idea of giving some man a similar kind of hold over her
was not something she anticipated.

With a slightly dejected shrug of her shoulders, she
trudged along the corridor to her door, fumbling in
her bag for her key, paying little attention to anything
else.

'Miss Mallory?'

The brusque, yet attractive, tones set her nerves jangl-
ing, and she spun round tautly, automatically clenching
her fingers round the strap of her bag, ready to use it as a
weapon if necessary. She had heard nothing, she had
thought the corridor was deserted, and looking up at the
tall stranger standing right behind her now, she realised
the vulnerability Simon was always speaking of. But the
man had spoken her name, so he could not be a villain,
could he? Why warn her of his presence, if he intended to
attack her?

Certainly he did not look like a thief, but criminals
were often plausible people. Where had she read that, or
heard that? On television, probably. They were always
warning women to be wary of any stranger, who might
threaten their lives or their property, and this man was
definitely a stranger. Her lips parted. Just because he was
tall and dark-skinned and attractive there was no reason
to doubt his duplicity, and her knees trembled violently
as she struggled to remain calm.

'What do you want?'

The involuntary question was a futile effort to gain
time, but the corridor remained obstinately empty. The
lift she had heard coming whined away past her floor,
and she was alone and helpless, and hopelessly de-
moralised.

'Relax, Miss Mallory. I'm not a thief or a rapist,' the
man assured her, in a crisp masculine drawl that had a
decidedly un-English accent. 'I'm sorry if I frightened you,
but I thought you'd heard my footsteps. This corridor
isn't exactly soundproof, is it?'

'Well, I didn't.' Rhia was trying desperately to regain
her composure. 'And—and one doesn't expect visitors
at—at eleven o'clock at night.'

'I know. I'm sorry about that, too. But my time scale

isn't the same as yours, and right now, I'm not too concerned about your reactions to my visit. I need to talk with you, Miss Mallory. Now. So do you invite me in, or do I state what I have to say out here?'

'Wait a minute . . .' Rhia clutched her bag like a lifeline. He was going too fast, much too fast. Who was he? What was he doing here? And what right did he think he had to demand speech with her?

'My name is Frazer,' he said now, anticipating her next question. 'Jared Frazer.' His lean mouth twisted in an expression of harsh satisfaction at her involuntary withdrawal. 'I see the name means something to you. It should.' He paused. 'I'm Glyn's uncle. And I'd be interested to hear your explanation as to how come you're so unconcerned that my nephew may be dying because of you!'

CHAPTER TWO

'THAT's not true!'

Rhia's denial was automatic, her pale cheeks flaming with hot colour as she faced his cold implacability.

'Then why aren't you at the hospital?' he demanded, raking her with a scathing glance. 'The least you could do is pretend you cared a damn for his life!'

'I—I do. At least, I care as—as much as anyone would care——'

'*Anyone?*'

'Yes, anyone.' Rhia glanced helplessly behind her. 'Oh, I—I think you'd better come in. You—you've made a mistake, Mr Frazer. I'm not who you think I am. Valentina is my sister. I'm Rhia.'

'*Rhia?*'

As she struggled to get her key into the lock, she heard him repeat her name with harsh incredulity. Then, as the key turned and the door swung open, she gasped in dismay as his hand at her back impelled her into the small hallway beyond. Panic flared once again, but it was short-lived as

he groped for the light switch and slammed the door
behind them.

'You lying little bitch!' he swore violently, iron-hard
fingers around her upper arm pressing her against the
wall. 'You'd better think of something else and quick,
Valentina. I met your sister Rhia when I came here
earlier this afternoon!'

Any thought of defending her sister died in Rhia at
that moment. 'Then—then you were misled,' she choked,
almost spitting the words at him. 'I—*I* am Rhia Mallory,
Mr Frazer. And I can prove it. Now will you please let
go of my arm? You're hurting me!'

She was aware that in the struggle, the neat coil of her
hair had become loosened and untidy strands of honey-
coloured silk were tumbling down about her ears, framing
the pale indignation of her face. Violet eyes, wide with
resentment, glared into the enigmatic darkness of his, and
she shook her head in fury as he continued to hold her
prisoner.

'Say that again,' he commanded, and she was so close
to him she could feel the warm draught of his breath as
he spoke. It was fresh and just faintly scented with alcohol,
as if he, as well as her sister, had taken time out from
visiting the hospital.

'I—I said, I'm Rhia Mallory,' she repeated unsteadily.
'I don't know who you saw this afternoon, but it certainly
wasn't me.'

'She said she was Rhia Mallory,' he insisted, and Rhia
could feel his frustration through the taut fingers gripping
her arm. 'She said you weren't home, and that I'd better
come back later. She didn't say when, so I came back—
at six, and again at eight o'clock this evening. This is my
fourth visit, Miss Mallory, and this time I don't intend to
leave until I know the truth!'

Rhia was trembling very badly, but somehow she
managed to sustain his angry glare. 'I don't care what she
told you, Mr Frazer,' she retorted tremulously. 'I imagine
she had her own reasons for telling you what she did. The fact
remains, I am Rhia, not Valentina, and I wish you would
stop behaving as if I'd committed some kind of crime!'

'And haven't you?'

'No, damn you!' Rhia caught her breath on a sob, the pain he was inflicting to her arm causing the blood to drain from it. 'For God's sake, let me go, can't you? You're taller, broader, and infinitely stronger than I am. Surely you're not afraid I might overpower you!'

The man regarded her malevolently for a long moment, and then, with a faint trace of admiration twisting his dark features, he opened his fingers and stepped back, allowing her to massage her injured arm with jerky movements. 'You're very cool, Miss Mallory,' he commented harshly. 'I should have expected it. But after meeting your sister, I'm afraid I was disarmed.'

Disarmed! Rhia couldn't imagine anyone who displayed a greater lack of such a weakness. But evidently Valentina had spoken to him, and succeeded in deceiving him. But why? What did she hope to gain by it? Surely she realised that by antagonising this man, she could only be making things more difficult for herself.

'You'd better come in.'

Pushing past him, Rhia led the way into the living room. For a moment, he resisted her attempt to pass him, but then, with a wry inclination of his head he allowed her to continue, and Rhia turned on the lamps with a feeling of mild incredulity. This couldn't be happening to her, she thought disbelievingly. But it was, and her unwelcome visitor's bulk uncomfortably reduced the generous proportions of the familiar room.

Glancing behind her to ensure herself of his whereabouts, Rhia emptied the contents of her handbag on to the dropleaf table in the window. Then, after finding what she was looking for, she held out several articles for his inspection: her banker's card, her cheque book, and not least, her driving licence.

'I think these will clarify the situation,' she declared, her voice breaking in spite of the iron determination she was putting on herself. 'And if any further evidence is required, I'm sure Simon—that is, the young man I was out with this evening—I'm sure he would willingly——'

She couldn't go on. It had all been too much for her. With a feeling of ignominy, she felt the hot tears overspilling her eyes, sliding down her cheeks in weak betrayal, and she quickly turned her back on him as she scrubbed her knuckles over her eyes.

If she had expected her tears to persuade him, she was wrong. As she stood there, struggling to control herself, she heard him flicking over the documents she had given him, in no apparent hurry to offer his apologies.

'Yes,' he said at last, 'I'm sure these are genuine. But why shouldn't I suspect their deliverer? If I was going to pretend to be someone else, I'd make pretty damn sure I had documentation, too.'

'Oh, you're impossible!' Rhia spun round helplessly, her breakdown made all the more humiliating by reddened eyes and a drip at the end of her nose. 'Why won't you believe me? Why would I lie?'

'Why would your sister lie?'

Rhia bent her head, rubbing her nose disconsolately. 'You tell me.'

There was silence for a few pregnant seconds, and then Jared Frazer moved, walking past her to the table and depositing the articles she had given him with the rest of her belongings. Rhia flinched away from him as he passed her, but he didn't touch her. After he had accomplished his mission, he returned to his position by the door, and when she looked up he was regarding her with something less than hostility in his brooding gaze.

In spite of their differences, Rhia could not deny that he was a disturbing man, disturbing both in his manner and his appearance. The hooded eyes with their heavy lids, that had raked her trembling defiance previously, were only part of his dark attraction. Set above a narrow intelligent face, with high cheekbones and a prominent nose, they only hinted at the sensuality that was evident in every line of his thin-lipped mouth. She had never seen Glyn, but if he was anything like his uncle she could quite see why Valentina had found him so attractive. Even the dark lounge suit he was wearing fitted his lean muscular body with unerring elegance, accentuating the narrowness of his hips and the powerful strength of his legs.

Yet, meeting his eyes, Rhia knew an uneasy sense of foreboding. It was strange, but now that the hardness of aggression was being erased from his features, she felt more—not less—anxiety. Why had he come here? What did he want? And why hadn't Glyn's parents made the trip?

'Okay,' he said, straightening from the indolent stance he had adopted, pushing back the lick of straight black hair that had tumbled across his forehead. 'Suppose I accept what you say: I guess that means it was Valentina I spoke to earlier.'

Rhia moved her head in a positive gesture.

'So—where is she?'

Rhia caught her lower lip between her teeth. 'At—at work, I suppose.'

'I assume you mean the hospital where she's a student nurse?'

'Naturally.'

'No.' He shook his head, folding his arms across the broad expanse of his chest, and Rhia's anxiety kindled into a hard core of apprehension.

'What do you mean, no?'

'Where do you think I've been this evening? Apart from a bar.'

Rhia frowned. 'But she must be there. She told me she was on duty at eight o'clock.'

His eyes narrowed. 'You've seen her?'

'Well—yes.' Rhia coloured. 'But it was at lunchtime. That—that was when I learned about what had happened——' She broke off uncertainly. 'How—how is Glyn?'

'Still in a coma,' said Jared Frazer flatly. 'The doctors say it may be hours or days before he comes out of it. There's nothing anybody can do until they know whether he's suffered any brain damage.'

'Oh, no!' Rhia felt sick.

'Oh, yes.' Jared Frazer was relentless. 'And I mean to find out how my nephew, who was a tolerably good driver, should have had the misfortune to wrap his automobile round a concrete post for no reason.'

Rhia moved her head. 'What—what did they tell you?'

'Who? The doctors, or the police?'

'The—police.'

'They're not happy with their investigations either,' he

replied, his eyes intimidatingly intent. 'They think someone else may have been with him. Your sister, perhaps. They know she was with him earlier in the evening.'

Rhia could not meet his eyes. 'I—I wish I could help you.'

'So do I,' he averred grimly. 'It would help to find your sister. Are you sure you have no idea where she might be?'

'No.' Rhia could be positive about that at least. 'I—at lunchtime when I left her I understood she was going back to the hospital to see Glyn. I can't imagine where else she would go.'

Jared Frazer pulled a wry face. 'You forget—she was here, wasn't she? I spoke to her at—oh, I guess it must have been about two-thirty.'

'Yes.' Rhia tried to think. 'But you've been to St Mary's since then and she's not there.'

'That's right.'

Rhia linked her unsteady fingers together. 'Then I don't know where she is, Mr Frazer. I—I wish I did.'

'Which leaves us with the original question, why should Valentina pretend to be you?'

Rhia nodded. 'I—I suppose—when she realised who you were——'

'——she panicked!'

'Panicked?' Rhia endeavoured not to betray her alarm. 'No, I—perhaps she was scared.'

'Scared!' He was scathing. 'And why should she be scared, if she had nothing to hide?'

'Oh, I don't know. Why are you catechising me?' Rhia's nerves were rapidly getting the better of her. First Valentina's confession, then the shock of meeting him at her door, and now this! She wasn't a criminal, but she was being made to feel like one, and the knowledge of what her sister had told her made everything that was happening like some awful nightmare.

Scraping her hand across her damp cheeks, she moved her shoulders in a dismissing gesture. 'I think you'd better go, Mr Frazer,' she said. 'I'm sorry I can't help you, but I'm sure Valentina will explain everything when she turns up.'

'When she turns up?' He glared at her. 'And when might that be? Is she in the habit of disappearing for nights on end? Aren't you worried about her?'

'Worried!' Rhia gasped. 'Of course I'm worried. And—and in answer to your question, no—no, Val is not in the habit of sleeping around, if that's what you're implying! But she's obviously not here, and I don't see what more I can tell you.'

Jared Frazer regarded her broodingly. 'Very well,' he said at last, after subjecting her to another penetrating appraisal, 'I'll go. I intend to spend the night at the hospital, just in case there's any change in Glyn's condition. If you do locate your sister, I'd be grateful if you'd contact me there. Otherwise, I've booked a room at the Westbury.'

'At—at the Westbury,' Rhia nodded. 'I'll remember.'

Jared Frazer hesitated only a moment longer, and then turned abruptly towards the door, preceding her along the narrow entrance hall with long powerful strides.

He pulled the door open into the corridor, then halted, glancing down at Rhia closely behind him. 'You'll be all right?' he asked, unexpectedly gentle after his earlier animosity, and Rhia caught her breath.

'I—yes,' she stammered awkwardly, and his lean mouth twisted into a wry smile.

'I'm sorry if I was brutal,' he offered, and she shrank back in alarm when he lifted his hand. But all he did was brush one errant tear from her cheek, his brown fingers light and cool against her overheated skin.

'I—will—will Glyn's parents be coming to England?' Rhia asked hastily, overwhelmingly conscious of the unwelcome intimacy promoted by that disturbing gesture, and to her relief he moved out into the corridor.

'Glyn's father was my elder brother,' he remarked, with resumed curtness, as if he was loath to explain himself to her. 'He's dead. I came on behalf of Glyn's mother, my sister-in-law. Since my brother died, I've accepted the role of Glyn's guardian.'

'Oh! Oh, I see.' Rhia cleared her throat. 'Well, goodnight, Mr Frazer.'

'Goodnight, Miss Mallory,' he returned politely, and she closed the door heavily as he walked away towards the lift.

With the safety chain in place, Rhia moved reluctantly down the hall again and into the living room. She was still trembling and for the moment she seemed incapable of coherent thought. Hardly thinking what she was doing, she gathered the contents of her handbag together and stuffed them all back inside, fastening the press-stud securely before looking round the living room.

It was not an unattractive apartment, with its patterned broadloom and neat three-piece suite, but she couldn't help speculating what Jared Frazer had thought of it, and wondered rather irrelevantly what his home was like. Probably ultra-smart and ultra-modern, she decided, wishing she knew more about Glyn's background. But Valentina's overtures on the subject had been short and apathetic, and Rhia had not been sufficiently interested to question her further. Besides, she had never expected the information to have any relevancy, and only now did she realise that apart from his name, and the college he attended here in London, she knew next to nothing about him.

With a sigh, she put up a hand to her hair, discovering to her dismay that it was almost completely loosened from its pins. What must Jared Frazer have thought of her? she reflected irritably. Remembering the elegance of American and Canadian women she had seen on television and in magazines, she decided that he had probably mistaken her for a slob. What with red eyes and a runny nose, and her hair looking as if it hadn't seen a brush in days, he had every reason to despise her; and even the brace skirt, which had looked so attractive this morning, was now creased beyond reason after the soaking it had taken at lunchtime.

Shaking her head, she turned out the living room lamps and went into her bedroom. In the light from an apricot-shaded bulb, she surveyed the damage. As she had expected, she did look a mess, her mascara smudged and uneven, and little, if any, make-up left on her face. Oh well, she thought bitterly, she had more important things to think about than her appearance. Where on earth was Valentina, and how could she hope to gain anything by hiding away?

Stripping off her clothes, Rhia went into the bathroom and erased the offending mascara, cleansing her face thoroughly and cleaning her teeth. Then, with her skin soft and glowing, she put on her cotton nightgown and sat down to brush her hair at the mirror before tumbling into bed. Her hair fell in a silken curtain almost to her waist, thick and smooth and lustrous, and completely straight. Only when she bound it in braids did it assume a kinky texture, but generally she preferred it as it was now, a skein of beaten gold. It was her best feature, she decided, ignoring the violet beauty of her eyes, and the generous width of her mouth. And Valentina had always made her feel overweight, comparing Rhia's more voluptuous curves to her own sylph-like figure. Where was Valentina? she asked herself again as she climbed into bed, but her emotional exhaustion soon eliminated even this thought from her mind.

It was light when she awakened, and a reluctant glance at the alarm clock informed her it was after nine o'clock. Not late, by Saturday standards, but anxiety, and her conscience, made her reach for her dressing gown.

It was chilly in the apartment, and she turned on the central heating before drawing back the curtains and going to plug in the kettle. Then, gathering the daily newspaper from the letter box, she made her way back down the hall.

On impulse, she opened her father's bedroom door, the room Valentina used while he was away. It was the smaller of the two bedrooms, their father insisting that as they were to share and have single beds, the two girls should have the larger room. While her sister was in residence, the room generally looked a mess, with discarded clothes left on the bed and Valentina's make-up adorning the dressing table, and after her visit yesterday, Rhia was quite prepared to find the place in disorder. But it wasn't. It was reasonably tidy, and what was more, the dressing table tray was empty of any cosmetics.

With a feeling of apprehension Rhia entered the room,

running her fingers over the surface of the chest of drawers where Valentina kept the nightwear and lingerie she used when she was at the apartment. Hardly aware that she was holding her breath, Rhia pulled open the drawers, one by one, her fingers quickening when she discovered they were empty. Only a discarded pair of tights still resided in the bottom of one of the drawers. Otherwise, all her sister's belongings had gone.

Expelling her breath on a gasp, Rhia hurried to the wardrobe, wrenching open the doors and standing back aghast when she found that here, too, her sister's clothes had gone, leaving only her father's spare suits and jackets hanging there.

Turning, Rhia surveyed the room blankly. So that was why Valentina had come to the apartment; that was what she had been doing when Jared Frazer interrupted her. No wonder she had panicked and lied. She must have been planning to leave all along.

But leave for where? Rhia's brain simply couldn't come up with a single idea. Surely she must have left a note, something, *anything*, to reassure her sister that she would be coming back. But although she searched the flat from hallway to bathroom, there was nothing to indicate where Valentina had gone.

The kettle had boiled and gone cold again while Rhia was conducting her search, and she switched it on again weakly, realising how suspicious her sister's disappearance would appear. The police were bound to want to see her, to ask questions, and if Valentina wasn't around, they might question her.

Might! Rhia's lips twisted bitterly. If Jared Frazer had anything to do with it, there'd be no possibility of improbability. He was not going to take this lying down, and who knew? Perhaps they would put out a bulletin for Valentina's arrest.

Rhia shook her head. Yesterday afternoon she had thought the situation couldn't get any worse, but it had. This man Frazer had arrived, practically breathing fire, and Valentina had disappeared. Dear God, what was she going to do?

It was while she was drinking her tea that she decided

she would have to talk to Simon. She had to talk to someone and there was no one else she could confide in. Simon would listen, she thought, with some relief, Simon would understand. But she couldn't wait until their date that afternoon. She had to talk to him now.

Tucking her legs under her, Rhia curled up on the couch and picked up the telephone, dialling Simon's number with fingers that persistently hit the wrong digits. She had to dial the number three times before she made the connection, and then, when the receiver was lifted, it was Mrs Travis, not Simon, who came on the line.

'Oh, Mrs Travis, is Simon there?' Rhia asked urgently, clutching the plastic handset tightly. 'I—er—I'd like to speak to him. It is rather—important.'

'I'm afraid he's not up yet, Rhia,' Mrs Travis replied firmly. 'He's had such a busy week. I'm sure the poor boy was exhausted.'

'Well, do you think you could get him up, Mrs Travis?' Rhia persisted anxiously. 'I—I wouldn't trouble you normally, but this is urgent.'

'What is it? Perhaps I can help.' Mrs Travis was evidently unprepared to wake up her son and bring him to the phone unless it was absolutely necessary, and Rhia sighed.

'No. No, I have to speak to Simon,' she insisted, hearing the older woman's cluck of impatience. 'Honestly, Mrs Travis, I wish you would just ask Simon to speak to me.'

'Oh—very well.' Mrs Travis gave in. 'But I trust it's something important, and not simply a ruse to get him to come round there. He's promised to set out some seedlings for me this morning, and I want him to do them while it's fine.'

Rhia didn't answer her. She couldn't, and with another sound of irritation, Mrs Travis went away.

It seemed ages before Simon eventually came to the phone. Rhia herself grew impatient, and she sat, drumming her fingernails against the vinyl arm of the couch, inwardly praying that he could help her.

'Rhia?' At last, Simon's unenthusiastic voice broke into her prayers. 'Mother says you insisted on speaking to me. What is it? Aren't you feeling well?'

'I'm—all right.' In truth, Rhia felt far from well, but it was not something an aspirin could cure. 'Simon, I have to talk to you. Could you come round to the flat—right away? I don't know what I'm going to do!'

Her voice broke on the final words, and Simon responded with a little more warmth. 'Look, Rhia, what is it, love? Can't you tell me now? You've got my undivided attention.'

'I can't discuss it over the phone,' Rhia insisted huskily. 'You've got to come round here, Simon. I'm sorry, I know your mother won't like it, but I've got to see you.'

'But I am seeing you—this afternoon,' Simon pointed out reasonably. 'Can't—whatever it is wait until then?'

'No.'

'Rhia——'

'Don't you dare tell me you've got some gardening to do!' Rhia almost screamed the words. 'Don't you understand, Simon? This—this is a matter of—of life and death! What do I have to say to make you believe me?'

'All right, all right.' Simon spoke hastily, trying to calm her down. 'Now, don't get in a panic. I'll come. I'll get there just as soon as I possibly can. Just—take it easy.'

'Take it easy!' Rhia choked back a sob. 'All right. But—be as quick as you can, will you?'

After Simon had rung off, Rhia went to get dressed. There was no point in hanging about in her dressing gown. And besides, the police could arrive at any moment. With her clothes on, she would feel infinitely more capable of facing them.

She put on jeans and a mauve silk shirt, and secured her hair at her nape with a leather thong. But she left it loose, having no patience for coiling it up into a neat roll today, and discarded the idea of make-up because her hands were too unsteady.

She was dressed and ready in half an hour, with her bed made and a pot of coffee perking on the ring. But it was fully another hour before Simon turned up, and she looked at her watch pointedly as she let him into the apartment.

'I know, I know.' Simon moved his Harris-tweed-clad shoulders half indignantly. 'But I'd promised Mother to put in some cabbages and cauliflowers——'

'Cabbages and cauliflowers!' Rhia almost choked over the words, but she said nothing more until they were both standing in the living room.

She couldn't help comparing Simon's broad-shouldered stockiness to the lean-limbed frame of the man who had stood there the night before. There was no similarity between them, and Simon's reddish-brown thatch bore no resemblance to Jared Frazer's night-dark head of hair. They were different in so many ways, and she wondered what Simon would say if she told him how savagely Glyn's uncle had treated her.

'Well?' Simon thrust his hands into the hip pockets of his twill trousers. 'I'm here. What was so urgent it couldn't wait until three o'clock?'

'It's almost that now,' muttered Rhia childishly, and Simon sighed.

'It's half past eleven,' he corrected her dryly. 'Hmm, is that coffee I can smell? I could do with a cup.'

'Haven't you had any breakfast?' demanded Rhia sarcastically. 'I'm sure your mother wouldn't send you out without the requisite number of calories.'

'I have had some toast and marmalade,' Simon admitted, somewhat defensively. 'Rhia, what is all this about? I knew something was wrong last night, but you wouldn't discuss it then.'

Rhia went into the small kitchen and poured two cups of coffee, curiously reluctant now he was here to actually broach what she had to say. How would Simon take it? Would he threaten to go to the police? How well did she really know him, when they were not even lovers?

'It's Val,' she said at last, carrying the coffee back into the living room and handing him a cup. Simon had made himself comfortable on the couch, but now he put the paper he had been scanning aside and gave her his full attention. 'She's disappeared.'

'Disappeared!' At least her words had the ability to cause Simon to halt in the process of raising his cup to his lips. 'What do you mean—she's disappeared? Has she been abducted—run away? What?'

'Not abducted,' declared Rhia definitely, perching on

the edge of the chair opposite. 'She's taken all her things—at least, all the things she kept here, at the apartment. I don't think a kidnapper would wait around for her to pack.'

Simon stared at her. 'And—you knew this last night?'

'No. No, of course not.'

'So what was upsetting you last night?'

Rhia sighed heavily. Then, in as few words as possible, she explained her meeting with Valentina the previous lunchtime, omitting only the fact that her sister had been driving the car.

'My God!' Simon was evidently stunned. 'And you think she's run away because she's afraid she'll be implicated?'

'Something like that.'

'But—what the hell! It wasn't her fault. I can't understand why she would feel the need to cut and run. It doesn't make sense.'

Rhia bit her lip. 'Perhaps—perhaps there's more to it,' she ventured.

'But what?' Simon was endearingly obtuse. 'It seems to me she'd have done far better to admit that she was with him when the accident happened. The police are bound to find out. They always do.'

'Do they?' Rhia looked at him anxiously.

'Of course they do. And in any case, it's a silly thing to do, running away. It encourages people to think the worst, to imagine you've got something to hide.'

'Perhaps she has.' Rhia hesitated. 'Perhaps—perhaps she was driving. How—how about that?'

'Don't be silly,' Simon sniffed. 'Val can't drive, you know that.'

'But—what if she was?' probed Rhia cautiously. 'I mean, young people do crazy things.'

'If I thought that, I'd have no sympathy for her,' retorted Simon grimly, shattering once and for all Rhia's hopes of confiding everything. 'No, no. Val may have been reckless, a bit of a tearaway when she was younger, but she wouldn't do a thing like that. Good heavens, that would mean she was guilty of manslaughter, if the chap dies.'

Rhia buried her nose in her coffee cup. She felt near to desperation herself, and now that Simon had proved so virtuous, where could she turn?

The sound of the doorbell ringing brought her head up however, and what little colour she had drained out of her face. Who was that? she wondered in dismay. The police! Having discovered Valentina was not at the hospital where she worked, had they come looking for her?

'Aren't you going to answer that?' Simon was looking at her in surprise. 'You did hear the doorbell, didn't you? Perhaps it's Val. Perhaps she's forgotten her key. Perhaps your fears were unfounded.'

Rhia had distinct doubts that this could be so, but she could not ignore the caller, whoever it was. If she didn't answer the door, Simon would; he was already half out of his seat, as if growing impatient of her hesitation.

Putting down her coffee cup, Rhia smoothed her damp palms down over the seat of her jeans and walked determinedly along the hall. As she went, she mentally rehearsed what she was going to say, deciding with resignation that she could not pretend she didn't know what it was all about. Valentina had disappeared, she would tell them that. What they chose to make of it was not her concern.

When she opened the door, however, it was not the blue uniform of a police constable that confronted her, but the grey suede waistcoat of a three-piece suit. And the man who was wearing it with such indolent assurance was the man who had briefly terrorised her the night before.

CHAPTER THREE

'Mr Frazer!' she breathed, glancing swiftly behind her, aware that Simon would be able to overhear what was said.

'Miss Mallory,' Jared Frazer returned equably. 'Can I come in? I need to talk with you.'

'*Again!*' Rhia pressed nervous lips together.

'Yes, again,' he confirmed, looking pointedly over her shoulder. 'Can I come in? I think you'll want to hear what I have to tell you.'

Rhia couldn't believe that she would. After the way he had behaved the previous evening, she had no wish to have anything more to do with him. He was too arrogant, too sure of himself; and how was she to explain his identity to Simon, when she hadn't even mentioned what had happened?

'Could you come back?' she asked at last, awkwardly. 'I—it's difficult for me to speak to you now——'

'Why?' His narrowed eyes sought and speared her anxious gaze. 'Have I come at an inopportune moment? Is Valentina here? Is that what you're trying so desperately to hide? Well, if she is, so much the better——' and thrusting Rhia aside, he strode determinedly into the flat.

Rhia was too shocked to stop him, and in any case, she doubted that she could. With a helpless shrug of her shoulders, she closed the door, and then hastened after him. Oh, lord, she fretted uneasily, what was Simon going to make of all of this? If only she had explained what had happened before Jared Frazer made his appearance!

Jared had halted in the middle of the living room, and when Rhia reached the doorway Simon had risen to his feet to confront the taller man. Rhia knew an almost hysterical desire to laugh at their conflicting expressions— Simon's blustering and indignant, Jared Frazer's hostile and suspicious.

'What's going on here?'

It was Simon who spoke, turning to Rhia in protest, his young good-looking face mirroring his confusion. If he had heard Jared Frazer's name mentioned, it had meant nothing to him, and Rhia spread her hands wearily as she came into the room.

'This—this is Glyn's uncle, Simon,' she answered him quietly, giving Jared a resentful look. 'You know—Glyn, Val's boy-friend; his uncle is here because of—of the accident.'

'Where is your sister?'

Jared was evidently in no mood to wait while Rhia

made the necessary introductions. With an expression of impatience he cast a quick look into the kitchen, then stood regarding her broodingly when she voiced an objection.

'She's not here,' she declared quickly, deciding that Simon's explanations would have to wait. 'Mr Frazer, I told you last night I didn't know where my sister was. I don't. And—and what's more, her clothes have disappeared.'

'Rhia——' Simon tried to intervene, but Jared wouldn't let him.

'You mean, she's run away,' he inserted harshly. 'That doesn't surprise me.' He shook his head. 'I suppose you've known all along that she was driving the car.'

Rhia gasped, and Simon took an involuntary step forward. 'Don't talk such rot!' he exclaimed, putting out a hand to Rhia and squeezing her fingers reassuringly. 'Val can't drive—she's never had the opportunity. I don't know what you're hoping to gain, Frazer, but blaming an innocent girl for your nephew's accident isn't going to help anyone.'

Jared ignored Simon, and addressed himself solely to Rhia. 'Let's not indulge in needless argument, Miss Mallory,' he suggested bleakly. 'Your sister was driving that car. I've no doubt the police will be able to prove it. But that's not important now. Glyn's come round. He's conscious. And—God help him—he's asking for your sister.'

'Oh!' Rhia pressed both hands to her cheeks.

'You really don't know where she is?'

'No.' Rhia shook her head. 'I—I wish I did.'

Jared nodded. Then after a moment's consideration he seemed to come to a decision. 'You'll have to do it instead.'

'Do it?' echoed Rhia faintly. 'Do what?'

'Pretend to be your sister,' said Jared flatly.

'Now, look here——'

Once again Simon tried to intervene, but this time Rhia overrode him: 'I can't do that! Glyn will know I'm not Val.'

'Not necessarily,' declared Jared heavily. 'From what I

can remember of your sister, you are not unalike in appearance.'

'But Glyn——'

'Glyn seems to be having some difficulty with his sight,' conceded her adversary bleakly. 'He's conscious, yes, but that's all. He didn't even recognise me at first.'

'But——'

'Voices can be deceptive,' he continued steadily. 'Sometimes a person doesn't really listen to a voice, only to who's speaking. Do you understand me? And your voice can't be so dissimilar from Valentina's. If you tell him you're her, he'll believe you.'

Rhia's lips parted to allow her tongue to appear. Then she looked helplessly at Simon, begging his approval.

'Why can't you tell your nephew the truth?' he demanded, ignoring Rhia's silent appeal. 'Surely he's got to know sooner or later.'

Jared Frazer's lips twisted, but with a shrug of his suede-clad shoulders, he dismissed what Simon had said. 'Get your coat, Miss Mallory. I'll drive you to the hospital. I'm sure you want to do all you can to ensure that Glyn recovers.'

'Rhia, wait——'

Simon tried to restrain her, but Rhia released herself from his impatient grasp with a regretful sigh. 'I've got to do it, Simon. Can't you see? It's not Glyn's fault that Val's run out on him.'

'It's not your fault either,' countered Simon irritably, eyeing the tall Canadian with evident resentment. Then, when it became obvious that Rhia was not going to take any notice of his objections, he exclaimed, 'Very well, I'll take you to the hospital myself. That way, I'll be there if anyone tries to intimidate you.'

'No,' Jared positioned himself squarely by the door, 'that won't be necessary, Mr—er——'

'Travis,' put in Simon shortly.

'Fine—Mr Travis.' Jared inclined his head politely. 'I suggest you wait for us here. I'll bring her back safely, don't worry.'

'Wait a minute——'

'I think you'd better go home, Simon,' said Rhia unhappily, re-entering the room, a blue corded jacket about her shoulders. 'I'll ring you as soon as I get back from the hospital. I'm sorry, but there doesn't seem anything else I can do.'

Simon's fair features were flushed with anger as he viewed her apologetic expression. 'I feel as if you've brought me here on a wild goose chase, Rhia,' he exclaimed. 'Why didn't you tell me last night that Frazer here had been to the flat? Even this morning, you've let me go on thinking it was what Val had said that had upset you, when all the while you've had this on your mind.'

'It wasn't like that, Simon,' Rhia began, but Jared was urging her towards the door, and she realised she didn't have time to explain anything now. 'I—I'll see you later,' she murmured, as they emerged into the corridor, and Simon contented himself with giving her companion a series of malevolent looks as they all went down in the lift together.

Simon left them on the forecourt of the flats, striding away angrily to where his Cortina was parked, leaving Jared to escort Rhia to his own vehicle. This was a Mercedes, sleek and powerful—a hire-car, he remarked dryly as he unlocked the door for her to get inside.

'I'm used to a longer automobile,' he added, levering himself into the seat beside her. 'But I know the Mercedes, and it seemed a reasonable compromise.'

Rhia bent her head. 'You don't have to explain yourself to me, Mr Frazer,' she said stiffly, and he cast her a half impatient glance.

'No, I know I don't,' he conceded, starting the engine. 'But I'd hate you to think I was trying to impress you. That wasn't my intention at all.'

'I'm sure it wasn't.' Rhia spoke hotly, then endeavoured to restrain her temper. It wasn't Jared Frazer's fault that Valentina had disappeared, and she could hardly blame him for her sister's part in the proceedings.

'Valentina was driving Glyn's car, wasn't she?' he said now, as they joined the stream of traffic in the Cromwell Road. 'She told you, didn't she? That's why you were so damn scared when I suggested she'd been with him when the accident happened.'

Rhia took a deep breath. 'Why—why should you think that?'

'Why?' He made a sound of impatience. 'Miss Mallory—oh, what the hell—*Rhia!* I can't go on calling you Miss Mallory—no way could Glyn's injuries have been sustained behind the wheel of that car. To begin with, there would have been some chest damage, bruising, at least, and there isn't. His injuries are consistent with those of a passenger, a passenger who, on the moment of impact, was impelled through the windshield.'

Rhia trembled. 'Did the police tell you this?'

'Not yet, but they will. It was Glyn's doctor who expressed his opinion, and I have to say, I agree with him.'

Rhia expelled her breath wearily. 'And—and is Glyn going to be all right? I mean, now that he's recovered consciousness.'

Jared shrugged. 'Let's hope so.'

'Was—was the injury to his head all that was wrong?'

'His face is pretty badly cut about, but I'm told the lacerations will heal. There doesn't seem to be anything else wrong with him. Apart from his suspected concussion—and the interference with his sight.'

'His eyes—of course.' Rhia shivered. 'What if he doesn't accept that I'm Val? What if he finds out I'm lying?'

'Why should he?' Jared's mouth was hard. 'Your sister—Valentina, that is—told me yesterday that she'd never met my nephew. Have you?'

Rhia shook her head. 'No.'

'So.' Her companion breathed more easily. 'Glyn has nothing to base his suspicions on.'

Rhia gazed anxiously out of the car window, hardly seeing the crowds of Saturday shoppers, the hectic jam of traffic heading towards the river. She was wondering where Valentina was, wondering how long she could last without any obvious means of support, wondering how much longer she, Rhia, could evade Jared Frazer's searching questions.

It took more than an hour to reach the hospital where Glyn was a patient, and it was after one o'clock when they walked the rubber-tiled corridor to the intensive care unit. There was an air of quiet competence about the place, a reassuring sense of skill and efficiency, that made Rhia believe that if anyone could help Glyn, these people could. She hoped so, she hoped so desperately. Not only for his sake, but for her sister's.

The Sister in charge of the ward greeted Jared Frazer cordially. Evidently he was already a familiar visitor, and his introduction of Rhia was brief and to the point. Happily, Sister Harris was content with the information that this was the girl Glyn had been asking for, and Rhia did not have to make any explanations before being shown into the side-ward.

Glyn Frazer was lying on a narrow hospital bed, his skin almost as white as the pillow behind his head. He was very still, and Rhia caught her breath at the mass of small cuts and scratches that etched his pale face. There was a bandage round his head, and there were tubes attached to his nose and his wrist; and Rhia's compassion was deeply stirred by the realisation of how helpless he was.

Glancing at Jared right behind her, she made an involuntary gesture, but Sister Harris had moved past them and was crisply dismissing the young nurse seated by the bedside. Then, bending close to her patient, she said: 'Mr Frazer! Mr Frazer, are you awake? You've got a visitor.'

'Val!'

Animation gave life to those mutilated features, and Rhia caught her breath as Glyn's eyes flickered open. They were not dark eyes like his uncle's, but blue, a clear transparent shade of blue, and when they turned in her direction, Rhia almost lost her nerve.

'Val?' Glyn said again. 'Val, where are you? Sister, you said I had a visitor——'

'Don't upset yourself, Mr Frazer.' The uniformed Sister beckoned Rhia forward. 'Miss Mallory's here, right beside me. Give me your hand—there,' she reached for Rhia's frozen fingers and entwined the two together. 'Now do you believe me?'

'Oh, Val——'

Glyn's voice cracked, and Rhia, acting under the silent instructions Jared's eyes were giving her, sank down into the chair the nurse had vacated, and moistened her dry lips. 'He—hello, Glyn,' she got out jerkily, as he pulled her fingers to his lips. 'How—how are you feeling?'

'I'm okay,' he exclaimed, and her breath escaped on a shaky gasp when she realised he had apparently accepted her identity. 'How are you? You're not hurt, are you? When—when you weren't here when I woke up, I—I thought you might be—dead!'

Rhia glanced helplessly round at Jared Frazer then, and as if realising she needed his assistance, he moved forward. 'You've been unconscious for more than twenty-four hours, old buddy,' he remarked, his tone light and deliberately cheerful. 'You couldn't expect—Val—to sit with you all that time. She had to sleep, too.'

'I know.' Glyn acknowledged this, his eyes turning again in Rhia's direction, evidently more interested in her than his uncle right now. Rhia, watching those light eyes, felt the hot colour surging into her cheeks. It didn't seem possible that he could look at her without seeing her.

'You're sure you're okay?' he insisted, holding on to her fingers. 'How—how do I look? Did they tell you about my eyes? I'm having some difficulty focussing.'

'You—you look fine,' Rhia assured him huskily. 'And—and I'm sure it's only a matter of time before your eyesight is back to normal.'

'I don't look like a freak, then?' Glyn persisted, his voice growing a little breathy as his strength drained away.

'No!' Rhia was swift to answer him. 'No, of course not.'

'Then why don't you kiss me?' he demanded, gazing up at her sightlessly, and Rhia could only do as he asked with Jared Frazer and Sister Harris looking on.

Glyn's lips opened beneath her tentative caress, creating an intimacy she had not expected. She half drew back in protest, and then, her startled eyes meeting his uncle's dominant gaze, she gave in and returned his kiss.

'You can do better than that,' Glyn whispered, when she would have returned to her seat, but to Rhia's relief, Sister Harris intervened.

'Not now, Mr Frazer,' she declared firmly. 'I think you should get some rest. Miss Mallory can come back later,

if she wants to, but for the present, I think she should
leave.'

'Oh, no . . .'

Glyn protested now, but Sister Harris was insistent, and
Jared assured his nephew that 'Val' wouldn't be far away.
'Give the girl a break, eh, Glyn. And yourself, too. We
don't want you overdoing things, do we?'

Glyn twisted a little restlessly beneath the thin sheet.
'You won't go away, will you, Val? I mean—you won't
leave the hospital.'

'I——' Rhia looked up at his uncle. 'I—no. No, I won't
go away. You—you get some sleep now. I'll see you
later.'

Outside in the corridor again, Rhia faced Jared with
only mildly concealed resentment. 'You knew that would
happen, didn't you?' she exclaimed. 'You knew Glyn
would react the way he did. How can I stay at the hospital? I have commitments of my own.'

'Then I suggest you try and work out where your sister
might have gone,' Jared responded dryly, falling into step
beside her as they walked back towards the lifts. 'But for
now, I suggest you let me buy you lunch. There's a bar
right across the road where they serve a passable hamburger.'

Rhia pressed her lips together frustratedly as the huge
lift glided smoothly down to the ground floor. He was
right, of course, Val would have to be found; and when
she was, she would have to be made to face up to her
responsibilities.

Installed in the pub, with a glass of lime and lemonade
beside her, and a sesame seed roll filled with hamburger
and cheese in her hand, Rhia regarded her companion
with slightly less hostility.

'He—he seems all right, doesn't he?' she ventured, as
Jared spread his legs to accommodate hers, as they sat
together on stools over a small circular table. 'I mean, at
least there hasn't been any brain damage.'

'No.' Jared conceded the point, taking a generous
mouthful of his own roll before adding: 'Your sister can
thank her lucky stars. That's one charge she won't have
to face.'

Rhia sighed. 'You really believe she was driving, don't you?'

'Don't you?' The dark, almost black, eyes narrowed.

'Will—will Val be arrested?' she ventured, avoiding a direct answer, and Jared Frazer frowned.

'That depends.'

'Depends on what?'

'Whether a charge is brought against her.'

'But won't the police——'

'The police? You seem obsessed with the police.' He shook his head. 'I guess they could act independently, but unless Glyn chooses to implicate your sister, it might not come to that.'

'But he will, surely he will!' exclaimed Rhia fiercely. 'I mean—when he finds out she left him——'

'How will he find out? Right now, I have no intention of hindering his recovery by telling him something like that.'

Rhia gazed at him. 'You mean—you mean you still approve of—of his relationship with—with my sister?'

'*No!*' Jared was adamant about that, his dark eyes sparkling with a sudden violence. 'No, I do not—*approve* of his relationship with your sister. The way she's behaved is nothing short of criminal, and she deserves everything that's coming to her! But—and it's a big but—until Glyn is strong enough to be told the truth, until he's fully re-covered, I intend to do everything I can to avoid un-necessary publicity.'

Rhia nibbled at her sandwich. That was all very well, she thought uneasily, but what if Valentina didn't turn up? What if Glyn didn't regain his sight? Surely Jared Frazer couldn't expect her to go on acting the part of her sister indefinitely.

'At least the first hurdle is over,' Jared remarked now, finishing his hamburger and swallowing half the lager in his glass. 'Glyn accepts you as Val. He's not going to fret over why she hasn't come to the hospital to see him. That's quite a relief.'

'But I can't go on pretending to be Val,' Rhia protested. She glanced at her watch and then gasped. 'It's half past two already. I'm supposed to be meeting Simon at three!'

'Well, you can't.' Jared was infuriatingly matter-of-fact. 'You'd better ring him and tell him you'll speak to him later. If he doesn't understand, blame your sister.'

Rhia caught her breath. 'You—swine! You don't care a damn about me, do you?'

Jared studied her resentful expression for a moment, then shrugged his shoulders. 'Should I?'

Rhia's face suffused with colour. 'You know what I mean.'

'I only know that my sister-in-law, Glyn's mother, is waiting desperately for word of her son. He's all she's got. And I'll do anything I can to ensure she isn't disappointed.'

Rhia held up her head. 'Including destroying anyone who stands in your way!'

Jared grimaced impatiently. 'I'm not destroying you, Rhia. Believe me, I'm being very patient. But don't push your luck, or you may not like the consequences.'

Rhia put down the remains of her roll. 'Are you threatening me, Mr Frazer?'

'Threatening you?' His gaze moved over her anxious face in narrow-eyed appraisal. 'I doubt you know the meaning of the words. And my name is Jared. Use it. Somehow I can't believe Valentina would be so formal.'

Nor could Rhia, in all honesty. In fact, she had the distinct suspicion that in her place, Val would have found Glyn's uncle infinitely more interesting than his nephew. She wondered how he would have handled that, then thrust the thought aside. Somehow she had the feeling that any complication of that kind would only stiffen Jared Frazer's resolve to bend her to his will. He might not be old enough to be Glyn's father, but he was certainly more experienced, and Rhia wondered for the first time what his wife thought of his evident attachment to his brother's widow.

'Tell me,' he said suddenly, arousing her from her reverie, and Rhia was glad he could not read her thoughts, 'are you going to marry Simon Travis? Is that why you're so anxious to appease him?'

'I—don't know.' Rhia answered unwillingly, startled by this unexpected invasion of her personal affairs. 'I don't think it's any concern of yours, Mr Frazer. How I choose to handle my life is not your problem.'

'Jared,' he inserted flatly, and then: 'I guess that means you're not sure about him. I can't believe he hasn't asked you.'

'Mr Frazer——'

'Jared. For Glyn's sake, hmm?'

'Oh, all right—Jared.' Rhia coloured anew. 'I don't see what my relationship with Simon has to do with you. I haven't asked you any personal questions. So why should you ask me?'

Jared finished his lager and regarded her with the faintest trace of humour in his eyes now. 'Fire away,' he commented laconically. 'I've got nothing to hide.'

'I've got nothing to hide either,' exclaimed Rhia, stung by his sardonic amusement. 'I just don't think it's relevant.'

'It might be.' Jared shrugged. 'But okay—if you'd rather not talk about yourself, tell me about Travis. What does he do? Is he a government employee? What is it you call them? Civil servants? Yes, I'd guess that was what he was.'

'Well, you'd be wrong.' Rhia was vehement. 'He—he's a teacher. And you shouldn't judge people by appearances.'

'That's for sure,' he conceded lazily. 'With your hair loose like that, I'd say you were the younger sister—if I didn't know better, of course.'

Rhia put up an involuntary hand to her hair, and then realising what she was doing, let it fall. 'You're playing for time, aren't you, Mr Frazer? So long as I'm sitting here, you know where I am.'

'That's a discerning conclusion,' Jared agreed dryly, and Rhia sighed frustratedly.

'I've got to go.'

'Not yet.' Jared's hand on her arm restrained her. 'Have another drink. I'll explain the situation to your fiancé.'

'He's not my fiancé,' declared Rhia impatiently, and then wished she hadn't sounded so vehement. 'And what makes you think he'll take it from you, any better than from me?'

'Because I can be more persuasive,' retorted Jared mockingly. 'What's his number? Or shall I find it in the book?'

Rhia hesitated, but realising there was no way she could reach Simon's home in Kensal Green before three o'clock, she knew the call would have to be made. 'I'll ring him,' she said firmly, getting to her feet. 'I shall tell him I'll see him this evening. I trust you have no objections to that?'

Jared moved his shoulders in an indifferent gesture, and Rhia left him before he could say anything else to dissuade her. But all the same, she had the unwilling feeling that if Glyn needed her, she would have to comply.

As expected, Simon resented very much the idea that Rhia should be made a scapegoat for her sister's short-comings. 'We were going to the Hohenmeister exhibition this afternoon, in case you've forgotten,' he exclaimed peevishly. 'What am I supposed to do now? Go on my own?'

Rhia sighed. 'It was only a tentative arrangement, Simon,' she protested. 'As a matter of fact, I ought to be buying some food for the weekend. There's nothing in the flat, and if Val comes back——'

'Val!' Simon's use of her sister's name was vituperative. 'Just wait until I see that young lady. I'd like to give her a jolly good shaking!'

'Wouldn't we all?' murmured a sardonic voice, near Rhia's ear, and she jerked round in alarm to find Jared Frazer lounging on the wall beside the pay-phone. He gave an apologetic grimace as her expression mirrored her indignation at this invasion of her privacy, but then Simon spoke again, and she had to give him her attention.

'Anyway,' he was going on, 'I don't like you associating with that man Frazer. The elder, I mean, of course. I think the best thing I can do is come round there and wait with you. At least then I'll know what's going on.'

The shaking of Jared's head made Rhia cast him an impatient glance, but common sense, and concern for her sister, made her give the denial. 'Don't do that, Simon,' she begged, irritated anew when Jared didn't hide his approval. 'I—er—I'll come over as soon as I possibly can. And don't worry about me. I—I can handle Jared Frazer!'

Jared made no comment when she slammed the receiver back on its rest, but Rhia couldn't wait to make her objections. 'How—how dare you?' she choked. 'Deliberately eavesdropping on a private telephone call! Have you no shame?'

Jared straightened away from the wall. 'Stop dramatising the situation, Rhia. Travis will get over his pique. And if all he can think to do with your sister is shake her, I shouldn't worry overmuch about any retribution he might reserve for you. Myself, I can devise a much more painful reprisal.'

'I'll bet you can!' Rhia was not appeased. 'You had no right to listen to what Simon was saying.'

'Perhaps not. But I did. Now, forget it. Let's get another drink.'

Rhia pursed her lips. 'I'm not thirsty. I—I suggest we go back to the hospital. I—I'll speak to Glyn again, and then I'm going home.'

'As you wish.' Jared's expression was unrevealing. 'Right.'

But Rhia wished she felt as determined as she sounded. Somehow she had the feeling she was getting deeper and deeper into quicksands.

However, when they got back to the side ward where Glyn was lying, it was to find that he was sleeping.

'He seemed calmer after your visit, Miss Mallory,' Sister Harris told her, with what she evidently thought was reassurance. 'He's resting peacefully now, but you can sit with him, if you'd like to. I'm sure he'll be delighted to see you when he wakes up.'

'Oh, but——' Rhia exchanged a pregnant glance with Jared, and then subsided. 'Yes. Yes, all right,' she agreed, a little flatly, realising she had said she would wait and speak to Glyn again. 'Thank you. I'd like to sit with him.'

'Mr Frazer?'

Sister Harris turned to Jared in polite enquiry, but to Rhia's relief, he shook his head. 'No,' he said. 'No, I don't think he needs both of us sitting by his bed. I—er—I

want to ring his mother, and I need a wash. I'll go back
to the hotel—*Val*. Ring me if you need me.'

Rhia's smile was frosty, a mere observance of the formalities for Sister Harris's benefit, and she knew he knew
it by the sudden twisting of his mouth.

'Okay,' he said. 'I'll see you later.' And with a wry
smile of acknowledgement, he left them.

A nurse brought her a cup of tea at five o'clock, indicating
that there was sugar if Rhia wanted it.

'No, thanks.' Rhia mouthed the words, but she took
the tea gratefully, and was glad of the diversion.

It had been a long afternoon, and after she had drunk
the tea and placed the empty cup on the plastic-topped
tray on its metal stand that was pushed to the end of the
bed, the minutes dragged on.

She supposed if she had been Glyn's girl-friend, or at
the very least, someone who knew him and cared about
him, this time spent watching him sleep would be a time
of rest and renewal. But he was a stranger to her. Even
though she had spoken to him, even though she had *kissed*
him, she knew next to nothing about him, and she felt
terrified at the thought that he might wake up and expose
her. He could do it in so many different ways—her voice,
her behaviour, her appearance! He had only to touch her
hair to realise that unless Val was wearing a wig, she was
not her sister, and her heartbeat quickened at the realisation that she had not considered this when she bent over
him. If her hair had brushed his face . . .

She brought herself up sharply at this point. It hadn't.
So far, Glyn did not suspect anything, and surely time
was on their side. Valentina could not keep out of sight
indefinitely, and when she returned . . .

Once again, her mind blanked out. She didn't want to
think about what would happen when her sister returned.
Val had Jared Frazer to face, as well as his nephew, and
she could have no idea how ruthless he could be.

Thinking of Jared Frazer was not conducive to her
peace of mind, and determinedly, she looked at the young
man in the bed. With his eyes closed and the scars the
glass had inflicted showing up strongly against his pale

skin, he looked drained and vulnerable, and Rhia wondered anew how Valentina could have abandoned him as she had. Didn't she want to know how he was? Didn't she care if he got better? Or was her own skin so precious to her that she was prepared to sacrifice anything to save it?

Frowning, she leant forward to study Glyn's features more intently. Surprisingly, the resemblance between him and his uncle was slight: a certain likeness in the shape of his cheekbones perhaps, a similarity in colouring. But whereas Jared Frazer's face had strength and determination, Glyn's was gentler—weaker, some might say, thought Rhia candidly—though she herself preferred the former connotation. He was good-looking, certainly, in spite of the splinter cuts around his closed eyes, and judging by his length in the bed, he was not far short of his uncle's six feet two or three inches.

Relaxing back in the chair again, Rhia tried not to think about Jared Frazer, but it wasn't easy. She couldn't help wondering what he had said to Glyn's mother about the situation here, what explanations he had made to her. Had he told her Val had disappeared, or like Glyn, was he prepared to let her believe that all was well? If he had no qualms about deceiving his nephew, why should he not deceive his sister-in-law? He could always appease his conscience with the thought that it would do no good to worry her unnecessarily.

Sighing, Rhia glanced at her watch again. Nearly seven o'clock. How much longer was she expected to stay here? How much longer was Glyn likely to sleep? Surely, even if she really was his girl-friend, no one could expect her to sit here indefinitely. Her spine was beginning to feel numb, and a certain resentment was rising inside her at Jared Frazer's prolonged absence. He wasn't spending his time sitting by his nephew's bedside. Oh, no, she thought indignantly, he was at his hotel, relaxing in far more attractive surroundings, secure in the knowledge that she was confined here, imprisoned by the fabrication he had invented.

The sound of a movement behind her brought her head round with a start, and she drew a deep breath as the object of her silent recriminations allowed the heavy door to swing closed behind him.

'Hi,' he greeted her softly. 'No change?'

'No change,' agreed Rhia shortly, without looking at him again. 'How good of you to come back!'

Jared Frazer strolled over to the bed and stood looking down at his nephew, his hands pushed deep into the pockets of a pair of dark green corded slacks. They were worn with a matching jacket over a cream silk sweater, and Rhia brooded on the time it had taken for him to change his clothes.

'Sorry I've been so long,' he remarked now, turning his head in her direction. 'Lisa wasn't home when I called the first time. I didn't get through to her until lunchtime.'

'Lunchtime?' Rhia looked at her watch again and saw that it was nearing half past seven.

'Yes.' Jared moved his shoulders indifferently as he walked round the bed to where she was sitting. 'I guess it's a little after noon back home right now. Mountain time.'

'Mountain time!' Rhia couldn't help the slightly scathing note that entered her voice. 'Do you live in the mountains, Mr Frazer?'

'Close by,' he conceded, not rising to her attempt at ridicule. 'A place called Moose Bay. I guess you haven't heard of it.'

'Should I have?'

He shrugged. 'I guess not. But you have heard of Calgary, I'm sure. That's not too far away.'

Rhia refused to be diverted by this discussion of his home town. Looking up at him angrily, her eyes wide and resentful, she exclaimed: 'How much longer do you expect me to sit here, Mr Frazer? I'm just wasting my time!'

His mouth hardened. 'You said you'd stay until Glyn woke up,' he reminded her. 'I didn't guarantee how long that might be.'

'But he could sleep all night!'

'I'm well aware of that—*Val*!'

Rhia bent her head. 'I need to use the bathroom,' she mumbled, avoiding his eyes.

'Do you?' He didn't sound convinced. 'You've got no plans of walking out on me, have you?'

'No!' Rhia was sulky. 'I have been sitting here for more than four hours, you know.'

'Okay.' After a moment's hesitation, he acknowledged the veracity of her claim. 'You'll find the washrooms just down the corridor.' He paused. 'Hurry back.'

Rhia said nothing. She merely rose rather stiffly to her feet and walked to the door, pushing it open firmly, and experiencing a distinct sense of relief when it glided shut behind her.

When she came back, Jared was lounging in the chair she had been occupying, but he got to his feet at her entry and came towards her.

'The night Sister has just been in,' he told her in a low voice. 'She's of the opinion that Glyn could sleep for another three or four hours. She suggests I take you for something to eat and come back later.'

'No!' Rhia stared up at him. 'I can't do that.'

'I'm afraid you're going to have to,' he averred flatly.

Rhia seethed. 'But—Simon——'

Jared put an impatient finger to his lips, indicating the man in the bed behind them, and Rhia was forced to stifle what she had been about to say.

'One day—is that too much to ask?' he enquired, impaling her with an ebony gaze, and with a weary sigh she shook her head.

'I can't go out with you like this,' she insisted, however. She felt hot and uncomfortable, and she badly needed a wash and a change of clothes. 'Let me go back to the apartment. I can take a taxi. If you're here, Glyn won't need me.'

'And you'll come back?'

'Afterwards, yes.'

Jared frowned, and then, after giving her suggestion some consideration, he shook his head. 'I'll come with you,' he declared. 'I'll wait and bring you back again. It'll be quicker that way.'

'What you mean is—you don't trust me to come back!' Rhia had the greatest difficulty in keeping her voice down. 'I don't lie, Mr Frazer. If I say I——'

'For God's sake, stop calling me *Mr* Frazer,' he muttered harshly. 'And I am coming with you, whatever you say. I don't want Travis turning up and persuading you to abandon the whole idea.'

'He couldn't do that——'

'Couldn't he?' Jared shrugged. 'Whatever—I'm coming too.'

Glyn was left in the capable hands of another nurse, whose sympathies were all with Rhia. 'Don't you worry,' she assured her warmly. 'We'll take care of him. You enjoy the break. You look as if you need it.'

'Do I?' murmured Rhia ruefully to herself, as they walked towards the lifts, and Jared gave her a wry look.

'You play the part very well,' he remarked, infuriatingly. 'I even begin to believe you care myself.'

'I do care,' exclaimed Rhia, stung by his cynicism. 'I'd care about anyone in a similar situation.'

'How much, I wonder?' he commented obscurely, as the lift took them to the ground floor, and all the way back to the flat, Rhia pondered this imponderable.

She was relieved to find there was no sign of Simon's car in the parking area. Obviously, he had taken her at her word and was waiting for her to contact him. She would have to ring him again, she supposed, not looking forward to it. If only Simon had been a little more understanding; as it was, she felt guilty on two counts.

It was quite a chilly evening, and going up in the lift Rhia was intensely conscious of the shabbiness of her surroundings and the absence of any heating. The walls of the lift were covered with scribbled comments and the overpowering smell of pine disinfectant, that was designed to disguise any more noxious elements, seemed to cling to her clothes. She was unutterably relieved to reach the comparative sanctuary of the flat, which at least mirrored her own personality, and not that of some faceless council employee.

Aware of Jared behind her, Rhia had her key ready when she reached the door. She had wondered on the way over here whether he would wait downstairs in the car, but evidently this had not been his intention. Instead, he followed her into the hall, almost tripping over her when she bent to pick up the envelope she found lying there.

It was a telegram, a plain unadorned telegram, with a London postmark and Rhia's name printed on the envelope. Immediately, her heart somersaulted. Who but Val could be sending her a telegram, and she glanced over her shoulder at Jared, as if seeking his confirmation.

Jared closed the door and leaned back against it, his nearness a disturbing reality in the confines of the hall. 'Aren't you going to open it?' he asked, as she turned the envelope over in her hands, and Rhia's nerves tightened in anticipation of what it might hold.

'Do you want me to do it?' he suggested after a moment, but Rhia could only shake her head. If he thought she was shocked, so much the better. The truth was, she was full of apprehension, and she dreaded the possibilities of what it might say.

Turning away from him, she stumbled down the hall, slitting the flap with her thumb and pulling out the single sheet of paper. It was very short, and very simple. It was from Val, as she had suspected. It read:

GONE TO JO'BURG STOP
DON'T WORRY STOP DADDY WILL
LOOK AFTER ME STOP VAL.

CHAPTER FOUR

JARED took the telegram from her unresisting fingers as Rhia sank down weakly on to the couch. There was no point in trying to hide it from him. He would find out soon enough. And besides, just at that moment, she had no strength left to try and bluff it out.

'I assume your father lives in Johannesburg,' Jared remarked at last, and Rhia looked up at him with dazed eyes.

'He—he works there,' she admitted, moistening her lips.

'But he's never asked either Val or myself to join him.'

'I doubt your sister cares about that,' answered Jared dryly. 'She's evidently only interested in her own skin. What I find hardest to take is the realisation that she didn't even wait to find out if Glyn was going to live or die.'

Rhia shook her head. That thought had occurred to her, too, and her sister's indifference was the most painful thing to confess. How could Val have acted so recklessly, knowing full well that Rhia would be forced to bear the brunt of her selfishness?

Jared tossed the telegram on to the table. 'Well, at least you now know where she's gone.'

'Yes.' The sigh Rhia expelled left her weak. 'What will happen now?'

Jared shrugged. 'Don't look so shattered. I'll think of something. Go and take a shower or whatever you planned to do, when we came here. Do you have any coffee?'

Rhia got unsteadily to her feet. 'Not proper coffee, just instant. Why?'

'You look as if you could do with some,' he responded laconically. 'Go on. I do know how to make coffee.'

Rhia went, primarily because she was too stunned to do anything other than obey. Valentina had gone: she had actually packed her things and left the country, without even leaving her sister a note to explain her whereabouts. Oh, she had sent the telegram, probably from Heathrow, but she had known that would not arrive until she was safely out of reach.

Bundling her hair inside a shower cap, Rhia turned on the taps and allowed the cascade of water to restore feeling to her numbed body. But even after towelling herself dry and feeling the blood circulating through her torpid veins, she was still in a state of raw bemusement.

She was searching through her drawer for fresh underwear when there was a tap at her bedroom door. For a moment, she was so caught up with what she was doing, she hardly realised who it might be, and her silence encouraged the man outside to believe that she was still in the bathroom. Her door opened, and she clutched be-

latedly for the towel as Jared entered the room carrying
an earthenware mug of coffee.

'What do you——'

Her startled protest was automatic, but Jared, after only
a momentary hesitation, set the mug down on the chest of
drawers. 'Okay. I'm sorry,' he said, his tone half impatient. 'But I thought when you didn't answer that you
must still be in the bathroom.'

'Well, as you can see, I'm not.' With a gradual return
of emotion, Rhia heard the rising note of hysteria in her
voice. 'Get—get out!'

'I'm going.' Jared turned obediently towards the door,
but in the aperture he halted and looked back at her. 'I
have seen the naked female form before, you know,' he
added, with infuriating mildness. 'Enjoy your coffee.'

Even when Rhia joined him in the living room some
fifteen minutes later, her colour had not entirely subsided.
It didn't help to find him lounging on her couch, one
ankle resting loosely across his knee, scanning the morning
paper. He had discarded his jacket and loosened his tie,
and he looked very much at home. He had the ability to
adapt himself, whatever his surroundings, she reflected
unwillingly, and dismissed the unwelcome awareness of
his unconscious sexuality as he turned to look at her.

'Ready?' he asked, thrusting the paper aside and getting
to his feet.

'Ready?' Rhia looked down blankly at the brown velvet
pants and amber knitted shirt she was wearing. 'Ready
for what?'

His expression narrowed. 'We don't have to go into all
that again, do we?'

'Mr Frazer——'

'Jared!'

'Jared, then—surely—Val's telegram alters everything.'

'In what way?'

'In what way?' she repeated. 'Why, in every way. Mr—
Jared!—Val's not coming back. You know that. And
unless they have extradition proceedings for driving
offences in South Africa, I don't see how you're going to
make her.'

Jared's nostrils flared. 'You're right. I can't.'

'Well then . . .'

'Well then—what? Are you telling me you're not going to come back to the hospital? That you're going to take the chance of Glyn's having a relapse when he discovers what your sister has done?'

'That's not fair!'

'Damn you, I know it's not fair. But was any of this fair?'

Rhia's lips trembled. 'Your—your nephew shouldn't have let Val drive his car.'

'Right.' Jared inclined his head. 'So for that, he's to be made to suffer?'

'No.' Rhia was confused. 'Jared, please—you must see I can't go on with this now!'

'Why not?' Jared's brooding gaze was disconcerting. 'It was never intended to be anything more than a temporary measure. Once Glyn regains his sight, obviously he's going to know you're not your sister. Is it so much to ask that you prolong the pretence until he's sufficiently recovered to bear the truth?'

Rhia moved her head from side to side. 'You don't know what you're asking——'

'I think I do.'

'Simon won't like——'

'No, I'm sure he won't,' Jared interrupted harshly. 'But Travis isn't hovering on a knife point between life and death!'

'Nor—nor is Glyn,' she protested.

'Not right now, no,' Jared agreed bleakly. 'But God help him, he loves your sister, Rhia. Are you prepared to tell him she's run out on him?'

Rhia had turned away, too strung up to know what to think, when the doorbell rang. It could only be Simon, she knew that, and her nerves prickled at the prospect of another encounter between these two. But she had to answer it. She had to let him in. And with a helpless little gesture she moved towards the door.

Jared moved, too, more swiftly than she did, insinuating himself in the aperture between her and the hall beyond. 'Well?' he said, in a low voice, his arm barring her way. 'What's your decision?'

'My decision?' Rhia looked helplessly beyond him. 'Jared, there's someone at the door.'

'Travis, I'd guess,' agreed Jared dryly, making no move to allow her to pass him. 'Rhia, I want to know what you're going to do before you open that door.'

Rhia shook her head. 'I don't know what I'm going to do.'

'Then think.'

'Jared, let me pass.' The doorbell pealed again, and she gazed at him incredulously. 'Simon will wonder what's going on,' she exclaimed, trying impotently to remove his arm, and only succeeding in eliminating what little space there was between them.

Jared was close, suddenly too close for comfort, the clean male smell of his skin filling her nostrils and making her overpoweringly conscious of the hard strength of his lean body. Where he had unbuttoned the collar of his shirt, she could see the shadow of fine dark hair against his brown flesh, and her own skin felt sensitised by that unwanted awareness. Dear God, she thought in sudden panic, if he touched her now, she wouldn't be able to stop him . . .

Her eyes turned helplessly up to his and in that night-dark gaze, she saw the reflection of her own awareness. Without a doubt he knew what she was thinking, and embarrassment flooded her being. Then, in a moment, she was free and unimpeded, facing an empty hall. Without a word, he had removed his arm, and himself, from her proximity, and not trusting herself a backward glance, Rhia hastened to open the door.

There was no one outside, but when Rhia looked out into the corridor, she saw Simon walking back towards the lift. For a moment she was tempted to let him go, but even as common sense caused her to speak his name, he glanced back.

'Rhia!' he exclaimed, coming back more quickly than he had left. 'Heavens, I thought I might have missed you!'

'Missed me?' Rhia felt hopelessly blank, but right now her mind was occupied with other things, things she would have preferred not to think about.

'Yes, missed you.' Simon followed her into the hall, and closed the door behind them. 'I rang the hospital, you see, and they told me you'd gone home——'

'They told you—oh, Simon! What did you ring the hospital for? Couldn't you wait?'

'Don't get upset. I didn't tell them who I was,' replied Simon, rather pompously. 'Honestly, Rhia, aren't you treating this matter a little too seriously? It's not your affair——'

'Simon, please——'

Aware of Jared in the room at the end of the hall, Rhia tried to shut him up, but Simon was determined to have his say. 'It's true,' he insisted, forcing her to lead the way into the living room. 'Val's problems are her own and no one else's. You can't keep on defending her. She's old enough to look after herself. And if half of what Frazer says is true—*Frazer*!'

'That's what I was trying to tell you, Simon,' Rhia murmured unhappily, noticing that Jared had put on his jacket again in her absence, and tightened the knot of his tie. 'We—er—we've just come from the hospital.'

Simon's mouth was a thin line. 'Really?'

'Yes, really,' said Jared flatly. 'And I've got to get back there. Coming, Rhia?'

Rhia thrust her shaking hands into the hip pockets of her pants, moving her shoulders helplessly. Then, without answering Jared, she addressed Simon again. 'There—there's been a telegram. From Val,' she murmured, nodding towards the buff-coloured sheet of paper lying on the table. 'Read it.'

Simon shrugged, but curiosity got the better of him, and picking it up, he scanned its contents. Then he turned to Rhia, red-faced with anger. 'The little devil!' he exclaimed, which she privately thought was a very mild interpretation of her own feelings. 'She's done a bunk!'

Rhia sighed. 'So it seems.'

'I suppose this is genuine.'

Rhia stiffened. 'I—I don't know——'

'Has her passport disappeared?' asked Jared, with flat practicality, and after Rhia had checked, she came back into the room nodding her head.

'She wouldn't have mentioned Daddy unless she intended to involve him,' she said, scuffing the toe of her shoe. 'She knows he'll ring me as soon as she arrives.'

'Well, at least that lets you off the hook, Rhia,' Simon remarked with some satisfaction, putting a familiar arm across her shoulders. 'There's not much point in flogging a dead horse, is there?'

Jared looked at Rhia, then shrugged his shoulders. 'Are you coming?' he asked, and her stomach fluttered unhappily, reminding her she had not had anything to eat since the hamburger at lunchtime.

'Of course she's not coming.' It was Simon who answered for her, sticking his chin out aggressively, staunch and protective. 'Look here, Frazer, we've both been pretty patient——'

'I asked Rhia,' declared Jared expressionlessly. 'Well, Rhia? It's your decision.'

But it wasn't, and he knew it, damn him, she thought impotently. If anything happened to Glyn now, she would never, ever, forgive herself.

'I'm sorry, Simon,' she said now, meaning it, but Simon, correctly defining her meaning, removed his arm from her shoulders.

'You're going with him?'

'I have to.'

'You don't *have* to do anything.'

'I do.' Rhia glanced unwillingly at Jared. 'For a little while longer I have to pretend. But once Glyn is out of danger, once he's well enough to be told the truth——'

'And how long might this take?' demanded Simon angrily.

'A few days,' inserted Jared evenly.

'A few days!' Simon snorted. 'And I'm supposed to kick my heels while Rhia plays the part of the grieving girl-friend!'

'Simon, it's the least I can do, can't you see?'

'Frankly, no. But then I don't much care what happens to Frazer or his nephew.'

Jared shrugged, but to Rhia's relief he did not appear to take offence. Instead, he moved politely towards the door and when her eyes met his, he inclined his head. 'I'll wait in the car,' he said, his tone eloquent with meaning, and Rhia nodded a jerky acknowledgement.

But when Jared had left them, Simon caught her by the shoulders. 'Don't do this, Rhia,' he pleaded urgently. 'For heaven's sake, you're wearing yourself out!'

'It's only a few days, Simon.' Rhia touched his cheek. 'Don't worry, I can take it. I'd rather. I don't want this family to be involved in any more trouble.'

Simon sighed. 'What about the concert?'

'What concert?'

'The Bartok concert,' exclaimed Simon impatiently. 'Don't say you've forgotten.'

'Oh—the Bartok concert.' Rhia made an awkward gesture. 'Well, that's not until tomorrow evening, is it?'

'And do you think you'll be free tomorrow evening?'

'I don't know.'

'That's what I thought.' Simon pursed his lips. 'Oh, well, I can see that you're determined. There's nothing I can say that will deter you. I just hope you know what you're doing, that's all.'

Rhia hoped so, too, and never more acutely than at eleven o'clock that night when Glyn awakened.

After leaving the flat—and Simon—Jared had taken her to a small restaurant not far from the hospital. She had assured him a sandwich would do, but he had insisted that she eat a proper meal, and over barbecued spare ribs and a dish of savoury rice, she had had to concede how hungry she was. Jared ate little, she noticed, although he did swallow the better part of the bottle of wine he had ordered to accompany the meal, and while she ate, he told her a little about Glyn's life here in London. He spoke sparingly, merely outlining his nephew's reasons for going to college in London, and relating where he lived and what his interests were. Aware of her sister's shallow personality, Rhia did not think Val would have paid much attention to Glyn's background anyway. Her main interests had seemed to be the vapid pursuits of entertainment and pleasure, and so long as Glyn could supply them, she would be content, until something—or

someone—more attractive came along. It was amazing
that someone so frivolous could have apparently evoked
such genuine emotion, and Rhia wondered how much
longer Glyn would have been deceived.

When he stirred, Rhia's mouth went unpleasantly dry,
and she thought how typical it was that Jared should have
chosen that minute to go and talk with the doctor. He
had been sitting with her, a silent observer in the corner
of the room, no doubt conscious of the fact that any conversation between them might be overheard. But only
moments before, the consultant in charge of Glyn's case
had come into the room, and after examining his nephew
had invited Jared to join him in sister's office.

'Val!'

It was disturbing that her sister's name should be the
first that came to his lips, and Rhia leant forward and
touched his hand. 'I—I'm here, Glyn.'

'Val.' He said her name again, more confidently this
time, and those clear blue eyes seemed to look right
through her.

'How—how do you feel?' Rhia glanced apprehensively
towards the door, wishing Jared would come back.
'You've slept for hours. Are you hungry?'

Glyn's lips turned back to reveal even white teeth. 'And
have you been sitting here all this time?' he asked, his
fingers sliding over her wrist and drawing her nearer.

'Some of it,' Rhia agreed, resisting his weakened grasp
without too much effort. 'Your uncle took me to get
something to eat, but apart from that, I've been watching
you sleep.'

'Not a pretty picture.' Glyn's lips twitched. 'But not
one you're unfamiliar with, hmm?' he added revealingly,
and Rhia had to stifle a gasp. She had never considered
that Val might have been sleeping with him. And yet
why not? she conceded wryly. Her sister was a grown
woman, after all. She had to remember that.

Her silence encouraged Glyn to speak again, and he
tugged rather ineffectively at her sleeve. 'Where's Jared
now?' he asked, and it took Rhia a moment to realise he
was speaking of his uncle. When she explained he was out
of the room at the moment, Glyn went on: 'He's quite a

guy, isn't he? We all depend on him a hell of a lot.'

Rhia hesitated. 'All?' she ventured faintly.

'Sure. Mom, and Pa, and the men——'

'I thought your father was dead!'

The words were out before Rhia could prevent them, but to her relief, Glyn seemed to notice nothing amiss. 'I mean Grandpa, of course,' he explained. 'Only he's always called Pa, and I forget people who don't know him don't understand.'

Rhia nodded, and then realising he couldn't see her, she said: 'Well, I'm sure all your family will be delighted to know you're going to be all right——' she began, and then broke off with a wince when Glyn's fingers tightened round her wrist with unexpected strength.

'Am I?' he hissed urgently, and she was alarmed by his sudden attack. 'Am I going to be all right?' he demanded. 'Have you heard anything? Is there anything I should know?'

Rhia shifted uneasily on her seat, but the door remained obstinately closed, and she was forced to try and reassure him. 'Of course you're going to be all right,' she exclaimed, endeavouring to sound confident. 'Your injuries are not serious. You've got a few cuts around your eyes, and you may have some concussion, but there's no reason——'

'But I'm blind!' he broke in raggedly. 'I'm blind! I can't see a damn thing. What are they going to do about that?'

'I—don't know.' And Rhia didn't know how to handle this. 'I—I believe sometimes—after a crash—this can happen——'

'Do you? Do you?' He wanted to believe her, and she thought how tragic it was that he had never once reproached her for her supposed part in the accident.

'I'm sure of it,' she said now, pressing his arm. 'It just takes time, that's all.'

'I haven't told them, you know,' he said suddenly, in a low voice, and Rhia guessed what he was talking about. 'I wouldn't do that. It wasn't your fault. If that cat hadn't scared you . . .' He moved his head inconsequently. 'I just wanted you to know. You don't have to worry.'

If anything, Rhia felt even worse, and she was un-utterably relieved when the Night Sister entered the room. 'So—our patient's awake, is he?' she remarked, with the cheerful familiarity of her profession. 'And how are you feeling this evening, Mr Frazer? Are you going to let Miss Mallory go home and get some sleep?'

'What time is it?' Glyn was disorientated, and Sister Bainbridge glanced at the watch pinned to her apron, as she checked his chart.

'It's nearly half past eleven,' she declared, coming round the bed to take his pulse. 'And Dr Singh will want to see you, now you're awake. I suggest you let Miss Mallory come back in the morning. By then you should be feeling a lot better.'

Rhia rose to her feet. 'Yes. Yes, I'll go, Glyn,' she said, smiling at the Sister. 'I'll come back tomorrow.'

'Will they let you?' Glyn held on to her fingers. 'I mean—don't you have to work?' Then, to Sister Bainbridge, he added: 'Val's a nurse, too, in her first year at St Mary's. So I'll be in good hands when I go home, won't I?'

Rhia's face flamed with colour, but Sister Bainbridge was too busy attending to Glyn's medication to pay much attention to her appearance. 'I know a Sister at St Mary's,' she remarked, without looking up. 'Margaret Fleming. Do you know her?'

Rhia didn't, *but did Val?* 'I—the name sounds familiar,' she murmured unhappily, and Sister Bainbridge laughed.

'It would,' she chuckled, examining the drip beside him. 'I believe she's got quite a reputation with student nurses. She doesn't suffer fools gladly, doesn't Margaret.'

'Well—I'd better go.' Rhia bent quickly and deposited a light kiss on Glyn's forehead. 'See you tomorrow, hmm? Be good.'

Glyn looked as if he was going to object to that fairly impersonal salutation, but Sister Bainbridge had already taken Rhia's place, and began pushing back the sleeve of his gown, preparatory to taking his blood pressure.

'Okay,' he said, his sightless eyes turning unerringly in her direction. 'I'll see you tomorrow. Or rather—*I won't—*—'

'Come now, Mr Frazer. That's no way to bid your girl-friend goodbye.' Sister Bainbridge was not deterred. 'Didn't Dr Singh tell you there was nothing wrong with your eyes? Give them time. They've had a shock. They're just reluctant to start working again.'

Rhia emerged into the corridor with an intense feeling of exhaustion. It was ridiculous. She had done nothing. And yet she could sense Glyn's frustration, and be affected by it.

Jared was standing some yards along the corridor, still deep in conversation with a dark-skinned man in a white coat. Dr Singh? Rhia speculated bleakly, and then stiffened instinctively as Jared saw her and beckoned her to join them.

'This is Miss Mallory,' he said, by way of an introduction. 'I've just been explaining the circumstances to Dr Singh.'

Rhia looked at him. 'You mean——'

'He means, he has told me that you are not the young lady Mr Frazer believes you to be, Miss Mallory,' the doctor informed her crisply.

'I see.' Rhia caught her lower lip between her teeth. 'And—and what is your opinion?'

'Of Mr Frazer? Or of your deception?'

Rhia shrugged. 'I—well, both.'

Dr Singh hesitated. 'Mr Frazer will recover,' he said slowly. 'His visible injuries are not considerable. Indeed, I would say he might be out of this hospital in one week or less.'

'Oh, thank heaven!'

'But,' he continued heavily, 'how soon he recovers his sight is another matter.'

'But I thought his blindness was only temporary!' exclaimed Rhia, glancing to Jared for confirmation, and he nodded:

'It could be.'

'What Mr Frazer is trying to explain is that the kind of blindness his nephew is suffering from is a—how shall I put it?—a spastic condition,' said Dr Singh quietly. 'Regrettably, we do not yet know sufficient about these nervous convulsions to be able to say with any confidence how soon the sight might return.'

Rhia gazed at him. 'You mean—it could last indefinitely?'

'Of that we can be certain,' said Dr Singh dryly. 'How long indefinitely may be is another matter.'

Rhia shook her head. 'And—and Val? Do you think he should be told about Val?'

'Not at the moment.' Dr Singh sighed. 'I realise how difficult this must be for you, Miss Mallory, but I have to say this is not the time to give Mr Frazer any more unwelcome shocks.'

Rhia quivered. 'But sooner or later he's going to find out.'

'I appreciate that,' Dr Singh nodded. 'I suggest we do as the Americans say, and "play it by ear", hmm? For the moment, he needs rest and reassurance. We must see that he gets it.'

Rhia was not so sure, and Jared chose that moment to break his own bombshell. 'You say Glyn should be out of here in a week?' he queried.

'About that,' agreed the doctor consideringly. 'Maybe ten days.'

'Well, I'm afraid I can't spare that amount of time. Not now I know Glyn's going to be all right.' Jared frowned. 'What I'd like to do, if you've got no objection, is fly back home on Monday, and come back again next weekend. Then, if Glyn's fit to travel, he can come home with me. I'm sure we can make some arrangements with the hospital in Calgary to continue any treatment he may be having.'

'Of course.' Dr Singh was thoughtful. 'I can see no reason why your nephew shouldn't make the trip. Providing he's well cared for. I'm sure the airline would be happy——'

'That won't be necessary.' Jared was abrupt. 'I have my own aircraft. Glyn will receive every care and attention.'

Rhia, who was still trembling at the realisation that Jared was going to leave her to cope with Glyn's recovery alone, felt a jolt of disbelief at this news. Jared had his own aircraft! She had never even met anyone who owned a private plane before, and for the first time she wondered exactly what kind of business he was tied up with. It was all getting far too complicated for her, and she realised Simon had been more right than he knew when he warned her that she would regret this.

She hardly heard the rest of the conversation that ensued between Jared and the doctor. She was too involved with her own state of mind, and when Dr Singh bade them both goodbye and walked away towards Glyn's room, she couldn't wait to express her misgivings.

'You can't go away and leave me to it,' she exclaimed, refusing to allow him to speak. 'I can't go on with this without your help. I mean—I don't know Glyn. I know nothing about him. How do you think I'm going to manage when he starts talking about things he and Val have done together—people they both know? It's crazy! It was crazy to begin with, and it's even crazier now.'

'Look, cool it, will you?' Jared expelled his breath wearily. 'Okay, I know it looks as if I'm putting the whole weight of this on your shoulders, but if Glyn's going to be fit to come home in a week's time, I've got to go back and prepare the way.'

'Prepare the way?'

'Yes, prepare the way.' Jared moved his shoulders in an indifferent gesture. 'I've got to see Lisa, I've got to tell her how it is. Right now, she doesn't know—everything.'

'You haven't told her Glyn's blind?' Rhia stared at him.

'You got it.'

Rhia shook her head. 'Couldn't you tell her on the phone?'

Jared made a negative gesture. 'No.'

Rhia sighed. 'Why not?'

'Because I can't.' He was abrupt. 'Look, we can't talk here. Let me tell Glyn I'm leaving, then I'll drive you home.'

'Don't bother.' Rhia was in no mood to be tactful. 'I'll get a cab. I'd rather.'

'You'll never get one at this time of night,' retorted Jared tersely. 'Don't be a fool, Rhia. Wait here.'

Rhia thrust her hands into the pockets of her jacket, as

she acknowledged he was probably right, about a taxi, at least. She wished she had the guts to walk home. Right now, she badly wanted to be alone to assimilate all she had learned, and to try and face the week ahead with something less that sheer blind panic. *Blind!* Her lips twisted bitterly. She had certainly been blind to walk into this so impulsively.

Jared was coming towards her again, and she watched his approach with covert eyes. In spite of the fact that he had had little or no sleep the night before, he did not look as exhausted as she felt. On the contrary, the slight pouches beneath his eyes gave him a slightly debauched appearance that was not unattractive, and there was no trace of weariness in his deceptively indolent stride.

'Let's go,' he said, and she had no choice but to obey. Somehow, she had the feeling he was well used to giving orders and being obeyed, and she couldn't understand why Glyn's mother should receive such individual treatment.

Happily, the streets were much clearer than earlier in the day, and they made good time. It was only a quarter to one when Jared brought the Mercedes to a halt before the block of apartments, and Rhia decided that whatever happened, she would not be getting up early on Sunday morning.

However, when she would have made to get out, he laid a restraining hand upon her arm. It was very comfortable in the car, with the heating purring and the voice of Randy Crawford issuing with soft insistence from the radio, and Rhia stiffened instinctively at the implied intimacy.

'I just want to—thank you,' he said, his features shadowy in the light from the street lamps outside. 'I do—appreciate what you're doing for us. And I promise you won't lose by it.'

Rhia, who had been briefly distracted by the attractive tones of his voice, knew a sudden sense of distaste. 'I don't want anything from you, Mr Frazer,' she retorted, removing her arm from his grasp and pushing open the door of the car. 'What I'm doing, I'm doing for Glyn, not you. Goodnight.'

'Rhia——'

She heard his impatient exclamation as she hurried into
the apartment building, but she didn't stop to find out
whether he was following her. The lift stood gaping on
the ground floor, and she stepped into it without a backward glance.

CHAPTER FIVE

DURING the week that followed, Rhia did her best to forget
what Jared Frazer had said. She did her best to forget
him, but it wasn't easy when Glyn frequently mentioned
his uncle. Perhaps he found reassurance in speaking about
his family, Rhia couldn't be sure, but she did not interrupt
him. It was a relief to her not to have to play any active
part in their conversation, knowing as she did how easy it
would be to make a clumsy mistake.

Jared had left for Calgary on Monday lunchtime, after
spending most of the morning with his nephew. Rhia
had had little to do with him on Sunday, arriving at the
hospital unaided in the morning, and arranging with
Simon to pick her up in the evening, so that they could at
least attend the latter half of the Bartok concert. It was
quite a relief to sit in the auditorium of the Festival Hall
and allow the music to sweep over her, even if the memory
of Jared's taut face when she told him her plans remained
an indelible memory. After all, she had her own life to
lead, she consoled herself, ignoring the fact that part of
her guilt stemmed from the way she had behaved the
night before.

Contrary to her expectations, she had no telephone call
from her father, but she did receive a second telegram,
from him. In it, he merely confirmed that Valentina was
with him, and promised he would write later with more
details. Rhia guessed this was her sister's doing. She would
not want Rhia regaling their father with her reasons for
leaving England so precipitately, and for the present Rhia
was too tied up to care.

Her working day was the most difficult thing to explain
to Glyn. He was used to Valentina working either days or
nights, or a split shift which entailed her being there
mornings and evenings. He was not accustomed to office
hours, and Rhia had had to lie and say that she had been
given a concessionary day-shift.

'Isn't it better that I come and see you in the evenings?'
she asked, when he first protested, and without much
alternative he had had to agree.

Her worst moments came when they were alone together and he wanted to get more intimate. She was
anxiously aware that her hair, confined though it was in a
knot on top of her head, would not remain in place if he
tried to run his fingers through it. In consequence, she
had to risk his believing she was too embarrassed to indulge in any heavy petting in the hospital, and appeased
her conscience with the thought that he might think she
was cooling off, which could only be for the best.

He was certainly getting stronger, and by the middle of
the week he was up and sitting in a chair beside his bed.
He was still in pyjamas and dressing gown, of course, but
it did mean he was more mobile and consequently more
hazardous to Rhia's peace of mind.

However, his continuing blindness was beginning to
take its toll. Whereas, at the beginning of the week, she
had been able to reassure him, as each day passed without
any improvement in his sight, his depression grew, and
she began to be less troubled about his discovering her
identity than worrying about his deteriorating state of
mind. He grew morose, and listless, and spent most of the
time when she came to visit him, questioning her about
his condition. He had accepted Jared's departure for
Calgary without anxiety, content in the knowledge that
when Jared returned, it would be to take him back for a
prolonged holiday. He had even spoken of Rhia—or Val,
as he believed her to be—accompanying them for a holiday herself, assuring her she would enjoy staying on the
ranch. Rhia had received the news that Jared Frazer
owned a ranch with some surprise. In her experience, far-
mers, as they were known in England, often found it hard
to make ends meet. They did not own private planes, or

fly back and forth across the Atlantic, as easily as they drove to market. But then she knew nothing about farming methods in Canada, and she supposed Jared could be a member of some farming combine.

Simon took the news of Glyn's depression without sympathy. 'Anyone who'd let that sister of yours drive his car deserves everything he gets,' he exclaimed one evening, when he had picked Rhia up from the hospital after visiting Glyn, and driven her to his mother's house in Kensal Green. 'The man must be a lunatic! She could have killed somebody!'

'That's true, Rhia,' said Mrs Travis, setting a tray containing a plate of biscuits and three cups of tea on the table beside her armchair. Then, subsiding into the chair, and spreading her slippered feet out before her, she went on: 'You seem to forget, that young man brought this whole affair on himself. While I'm not excusing your sister—running off like that, quite unforgivable—I can't help thinking you're treating the matter far too lightly.'

'Lightly!' Rhia gazed at her aghast.

'Well—lightly in the respect that you're saving all your sympathies for Glyn Frazer, when you might conceivably consider what the consequences might have been.'

Rhia sighed. 'There's not much point in that, is there, Mrs Travis? I mean, all right, I admit Glyn shouldn't have let Val drive his car. But I know my sister. She can be very persuasive. And as Glyn obviously thought—thinks—a lot of her, he probably wanted to please her. It was wrong, we all know that, but he's the only one being made to suffer. Don't you think that's sufficient punishment for anyone?'

Mrs Travis sniffed, and Simon leant forward to help himself to a biscuit. 'Well, I tend to agree with Mother,' he remarked, not entirely to Rhia's surprise. 'And I think Frazer has taken advantage of your generosity.'

'Glyn! He doesn't——'

'No, not Glyn,' declared Simon tersely. 'I mean his uncle, naturally. Clearing off like that and leaving you to bear all the responsibility—it's not right.'

'And it's not very nice for Simon either,' put in his mother, nodding her head. 'How do you think he feels when friends come up to him and ask him why you were at the hospital? People talk!'

'Friends?' Rhia looked to Simon for confirmation. 'Who?'

'It was Toby Richards, actually,' muttered Simon, not entirely happy with his mother for bringing it up.

'Toby Richards!' Rhia gasped. 'Well, honestly, Simon, you can hardly call Toby Richards a friend!'

'No. But he is a colleague,' said Simon defensively, and Rhia shook her head.

'You see him about twice a year.'

'Yes, but he knows you. By sight, anyway.'

'And he saw me at the hospital?'

'Last weekend.' He paused. 'With—er—with Frazer, actually.'

'With Glyn!'

'Are you being deliberately obtuse, Rhia? No, of course not with Glyn. With his uncle, of course. Toby was going into the hospital, to visit his mother, just as you and Frazer were coming out.'

'Oh, I see.' Rhia was beginning to understand. It wasn't so much her visiting Glyn that Simon objected to, as being seen with another man. She knew of Toby Richards' reputation, and she could quite imagine the interpretation he had given Simon.

'So, how is he this evening?' Mrs Travis interposed quickly, noticing the indignant sparkle that had come into Rhia's eyes, and unwilling to be accused later of starting an argument. She could never be sure which side Simon was going to take. Even when her claims were justified, he often took Rhia's part, and she had no wish to fall out with him.

Rhia, tempted to ignore the question and pursue the matter of Toby Richards further, gave in. She had no real desire to fall out with Simon either, and schooling her features, she forced a faint smile.

'Physically, apart from his eyes, that is, he seems to be getting stronger. But this obstruction of his sight is the real problem.'

'Can't he see anything?' asked Mrs Travis curiously.

'I'm afraid not.' Even thinking about it made Rhia feel

so helpless. 'Poor Glyn, I feel so sorry for him.'

'And Frazer's playing on that,' exclaimed Simon, losing patience. Getting to his feet, he surveyed her frustratedly. 'When is he coming back? When can we expect to be free of this—this duty? Rhia, I've been very tolerant, but I'm beginning to feel stifled by it all.'

'I'm sorry you feel like that, Simon.' Rhia put down her teacup and folded her hands. 'What would you have me do? Stop visiting him?'

Simon hunched his shoulders. 'You make it sound like a crime!'

'And wouldn't it be? Cruel, anyway.'

Simon drew a deep breath. 'Okay. But when his uncle gets back——'

'When his uncle gets back, he's going to take him home,' declared Rhia firmly, and stifled the realisation that for all her misgivings, she was going to miss Glyn.

On Thursday evenings she didn't see Simon, and she arrived home from the hospital at about half past nine to hear the telephone ringing in the apartment. Expecting it to be him, Rhia didn't hurry, but when she eventually lifted the receiver she had the strange sensation that she was listening to space. Immediately, her mind jumped to her father, and the possibility that he had decided to ring after all, but then another voice spoke, deep and vibrant, and she realised it was Jared Frazer.

'I didn't get you out of bed, did I?' he enquired, after she had answered his greeting, and Rhia made a sound of indignation.

'I've been at the hospital, visiting your nephew,' she retorted, taking her bag from her shoulder, with fingers that were not quite steady, and dropping it on to the couch. 'Where—where are you calling from?'

'Moose Bay,' he replied flatly, his voice echoing hollowly on the line. 'I just wanted to ask you how you think Glyn is progressing.'

'If you rang the hospital——' began Rhia quickly, unsure why he should be calling her, but Jared cut her off.

'I have rung the hospital,' he declared. 'And spoken with Glyn, as it happens. I guess it must have been just after you'd left. That's why I'm ringing you.'

Realising her palm was sticking to the receiver, Rhia herself sank down on to the couch, and shifted the phone into her other hand. 'But why?'

'You know why, Rhia. Glyn's not responding to treatment, is he? And according to Singh, he's in a pretty low state of mind.'

Rhia sighed. 'I'm afraid that's true.'

'He hasn't guessed—he doesn't suspect——'

'Me?' Rhia shook her head. 'No. No, I don't think he suspects anything like that. But he is upset because his sight isn't returning.'

'So I believe.' Jared sounded grim. 'God knows how he's going to adapt to an indefinite period of blindness!'

Rhia made a helpless gesture. 'It may not come to that, Jared. I mean—give it a little longer before you start jumping to conclusions. Nerves are funny things. Maybe he just needs to relax, away from the hospital.'

'You're very reassuring,' remarked Jared dryly, his wry humour stirring her unwilling pulses. 'What a pity you're not a nurse, instead of your sister. I think you've missed your vocation.'

Rhia had to laugh, and Jared gave a rueful sigh. 'You should be here, you know that?' he added, bringing an uneasy flutter to Rhia's stomach. 'I could do with your support.'

'W-why?' Rhia paused. 'Did you tell your sister-in-law?'

'About Glyn's blindness? Yes, I told her. She took it pretty badly, as I knew she would. Even my father feels the strain.'

'I'm sorry.' The words were trite, but Rhia couldn't think of any others. 'I—when—when will you be back?'

'Why? Have you missed me?' he asked, half teasingly, and Rhia's own nerves quivered.

'Naturally—naturally Glyn has missed you,' she said, avoiding a direct reply. 'I—I think he'll feel better when he leaves the hospital.'

'Do you?' Jared did not sound convinced. 'And I guess Travis will feel better too, won't he?'

'My visiting Glyn is not hurting Simon,' Rhia replied

firmly, not quite knowing why he was bringing this up.

'Good.' Jared essayed his approval. 'Well, I'm flying back Friday night. I'll give you a call Saturday morning, if that's okay.'

'Of—of course.' Rhia felt a ripple of anticipation slide along her spine.

'Okay.' Jared prepared to ring off, and then, just as Rhia was about to offer her goodbyes, he said: 'About the other night—I want to apologise——' And when she tried to protest, he added: 'Listen. I didn't mean to offend you, I just wanted to show my gratitude.'

'It's all right. Really.' Rhia was embarrassed, but Jared did not spare her blushes.

'I don't know what either. Glyn—or I—would have done without you,' he said, his voice low and resonant. 'See you Saturday. Goodnight.'

Rhia replaced the receiver carefully, sitting for several minutes just staring at the phone before getting up and taking off her coat. She realised she was feeling decidedly shaky, and she chided herself for being affected by the unconscious charm of the man. He was being polite that was all. His reasons for calling her had been painfully obvious. He was worried about his nephew, and after speaking with Glyn, he had needed reassurance that his anxieties were not misplaced. Nevertheless, she could not deny that he was an attractive man, and she thought it was just as well it was Glyn, and not Jared, who was needing her help. The idea of sitting with him for hours on end was a disturbing one, and to imagine kissing him, as she was getting used to kissing his nephew, evoked a sudden pain in the pit of her stomach. Jared had such an attractive mouth, narrow-lipped and faintly cynical, and the idea of feeling those firm lips parting hers brought a wave of heat surging through her body.

Her foolish emotions irritated her, however, and she hung up her coat with impatient hands. It wasn't as if she was a schoolgirl, attracted by the first man who showed an interest in her, she thought irritably. Heavens, she was twenty-one years old; she had had boy-friends since she was sixteen, and she and Simon had been going out together now for almost three years! She was letting the emotions she felt for Glyn get mixed up with her feelings towards his uncle, and the sooner both of them got out of her life, the better.

Nevertheless, she could not prevent the sense of anticipation she felt on Saturday morning, when she awakened to the awareness that Jared was probably already back in England. Making her morning tea and taking a cursory glance at the newspaper, she was overwhelmingly aware that she was waiting for his call, and when the phone rang, she practically leapt to answer it.

It was Simon, and trying not to reveal her disappointment, Rhia endeavoured to concentrate on what he had to say:

'As Frazer will probably be leaving in the morning, I thought we might drive over to Reading for the day,' he suggested. 'Mother would like to see Aunt Edna, and I thought, after lunch, you and I might spend the afternoon at Henley—what do you say?'

The idea of Sunday lunch with Simon's Aunt Edna was not particularly appealing. She was Mrs Travis's sister, and like Simon's mother she enjoyed nothing better than discussing her ailments. The two of them would happily spend the lunchtime period talking about their various operations, while Rhia would have the greatest difficulty in swallowing roast beef and Yorkshire pudding in company with glandular complaints and gallstones.

'Oh, Simon,' she said now, 'could I think about that? I'm not sure when the Frazers are leaving, and I'd really like tomorrow free, to catch up on my housework. With going to the hospital every evening, I've done practically nothing, and I've a load of laundry waiting in the washer.'

'I shouldn't have thought one more day would make much difference,' Simon replied crisply, and Rhia sighed.

'But I'll be back at work on Monday,' she explained. 'Weekends are the only time I'm really able to get on.'

'That wasn't what you said last weekend, when Frazer had you spending the whole day at the hospital.'

'That was different,' Rhia insisted resignedly. 'Look, Simon, I'm sorry, but I'm going to have to leave it for now. I'll see you this evening. We can discuss it then.'

'We can't. Aunt Edna will need to make provision, if the three of us are joining her and Sybil for lunch.' He paused, and when she made no comment, he added: 'Very well, then, Mother and I will go alone. I'm sorry, Rhia, but you can't expect me to hang about on the offchance that you *might* be free.'

Rhia felt mean for disappointing him, but unutterably relieved that she would not have to listen to another recital of Aunt Edna's thyroid operation. 'I'll see you tonight, then,' she said, feeling contrite, and with a curt word of agreement, Simon rang off.

The phone rang again as she was getting dressed, and pulling her shirt over her shoulders, she hurried to answer it. This time it was Jared, and her stomach wobbled at the familiar drawl of his voice.

'Hi,' he greeted her lazily. 'When can we meet? I wondered if you'd care to join me for lunch. You and— Travis, if he's around.'

'I'm not seeing Simon until this evening,' confessed Rhia breathily, mentally going over the contents of her wardrobe. 'But—lunch would be fine. When, and where?'

'Do you know a restaurant called The Gondoliers?'

Rhia's lips parted. She had heard of it, of course. Who hadn't? 'Yes,' she said, crossing her fingers, and Jared sounded relieved.

'Okay. We'll meet there at—let me see—one o'clock, right? We can visit Glyn afterwards. Then I'll fetch you home.'

'Fine.' Rhia swallowed. 'One o'clock.'

'One o'clock,' he agreed, and rang off before she could ask what kind of flight he had had.

While she took off her clothes again and took a shower, Rhia wondered what kind of plane it was that took him back and forward across the Atlantic. Who flew it? Surely he didn't fly it himself. It didn't seem credible that he could fly over four thousand miles and still have the energy to take her out for lunch.

Choosing something to wear presented a problem. She didn't want to disgrace him, but equally, she didn't want him to think that she was trying to attract his attention,

and inevitably she came up with the realisation that that
was exactly how she was behaving. It sobered her, that
knowledge, and schooling her chaotic thoughts, she chose
a plain black suit made of a fine mixture of polyester and
wool, that she had bought to attend a conference with Mr
Wyatt the previous November. It was neat and businesslike, and her only concession to fashion was a plain cream
blouse, with a cascade of cream lace at the neckline.

Her hair coiled into a smooth roll, and she allowed
several errant strands to tumble by her ears, softening the
severe style. She was aware that the black suit formed a
startling contrast to her blonde colouring, but she was
pleased with her appearance, and refused to reconsider
the advisability of her choice.

She took a taxi to the restaurant, primarily because she
wasn't absolutely sure where it was, and she was glad she
had when the driver wove his way in and out among the
streets surrounding Claridge's. But eventually he deposited her on the pavement outside the rather ordinary-
looking façade of The Gondoliers and Rhia hastily paid
him before watching him drive away.

She had expected Jared would be waiting outside for
her. It was already ten minutes past one, the cab having
become snarled up in the lunchtime traffic, and she looked
about her doubtfully, before entering a green-shadowed
lobby. A uniformed commissionaire came towards her,
and taking a deep breath, Rhia asked him whether a Mr
Jared Frazer had been there.

'Yes, Mr Frazer's here, miss,' the man answered, not at
all surprised by her enquiry. 'You go on in and ask for his
table. The maître d'hotel will see that you're all right.'

'Thank you.'

Smiling her gratitude, Rhia passed through the door
he held open for her into a moderately-sized restaurant,
artificially lighted by a series of conically-shaped lamps.
The tables were set well apart, and the lamplight glinted
on fine napery and polished cutlery. Rhia found herself
standing beside a desk, where the head waiter was idly
scanning the list of bookings, but he turned at her appearance, and made himself polite.

'Mr Frazer's table,' he said, his accent more cultivated

than cultured, Rhia suspected, but then she saw a man threading his way through the tables towards her. It was Jared, even in the discreet lighting of the restaurant his tall frame and dark countenance were unmistakable, and Rhia's fingers tightened round the bag she was clutching until her knuckles ached.

'It's okay, Luigi, the lady's with me,' he remarked, as he approached, and the man beside Rhia bowed his head in silent deference.

'I'm sorry if I've kept you waiting,' she began, not sure whether or not he expected to shake hands with her, and when he didn't, hastening on: 'The taxi got stuck in the traffic, and then when I got here, I thought you might have gone——'

'I wouldn't do that,' Jared interrupted her dryly, and she realised she was babbling on like some excited teen-ager. 'Come on, our table's over here. We can have a drink before we decide what we're going to eat.'

Rhia managed an awkward smile, going ahead of him when he directed her, overwhelmingly aware of him behind her, watching her every move. Heavens, this was ridiculous, she thought impatiently, trying to still her tumultuous emotions, but seeing him again was disturbing, more disturbing than she had anticipated, and her eyes turned back to his lean face in helpless fascination.

But he was not looking at her, he was looking beyond her, and when she was forced to pay attention to where she was going, she saw that someone else was sitting at the table they were making for. It was a woman, she saw with apprehension, a young woman, older than herself, but not that much older, perhaps in her late twenties or early thirties, a slim dark woman, with delicately pointed features.

Rhia's head spun round to look at Jared again, half prepared to believe that he had made a mistake, and that this really wasn't their table, but this time his dark gaze met hers and she knew that he had apprehended her confusion.

'Allow me to introduce you to my sister-in-law,' he said, inclining his head politely. 'Lisa, this is Valentina's sister, Rhia.'

Lisa Frazer's skilfully defined lips revealed even white teeth. 'I'm so pleased to meet you, Rhia,' she declared with easy informality, holding out her hand. 'Jared's told me what you've done for my son, and I really am extremely grateful.'

Rhia took the hand that was offered.

'I—it's nothing,' she murmured, subsiding into the chair Jared held for her, hardly able to believe that this woman was Glyn's mother. She didn't look old enough, she didn't even look old enough to be a widow, and with this thought came the uneasy realisation that Lisa was looking at Jared with a far from sisterly affection.

'What will you have to drink, Rhia?' Jared asked, taking his own seat again, and she sought about confusedly for her reply.

'Oh—just a dry Martini,' she answered, trying to instil her voice with some enthusiasm, and as he raised his hand for the waiter, she said: 'Have you seen Glyn yet, Mrs Frazer?'

'Yes.' Lisa picked up her own glass and surveyed its contents thoughtfully. 'We went straight to the hospital from the airport.'

'And—how was he?' Rhia felt obliged to ask, even though she had seen Glyn herself only the night before.

'He was—morose, uncommunicative,' declared Jared, before his sister-in-law could reply, and Lisa's lips pouted prettily.

'Don't say that, darling,' she exclaimed, patting his sleeve with expertly-lacquered nails. 'Rhia will think Glyn wasn't pleased to see me, and you know he was.'

'Rhia's not a fool, Lisa. She knows the the state Glyn's in better than anyone,' Jared retorted, thanking the waiter for delivering Rhia's drink. 'We might as well be honest about this: the prognosis is not optimistic.'

'Oh, come now, Jared.' Lisa's fingers curved possessively round his sleeve. 'Once Glyn's back home, once he's able to get on his horse, and feel the wind in his face——'

'You're not being realistic, Lisa.' Jared's tone was flat. 'Who do we think we're kidding? Glyn left Moose Bay because he wasn't interested in the ranch or in farming in general——'

'That's not true.' Lisa looked hurt, and Rhia began to wish that she had not accepted this invitation after all. 'Jared, Glyn needed to get away for a while, that's all. To spread his wings. You know as well as anyone how confining the ranch can be. Why, when Angus was alive, I remember you and he didn't always see eye to eye.'

'Maybe.' Jared cast a brooding glance in Rhia's direction. 'But the fact remains, I stayed. I rode the rough patches and made it. I don't know whether Glyn even *wants* to make it.'

'He wants to please you,' Lisa insisted, eyes of a peculiar light grey colour gazing into his. 'Jared, be patient. Glyn will see sense. And once he's home . . .'

'Lisa, Glyn's not going to see anything for the next few weeks, possibly even months,' Jared exclaimed brutally, and Rhia bent her head to avoid looking at the other woman. 'But I agree, we have no option but to take him back to the ranch. However, I also think we should consider his suggestion seriously.'

'Oh, Jared!' Lisa withdrew her hand abruptly, and Rhia wished herself miles from here as Jared turned to her.

'It's you,' he said, and Rhia's colour came and went beneath his steady gaze. 'He wants you to come back with us,' he explained, causing her breathing to become constricted, somewhere in the back of her throat. 'I told him it was impossible, that you had a job of work to do. But he insists that you and he have discussed it, and you didn't offer any objection.'

'I—I——' Rhia couldn't answer him. It was true, Glyn had mentioned that she should visit the ranch, but they had hardly discussed it; and in any case the invitation was not to her, but to Val!

'It's obvious Rhia knows nothing about it,' declared Lisa shortly, her sharp nails plucking impatiently at the handle of a piece of cutlery. 'And in any case, the whole idea is ridiculous. Glyn needs a nurse, not a girl-friend!'

'But you forget, Glyn thinks Rhia—or rather, Valentina—is a nurse,' replied Jared tersely. 'And it's not such a crazy idea as it may seem. Okay, Glyn needs a rest, he needs to relax; but will he, with only you and me for company?'

'There's your father,' Lisa protested, but at this point, Rhia had to intervene.

'I—I don't know what Glyn's said to you, Mr Frazer——'

'Jared!' he said doggedly, and she flushed.

'Jared, then. But—well, I couldn't possibly accompany him to Canada. I—why, the idea's ludicrous!'

'Is it?' Jared held her wavering gaze. 'Even if it might make the difference between Glyn's success or failure?'

'Don't be melodramatic, Jared.' Lisa gave Rhia a vaguely impatient look. 'What can she do that we can't?'

'Well, to begin with, she can bridge the gulf between his life here and the life he'll be forced to lead in Moose Bay,' essayed Jared crisply.

'You forget——' Rhia spread her hands, 'I'm not Val.'

'Glyn thinks you are. That's what's important.'

Rhia shook her head, too bemused by this whole conversation to be able to think coherently. Jared couldn't seriously believe she might be persuaded to give up her job and accompany them back to some unknown place in the Mid-West of Canada, could he? It wasn't logical. And aside from everything else, she could imagine what Simon would say!

'Listen to me, Rhia.' Jared was speaking again, while his sister-in-law lay back in her chair, sipping her drink with evident dissatisfaction. 'I'm not asking you to give up your life here, or anything dramatic like that. You have holidays, don't you? All I'm asking is that you consider taking your holiday now—and with us.' He paused. 'I'd offer to pay you, if you weren't so damn touchy, but if that offends you, at least believe you'd enjoy every comfort we could supply.'

Rhia moistened her lips. 'You don't seem to understand. It's not just—that. Glyn's on his feet now, he can move around. Oh, at present, as you say, he's too wrapped up in his own misery to pay too much attention to me. But—but if he was home, if he began to gain confidence, he—well, he'd soon discover I wasn't who I said I was.'

'How?' Jared ignored his sister-in-law's discontented

face and gave Rhia his full attention, and she sighed.

'Well—my hair, for one thing. Val—Val's hair is short, and—and curly. But you know that. Mine—mine isn't.'

'You could always cut your hair,' inserted Lisa shortly, stung by Jared's continued rejection. She snorted. 'If it weren't all so ridiculous, I've no doubt a haircut and a perm would solve the problem.'

'But I don't want a haircut and a perm, Mrs Frazer,' Rhia replied stiffly, her hand going protectively to her nape.

'You could wear a wig,' remarked Jared quietly. 'And I'd try to see there weren't that many occasions when wearing it was a necessity.'

Rhia shook her head, and Lisa leant her elbows on the table. 'Can't you see, she doesn't want to do it, Jared, and I don't blame her. I'm sure a girl as—attractive—as Rhia has friends—*boy*-friends of her own. You can't expect her to give them up——'

'I'm not asking her to give anything up,' retorted Jared curtly, and then looked up impatiently when the waiter appeared silently at his side. 'Oh—yes. Yes, we'll have the menu now. We can continue this conversation after the meal.'

Rhia knew the food was delicious, but she didn't enjoy eating it. Smoked salmon served with prawns, a juicy fillet steak: she knew she had never been served anything nicer. But she was overwhelmingly aware of the atmosphere around the table, the conflicting emotions that gave their features expression; and although there was no dearth of conversation, what there was was stilted and strained.

Refusing a dessert, Rhia accepted coffee, but no liqueur, the wine Jared had had served with the meal more than enough to make her feel heady. And she needed to keep her wits about her in this society, she thought rather tensely, waiting with bated breath for Jared to pursue his argument.

But he didn't. Instead, while Lisa carried on an apathetic, if polite, discussion with Rhia over the relative attributes of various kinds of fabric, he sat and stared into his drink, responding in monosyllables every time his sister-in-law endeavoured to draw him into the conversation.

It was nearly three when they left the restaurant, and explaining that he had left his car at the hospital, Jared summoned a cab to take them across London. In the cab, as in the restaurant, he said little, and it was left to Rhia and Lisa to bridge the awkward gap his silence created.

'Darling, aren't you being a little unkind?' Lisa asked once, laying her hand familiarly on his knee. 'I think Rhia's done a wonderful job. But it's natural that she should want to lead her own life.'

Jared inclined his head, neither acknowledging nor negating her comments, but his dark gaze slid broodingly over Rhia, and she was made uncomfortably aware of his censure.

Glyn was waiting for them, and Rhia was embarrassed when he insisted on kissing her in front of his mother and his uncle. 'Isn't she beautiful?' he asked his mother proudly, keeping Rhia's hand tight within his own. 'I'm crazy about her, and she knows it. I don't know what I'd have done without her this past week.'

Lisa's smile was a little frosty as she seated herself beside her son, and he was forced to relinquish Rhia's fingers when his mother insisted on taking both his hands in hers.

'You're coming home with us,' she told him huskily, holding on when he would have released himself. 'Once you're home, all this will seem like a bad dream. You'll see. In no time at all, you'll feel entirely different.'

'Will I, Mom?' Glyn did pull himself away from her now, getting up from his chair and walking unsteadily across the room. Rhia saw the trolley in his way, but she was too late to prevent him walking into it, and he grasped it for support before shoving it savagely out of the way.

'Oh, yes,' he muttered, and Rhia cast Jared a painful glance as she supported Glyn back to his chair, 'I'll feel different all right. The only difference will be that I'll have plenty of space to fall about in.'

'Glyn, you won't fall about.' It was Rhia who spoke, Rhia who stood beside his chair and allowed him to hold on to her hands. 'Believe me, you're going to get better. Just give it time. Give it time!'

Glyn shook his head, looking up at her with those tragic sightless blue eyes. 'I'm frightened, Val,' he said, and her heart plunged at his painful vulnerability. 'I want to go home——'

'Of course you do,' Lisa exclaimed, but Glyn ignored her.

'I want to go home,' he repeated, 'but I don't want to go alone.'

'You won't be alone,' his mother protested, but this time a look from Jared silenced her.

'I want you to come with me, Val,' Glyn continued, as if Lisa hadn't spoken. 'I want you to come to Moose Falls. You will come, won't you? If—if you don't, I won't go either!'

CHAPTER SIX

'YOU knew that would happen, didn't you?' Rhia faced Jared in the living room of the apartment, her lips trembling as she endeavoured to articulate her indignation. 'You knew what Glyn would say. You knew how he would react, as soon as his mother mentioned taking him home. Oh, how could you? How could you? You're despicable!'

Tears were very close, and Rhia turned abruptly away, unwilling for him to see how emotional she felt. Perhaps it would have been better if they had not had this opportunity for conversation, she thought. Given time, she might have been able to marshal her arguments better. As it was, she was too shocked and helpless to offer any coherent objection, and she knew how easily she could say something she would regret.

Shrugging his shoulders, Jared flung himself on to her couch, and glancing round at him Rhia thought again how easily he could adapt to his surroundings. Compared to someone who flew the Atlantic in his own aircraft, this apartment must seem very drab and ordinary, and yet he used its accoutrements with the minimum amount of fuss.

They had left the hospital three-quarters of an hour ago, and after dropping Lisa at the hotel, Jared had driven

Rhia home. She had wanted to take a cab, wanted this
time to herself, but he wouldn't hear of it. And in spite of
his sister-in-law's evident pique, he had got his own way,
as usual, and once here he had insisted on accompanying
her inside.

'Okay,' he said, when she persisted in keeping her back
to him. 'So I knew how Glyn would react.' He loosened
the knot of his tie. 'You must have known it, too, if he has
discussed it with you.'

Rhia swung round. 'He didn't—discuss it with me,' she
declared hotly. 'He just said—he just said I would enjoy a
holiday at the ranch. That was all—I swear it.'

'Okay, okay.' Jared's night-black eyes showed he
believed her. 'Don't get so steamed up. You would—you
will—enjoy visiting the ranch——'

'I won't!' Rhia clenched her fists. 'I won't, because I
won't be coming!'

Jared gazed up at her intently for several seconds, then
got to his feet again, tall and broad and distinctly threatening. 'What do you mean—you won't be coming?' he
demanded. 'You told Glyn you would.'

'I know what I told Glyn.' Rhia put up an unsteady
hand to her head. 'But—but I can't. You must see that I
can't. Jared, please, don't look at me like that. I—I can't
go through with it.'

'Why not?' Jared took a step nearer to her, and although she was a tall girl, she had to tilt her head to look
up at him.

'I—I—because I can't.'

'You can take a holiday, can't you? Or leave of absence?
I've told you, I'd reimburse you for any expense——'

'It's not that.'

'Then, for heaven's sake, what is it?' Jared's face contorted with impatience, and his hands descended painfully
on her shoulders, imprisoning her within his grasp. 'Rhia,
I don't believe you're so insensitive you don't know what
you're saying. If you don't come with us, Glyn will refuse
to leave, too, and that will break his mother's heart!'

Rhia doubted anything to do with her son would truly
break Lisa Frazer's heart. Jared, yes. It was obvious from
the way she treated him, from the way they behaved with

one another, that their relationship possessed an intimacy only lovers could share, and Rhia's resentment was fuelled by the awareness that Jared's concern was as much for Lisa as for his nephew.

'I'm sorry,' she said now, keeping her head down, concentrating on the top button of the dark brown waistcoat that matched the rest of his suit, but she could sense his frustration.

'It's Travis, isn't it?' he snapped angrily, bringing her head up in protest as his fingers bit into her bones.

'No,' she exclaimed, 'that isn't the reason. If you must know, I can't go through with it because of Glyn.'

'Glyn?' Jared's eyes narrowed. 'What has he done?'

'It's not what he's done,' retorted Rhia, wincing at his continued violence. 'Jared, you're hurting me!'

'Tell me how Glyn presents any obstacle to you,' he commanded, and realising he was not going to let her go until she did, Rhia drew a deep breath.

'He—he and Val had—had a relationship.'

'God, I know that.'

Rhia gasped. 'And that doesn't suggest any obstacles to you?'

'Not insurmountable ones, no.' He sighed. 'Rhia, I've seen him kiss you, and you don't exactly object——'

'You—*bastard!*' Rhia gazed up at him resentfully, and Jared's face darkened with hot colour.

'Am I?' he muttered, looking down at her with smouldering impatience. 'Because I tell it how it is, you call me a bastard.'

'That's not how it is,' cried Rhia fiercely. 'I—I don't like it. I don't want him to kiss me. But I have no choice.'

'You're not frigid, are you?' he asked, his voice harsh and insulting, and Rhia caught her breath, hardly capable of believing this was happening.

'I don't know whether I'm frigid or not,' she declared proudly. 'I haven't felt the need to find out. I'm not in the habit of indulging in promiscuous relationships——'

'Then let's find out, shall we?' Jared muttered, jerking her towards him, and before she had a chance to offer any protest, his searching lips had captured hers.

It was not as if she had never been kissed before, Simon

had kissed her many times, but he had never aroused the wild singing in her ears that Jared aroused. Although his lips were hard and angry, she responded without volition, her mouth opening under his and evoking an intimacy he could not have expected.

With a groan of anguish, he moved his hands from her shoulders to her throat, and for a heart-stopping moment she thought he meant to strangle her. But instead his palms cupped her nape and held her closer, his mouth softening and gentling to a blinding sweetness.

Weakness made Rhia's knees sag, and she clutched at him helplessly, her arms sliding beneath his jacket to en- circle the leanness of his hips. Her action brought the lower half of his body closer to hers, and with a trembling sense of recognition she felt the swollen hardness of muscle probing against her.

'God—*Rhia!*'

Before her own scattered senses could form their own assessment of what was happening, Jared had propelled her away from him, raking back his hair with shaking fingers. 'I think we can safely say you're not frigid!' he muttered, with a bitter attempt at humour. 'God, Rhia, I'm sorry. I didn't mean to do that, and God help me, I didn't expect it to go as far as it did. I'm sorry.'

Rhia said nothing. She felt too stunned, too numb, to make the kind of casual comment he no doubt expected of her. Perhaps he was doubting her earlier protestations of innocence. Certainly, he had every reason to do so. She had not acted like an innocent, and she could hardly tell him that he was to blame, that until he kissed her she had not believed herself capable of emotions like she was ex- periencing now. He was prepared to accept responsibility, and she had to let him, even while her body ached for him to touch her again. Her eyes drifted down, over the taut muscles of his thighs, and her senses reeled.

'Don't look at me like that,' Jared said harshly, tipping back his head, as if the muscles at the back of his neck ached. 'Rhia, I have got to go. Lisa,' she thought he said the name deliberately, 'Lisa will be wondering where I am.'

'Of course.' Rhia got the words out with difficulty.

'Don't—don't let me detain you.'

'*Rhia!*' The near-black depths of his eyes were tormented as they sought hers. 'Don't make this any harder than it already is. I guess I've done enough damage for one afternoon, don't you?'

Rhia turned abruptly towards the door, but he caught her arm and swung her back to face him. 'I suppose there's no way you could not let this influence you, is there?' he demanded, and his lean face had a disturbingly defeated vulnerability.

'I—I did say I couldn't—go,' she said jerkily. 'Be—before you touched me.'

'Yes, but for God's sake, Rhia, Glyn needs you! We all—need you!'

Rhia pulled away from him. 'I—I think you'd better go——'

'*Rhia!*'

'I can't go with you,' she insisted. 'You can't make me!' But when he gave her one last brooding look before striding out of the flat, she knew he would not give up that easily.

She was expected to go to the hospital that evening, and unable to disappoint Glyn this last time, Rhia rang Simon and asked him if he would take her.

'And then what am I supposed to do?' he demanded. 'Sit outside like a banana, while my girl-friend plays nursemaid to a spoilt little rich boy!'

'Oh, Simon, Glyn's not spoilt—at least, not a lot anyway. And it will only be for an hour. We had arranged that you should pick me up there, hadn't we?'

'And so I will,' agreed Simon pedantically. 'Eight o'clock, didn't you say?'

Rhia's nerves tightened and her patience, drawn to a feverish thread by what happened between her and Jared, snapped. 'Don't bother!' she said tersely. 'I'll take a bus there, and home. That way, you won't have to leave the comfort of your mother's fireside!'

'*Rhia!*' Simon sounded hurt now. 'There's no need for you to take that attitude. I think I've been very patient this last week, putting up with all these unnecessary visits to the hospital. You can't expect me to play chauffeur every time you need me.'

'This is the first time I've asked you,' declared Rhia tensely. 'And they haven't been unnecessary visits. Glyn's blind! Can't you at least try to imagine how he must feel? And how I feel, too, knowing my sister was responsible!'

'I think you've flogged that particular horse to death,' retorted Simon, recovering his indignation. 'As Mother says, your sister appears to mean more to you than I do.'

'Oh, Simon!' Rhia felt an intense weariness. Then, remembering the rapture she had felt in Jared's arms, she nodded to herself. 'Perhaps—perhaps you're right,' she agreed heavily. 'Maybe it would be an idea to give our relationship a breathing space.'

'What do you mean?' Simon was anxious now. 'Look, Rhia, just because I've made a bit of a stand about being made use of, it doesn't mean you have to go off the deep end!'

'I'm not.' Rhia felt incredibly weary suddenly. 'I accept what you say. I have expected a lot of you. I'm sorry, I didn't mean to hurt you.'

Simon made a sound of impotence. 'You haven't *hurt* me, Rhia,' he protested. 'Angered me, yes, but that's nothing new, is it? It's not the first time you've annoyed me over Val, and I don't suppose it will be the last.'

'What do you mean?' Rhia was confused. 'How have I annoyed you over Val?'

'It doesn't matter.' Simon was irritatingly smug.

'It does matter.' Rhia insisted on knowing. 'What did I do? I want you to tell me.'

'Well——' Simon drew the word out, 'it's just the way you make yourself responsible for her. I mean, when she was younger, running around with that fast crowd, I used to get really angry when you went chasing off to get her out of one scrape or another. I mean, it's not on, is it? You're not her mother. And what's your father doing, that's what I'd like to know!'

It was amazing, thought Rhia incredulously, how by setting one pebble rolling one could cause an avalanche. She had never suspected that Simon seriously objected to her taking care of Valentina, or that he considered her father less than responsible by leading his own life.

'I think this conversation has gone far enough, Simon,' she said now, the coolness in her voice unmistakable. 'Obviously, we both need some time to think about the situation. I suggest I give you a ring when I've got things into perspective. I don't think raking up old scores is going to help either of us.'

'You're not serious!'

'I am serious.'

'You're saying, we shouldn't see one another any more?'

'Not right now, no.'

'I won't let you do this.' Simon snorted. 'It's the Frazers, isn't it? They've put you up to this. I might have known Jared Frazer had some ulterior motive for persuading you to pretend to be Val. What do they want you to do? Go back to Canada with them?'

For once, Rhia was astounded by his perception, but perhaps it wasn't so extraordinary after all; as Glyn hadn't regained his sight, it was a not unnatural conclusion.

'I don't think there's anything more to say, Simon,' she averred firmly. 'And anything I've done for Glyn, I've been happy to do. Remember that!'

When she rang off, she was half afraid Simon would try to phone her again, but while she went into the bathroom and rinsed her hot face with cold water, the telephone remained blessedly silent. However, his defection did mean that she had less time than she had expected to get to the hospital, and without stopping to get anything to eat, she restored her make-up and hurried out into the Fulham Palace Road to hail a taxi.

To her surprise, Glyn was alone when she entered his room, and after exchanging the increasingly urgent kiss he seemed to expect, she sought the chair that was situated some yards from him. His small side ward had gradually gained the appearance of a sitting room, with two armchairs, two upright chairs and a table, as well as the usual fitments of bed and trolley-type units.

'Well?' he said, after she had seated herself and folded her hands together in her lap. 'What's your decision? You

are coming with me, aren't you? If you don't, I don't
know what——'

'Oh, Glyn, don't say it!' Rhia drew an unsteady breath.
'I—I can't come with you. You know I can't. I'm—I'm
in the middle of my—training.'

'Don't I mean more to you than your bloody career?'
he demanded, his hands curving and uncurving over the
arms of his chair. 'Val, I *need* you. I never thought I'd
ever say that to anyone, but I'm saying it to you.'

'Glyn——'

'All right, all right.' He held up one hand. 'Look, I
didn't want to have to say this, but—well, don't you think
you—*owe* it to me?'

Rhia closed her eyes in despair. 'Glyn——'

'No, listen: it's true. I—I've never involved you in any
of this, but that doesn't alter the fact that you *were* driving,
weren't you?'

Rhia raised her eyes heavenward. 'You—you shouldn't
have let me!' she protested.

'Agreed. But I did, and now look at me! At least *you* can!'

Rhia quivered. 'I—I can't give up my job——'

'I'm not asking you to. Like Jared says, you have
holidays, don't you?'

'Jared—Jared said that?'

'Sure he did. And you do, don't you? Everybody does.'

Rhia shook her head. Of course she had holidays, but
after what had happened this afternoon, she had even less
reason to want to go with them. It was worse than mad-
ness to consider living in the same house as a man who
could evoke such an emotional response inside her, and
yet who evidently shared a similar relationship with his
sister-in-law. And surely by persisting in this charade, she
was only compounding an impossible situation.

'Glyn, it's not that easy.'

'Why isn't it?' Responding to the sound of her voice, he
got up from his chair and groped his way to hers, sinking
down rather heavily on to the arm and putting his arm
about her shoulders.

Immediately, Rhia froze. Just one movement of his
hand in the direction of her hair, and it would all be
over. He had only to brush the silken coil that circled her

head like an amber halo to realise it was not the bouncy, bubbly style Val had adopted, and in those revealing moments she realised that she didn't want him to find out.

'All right,' she said, the words spilling from her lips in her haste to evade discovery. 'All right, I'll come with you. But just for two weeks!'

'Four,' he said huskily, his hand groping for her chin, turning her face up to his, and Rhia trembled.

'Compromise,' remarked a dry voice behind them, and to Rhia's intense relief Glyn got to his feet to greet his uncle and his mother.

'Okay—three,' he agreed, pumping Jared's hand with vigour. 'Hey, did you hear that, Mom? Val's going to come with us. Isn't that great news?'

'Great,' echoed Lisa Frazer without enthusiasm, and Rhia, meeting her chilly eyes, knew there was one person who would not welcome her to Moose Falls.

Jared's feelings were less easy to define. He was evidently relieved that she had agreed to come for Glyn's sake, but she suspected he was not indifferent to the complications that the afternoon's events might create. But he needn't worry, Rhia thought tautly, meeting his guarded gaze with cool hostile eyes. She had no intention of remembering that particular incident. It was over, it was done with; and she wanted to forget it . . .

Leaving England was easier than she had imagined, or perhaps it was Jared Frazer's influence that only made it seem so. It was he who went to see Mr Wyatt and arranged for Rhia to take two weeks of her holiday immediately, commencing Wednesday, with the added bonus of a further week's leave of absence. Her boss was unexpectedly understanding when Rhia attempted to explain why she needed this holiday so urgently, and she could only assume that Jared possessed some authority she was unaware of.

All that remained was for her to tie up the loose ends of her life, like cancelling the milk and papers, and making arrangements with her neighbour to keep an eye on the apartment for her. Of Simon, she saw nothing, and she was relieved. The last thing she needed right now was for him to come poking around and discover she was doing what he had accused her of. It was a job of work, she told herself severely, but she could not entirely dispel the sense of anticipation the trip engendered. After all, she had never been to Canada, she had never crossed the Atlantic before, and the idea of spending three weeks in the open spaces of the Mid-West was doubly appealing after the confines of the city.

Because she was going with them, Jared had delayed their return until Wednesday, and Glyn had remained in the hospital. He could have gone to the hotel, but he had not wanted to, and Rhia understood his aversion to finding his feet in the public rooms of such an establishment.

On Wednesday morning, a taxi arrived at nine o'clock to take her to Gatwick, and as the driver stowed her suitcases in the front of the cab, she knew a sudden shiver of apprehension. She really was living dangerously, she thought, whatever way she looked at it. And even the curly blonde wig residing in her suitcase did not give her the reassurance that perhaps it should.

The Frazers were waiting for her at the airport. They had been shown to a private room, in deference to Glyn's condition, and waiting on the tarmac was the sleek executive jet that was to transport them to their destination.

'Do you like the Learjet?' asked Glyn, groping for her hand as she seated herself rather nervously beside him. 'Powerful little machine, isn't she? She's got a maximum speed of nearly five hundred and fifty m.p.h., almost as fast as some of the bigger jets, and she handles like a dream!'

Rhia tried to keep calm. Her experience of flying had been limited to a package trip to Spain aboard a BA 1-11, and this aircraft seemed awfully small to be capable of crossing the Atlantic.

'You—er—you've flown the plane?' she ventured, trying not to sound as apprehensive as she felt, but Glyn shook his head.

'No,' he averred. 'But Jared has. Although he employs a pilot for these long trips, because they're so boring.'

'Boring!' Rhia's voice rose slightly at the end of the

word, and Jared, who had been in consultation with another man at the far side of the room, finished his conversation and came to join them.

'Ready?' he asked, and Rhia glanced up at him reluctantly.

'I suppose so,' she said, keeping her breathing steady
with an effort. But she was intensely conscious of his nearness, and the fact that he seemed to have succeeded in
dismissing what had happened between them without
apparent effort.

'Good.' His smile was impersonal. 'Vince says we can
get on board.'

Lisa insisted on helping her son across the tarmac and
up the steps into the plane, and for a brief spell Rhia and
Jared were alone. It was the first opportunity for private
conversation they had had since that afternoon at her
apartment, but Rhia could have wished it had come at
some other time.

'Don't be nervous,' he remarked, as they followed the
others towards the plane. 'It should be a smooth flight.
Most likely you'll fall asleep, as soon as we've reached our
cruising height.'

Rhia stiffened. 'Don't worry about me,' she said tautly.
'I'll be fine. So long as Glyn's all right, that's all that
matters.'

'As you say.' Jared's mouth tightened at her implica-
tion, and for a few moments there was silence between
them. Then, as she was about to climb the steps leading
up into the plane, his hand on her sleeve detained her.
'Thank you for coming,' he said. 'I haven't had a chance
yet to thank you, but I want you to know, I do appreciate
this. Particularly after—well, particularly after I almost
blew it!'

So long as I don't blow it myself, thought Rhia bitterly,
mounting the steps without answering him. Her attraction
towards him had not decreased—quite the reverse; and
three weeks spent in his company was going to put an
intolerable strain on her emotions.

The interior of the jet was laid out like a luxurious
lounge, with deep armchairs, and polished tables, and a
thick pile carpet upon the floor. There were lockers to

store those bags that had not been stowed in the hold, and a white-coated steward to attend to their needs.

'There's even a bedroom aft, where Jared sleeps when he flies overnight,' Glyn told her, assuring himself that she took the chair next to his, and Rhia's skin prickled with the unpleasant task of conjecturing whether Lisa had shared it with him on the outward flight.

She was introduced to the two pilots who, along with Jared himself, would navigate the plane. 'Maybe later on you'd like to come and join us and see how it's done,' Vince Harding offered with friendly irreverence, but Rhia doubted she would leave her seat once they were off the ground.

Take-off was smooth and uneventful. Jared remained in the cabin as they taxied along the runway, and Rhia noticed Lisa's scarlet-tipped nails digging into his fingers as the light aircraft rose into the murky skies above London.

For a time, cloud enveloped them, but then they emerged into the brilliant sunlight above the clouds, and Rhia relaxed as the initial strain on the engines was eased. They were actually on their way, she thought, feeling an irresistible surge of wellbeing, that was only partly doused when she encountered Jared's gaze as he rose from his seat.

'Okay?' He addressed himself to Glyn, squatting down beside his nephew and attracting his attention.

'What? Oh, yeah—I'm fine,' Glyn nodded, swallowing a little tensely, and Rhia realised for the first time how unnerving it must have been for him, being unable to see or look out for himself.

'Do you want a drink?' his uncle suggested, squeezing Glyn's arm by way of approval, and Glyn nodded a little jerkily.

'Scotch,' he agreed huskily, emitting a short laugh. 'How about you, Val? Are you going to join me?'

Rhia looked doubtful, and the steward, emerging from his compartment at that moment, made another suggestion: 'Perhaps the young lady would prefer some coffee,' he remarked, and Rhia gave him a grateful smile.

'Yes. Yes, coffee would be lovely,' she agreed, and Jared

inclined his head politely, before leaving the steward to his task.

Lunch was served as they passed over the northernmost tip of Britain, and Rhia found herself enjoying the rich salmon bisque, and plump Aylesbury duckling, served in a delicious orange sauce. Bates, as the steward was called, was certainly an expert chef, she reflected, and then grimaced at Glyn when he explained everything was prepared before it came aboard.

'Oh, it's not the rubber food they serve on the airlines,' he agreed. 'It's freshly cooked and served. But don't imagine Bates puts on his apron and starts peeling potatoes himself, because he doesn't.'

Jared spent the early part of the flight seated at one of the tables, studying some files he had taken from a briefcase. He was interrupted from time to time by Lisa, who evidently resented his absorption in the papers, and Rhia couldn't altogether blame her when Glyn paid his mother so little attention.

After lunch, Rhia did indeed fall asleep, much to her astonishment afterwards. The restless night she had spent combined with the nervous energy she had used up preparatory to take-off had been exhausting, and, comfortably fed and watered, she found it pleasant just to close her eyes.

She awakened to the not so pleasant awareness that they were losing height, but when she cast a hasty look out of the window, she was relieved to see buildings below them.

'Are we there?' she exclaimed, turning back to Glyn, and he chuckled amiably at her obvious naïveté.

'No,' he said. 'This is Reykjavik, Iceland. We're just coming down here to refuel.'

'Iceland!' Rhia stared disbelievingly out of the window. 'I didn't know we were going to land in Iceland.'

'Why should you?' observed Lisa, from her seat across the cabin. 'I don't suppose you're a very seasoned traveller—Val. Or am I mistaken?'

'No. No, I'm not a seasoned traveller,' Rhia answered quietly, and had returned her gaze to the window again when Jared spoke.

'We're making a curve that takes us up close to the Arctic Circle,' he said, to the cabin in general, but to Rhia in particular. 'Then we fly south over Greenland and the North-West territories to our eventual touchdown at Moose Bay.'

Rhia's brow furrowed. 'But I thought we were flying to Calgary.'

'It's easier to use that for definition,' explained Glyn. 'But we have our own airfield at Moose Bay, which is only a few miles from our spread.'

'I see.' Rhia shook her head. It was all so much more sophisticated than she had anticipated, and her own ideas of Canada shrank in comparison.

After they had left Reykjavik again, Jared disappeared into the pilot's cabin, and after a while Vince Harding, the more senior of the two pilots, appeared and invited Rhia into the cabin.

Although she demurred, Glyn was enthusiastic. 'Go on. Go!' he said, urging her out of her seat. 'You can come back and tell me what it's like.' His lips twisted, and although she knew he had made a concerted effort not to let his condition spoil the trip for her, his features mirrored his frustration. 'Go, Val, don't be afraid. Sitting in the pilot's seat is the most self-glorifying thing in the world!'

Rhia was not so sure, but aware of Liza Frazer's amused eyes upon her, she accompanied the man forward, bypassing Bates's kitchen, and into the pilot's cabin.

Jared was sitting in the co-pilot's seat, having a casual exchange with Bruce Fairchild, the other pilot, but when Rhia entered he got to his feet, indicating his chair with mocking insistence.

Rhia did not immediately take it. She was too enthralled by the sensation just standing there was giving her. It was like stepping into a vacuum; there was nothing above or below them, and her stomach quivered in consternation. Sitting in the passenger cabin was so much different. There, she could deceive herself that she was not actually off the ground, and the carpet of broken cloud below them seemed to propound that illusion. But here, there seemed nothing between her and deep space, and she felt paralysed with fright.

'Come on, sit down.' Jared seemed to sense that she had frozen, and she was grateful for his hand to support her as she stepped towards the bank of instruments.

'Are—are you sure it'll be all right?' she stammered, although she sank weakly into the co-pilot's chair, as if contradicting her statement, and Jared exchanged a wry glance with Bruce Fairchild.

'Sure,' he answered her, squatting down beside her and fastening the straps about her. 'No one's asking you to fly the plane. Just get the feel of it.'

In the event, it was all incredibly exciting. Once her initial fears had fled, she began to enjoy herself. The powerful little jet inspired her confidence, and there was something thrilling in the knowledge that she was actually flying several miles above the earth.

When she returned to her seat, her legs were like jelly, and Glyn grunted at the sigh that seemed to emanate somewhere near her ankles. 'Nothing to it, is there?' he remarked, when she had recovered her composure. 'Do you know, the big jets almost fly themselves. They can even land, too, totally on automatic, though I don't believe they'll ever take off in the same way.'

'When they do, I shall stop flying with the airlines,' put in Lisa dryly, examining the colour of her nails. 'Once the pilot stays on the ground, so will I.'

It was early evening local time when the jet touched down at the little airfield of Moose Bay. For the past couple of hours they had been flying south over country mirrored with a thousand lakes, both large and small, and Rhia was glad Glyn had fallen asleep so that she could enjoy the view without feeling guilty. For her, it was all totally new and exciting, and although she knew that, by the time she was used to, it was already after midnight, she wasn't particularly tired. Of course, the sleep she had had earlier had refreshed her, and after Bates had served a delicious afternoon tea, she had dozed again. But she guessed it was the adrenalin running through her veins that made her feel so energetic, and she could hardly wait for their arrival.

Acres of virgin forest spread themselves among the lakes, their rich green foliage looking dark and mysterious

as the sun sank towards the west. It was a little unnerving
to think about the vast distances they were covering, and
to realise that if the plane came down, it could be weeks
before anyone discovered their whereabouts.

She saw the small town of Moose Bay from the air,
nestling on the edge of Moose Lake. Glyn told her it was
Moose Lake, awake now, and as impatient as she was for
their arrival. It looked different from small towns back in
England, the houses of no apparent uniformity, the various lots sporting lakeshore moorings or swimming pools.
As the Learjet made its approach to the airfield, she
glimpsed the purple-shrouded peaks in the distance, and
realised, with a feeling of awe, that she was within sight of
the Rockies.

The formalities of disembarkation were soon dealt with.
The Frazers were evidently well known in the area; but
Jared kept their well-wishers at arm's length, skilfully
guiding Glyn through the familiar routine, and avoiding
any over-enthusiastic overtures of sympathy.

Rhia, a little dazed by the bright lights of the airport
buildings and chilled by the air, which was suddenly
several degress below what she was used to, simply
followed the others. She was enveloped by an unexpected
feeling of weariness, as a sense of anti-climax replaced her
earlier exhilaration, and her surroundings seemed strange
to her, harsh and unwelcoming, and disturbingly alien.

They emerged on to a concrete parking lot, whose stark
environs did little to lift Rhia's spirits. Everywhere seemed
flat and uninviting, and beyond the wire fence that
enclosed the airstrip there appeared to be nothing but
barren land. Where was the lake she had seen from the
air, she wondered, the great pine forests that had stretched
for miles and miles? All she could see right now was an
expanse of unfriendly concrete, with nothing beyond but
the gathering shadows of evening.

CHAPTER SEVEN

A DUST-SMEARED station wagon hove into view, accelerating along the road that bordered the parking area, its wheels squealing noisily as it swerved through the gates and raced towards them. Powerful brakes brought the huge vehicle to a halt in front of them, and a gum-chewing teenager swung out of the driving seat, giving Jared a rueful grimace.

'Hi there, Mr Jared, sir—ma'am,' he added, including Lisa in his salutation. 'Sorry I'm late, but I didn't know until a half hour ago that I was to come meet you. D'you have a good trip?'

Jared's mouth drew into a wry line. 'It was fair, Troy, it was fair,' he conceded flatly. 'Where's Mr Frazer? He knew what time we were expected.'

The boy flushed, tipping the baseball hat he was wearing back on his unruly blond head. 'Y'know how it is, Mr Jared,' he muttered, picking up Rhia's two suitcases and heaving them into the luggage rack at the back of the station wagon. 'I guess Mr Frazer just didn't know the time.' His eyes flickered from Jared to Glyn, and he grinned a little awkwardly. 'Hi there, Glyn. How are you?'

'I'm okay, Troy.' Glyn remained where he was, gripping Rhia's arm, and with a thoughtful expression Jared turned to Lisa.

'Okay, let's move it,' he said, the edge of impatience evident in his tone, and with a pout of indignation Lisa took Glyn's free hand.

'Come along, darling,' she said. 'Let me help——'

'I can manage,' declared Glyn, releasing himself abruptly, and causing Rhia's heart to somersault as he lurched towards the car. But happily, his fingers encountered the door Jared had swung open at his approach, and he levered himself inside, with the minimum of difficulty. 'You sit up front, Mom, like you usually do,' he added, making himself comfortable. 'Val, Troy and me will take the back.'

Jared drove, with Lisa beside him, her arm casually draped along the back of his seat. Rhia, squashed between Glyn and the boy Troy, found her eyes glued to the back of Jared's head, and she could not help but observe Lisa's fingers when they strayed possessively over his collar. It was as if the other woman couldn't keep her hands off him, and Rhia's blood pounded heavily in her veins as she watched that intimate caress.

Once, she encountered Jared's eyes, reflected in the rear-view mirror, but she could gauge nothing from them. They were narrowed against the headlights of oncoming vehicles, illuminated in the gathering dusk, and guarded, as if unwilling to share his most private thoughts.

There was little to see beyond the road ahead, but as they left the airfield behind, there were at least signs of habitation. Rhia glimpsed flatboard houses, set back from the road, but without the little hedges or fences she was used to. Lights gleamed from shuttered windows, dogs barked, and in every driveway, a vehicle of a similar size to the one they were driving in seemed to be parked.

'This is Highway 49,' Glyn told her, as darkness descended. 'It goes south to Willow Creek. We turn off it just along here, and then we're on Frazer land, all the way.'

Jared said little on the journey, apart from exchanging a muffled word or two with his sister-in-law. Since the boy Troy's arrival at the airport, he had become grim and morose, and Rhia could only assume it was because his father had not come to meet them. Perhaps Mr Frazer had something more important to do, she reflected, not altogether certain of what that something might be. But somehow she sensed Jared's anger stemmed from more than mere pique at his father's defection, and she sensed that the others knew what was wrong. It made her feel even more of an outsider, and even Glyn's attention could not prevent her from feeling isolated.

They seemed to drive for a long time after leaving the main highway, and she decided Jared must be taking a circular route. They appeared to be crossing a vast expanse of open land, although Rhia could see little beyond

the car's windows, and in consequence could only guess
what lay ahead. But eventually, lights appeared ahead of
them, and Jared stopped so that Troy could get out and
open up a wide-railed gate for them to pass through.

They drove past sheds and stables, a long building,
which Jared indicated was the bunkhouse, and finally
braked to a stop below a sprawling half-timbered building, that seemed to spread over an enormous area.

'Welcome to Moose Bay,' said Glyn, squeezing her
hand, as Rhia gazed in amazement at the ranch-house.
'What do you think? It's some place, isn't it?'

An hour later, Rhia felt more equipped to agree with
him. Standing in the huge apartment that had been
provided for her use during her stay, she felt a helpless
sense of wonderment at the beauty of her surroundings.
Whatever she had imagined, whatever luxuries she had
dreamed of, nothing had prepared her for the simple elegance of Glyn's home, or the sense of spacious living its
uncluttered rooms compounded.

And it was its sheer size that had impressed her first: its
huge hall with a deliciously-smelling pine log fire glowing
in the massive grate, which Glyn told her was used for
parties; the curving oak staircase, leading to the upper
floor, its polished balustrade gleaming; and the high, wide
corridors, carpeted in a richly-patterned cream carpet,
that seemed big enough to mount a rugby scrum.
Everything was on the large scale—from the handful of
sofas needed to furnish the hall, to the great rectangular
window that almost filled the wall of the first landing, its
long velvet curtain gleaming regally in the light from a
dozen different lamps.

They had been met by a tall thin woman, with iron-
grey hair, whom Jared addressed as Maria. Her features
were dark and sharply defined, and from her appearance,
Rhia judged her to have Indian blood in her veins.
However, her expression was open and friendly, and she
greeted Glyn with genuine affection, even if she reserved
her warmest welcome for Jared.

'You're late,' she said. 'I was beginning to get worried.
A man wasn't intended to fly back and forth across the

ocean, like a hawk that can't decide which side of the
mountain to build its nest.'

Jared, much to Lisa's evident chagrin, enfolded the
elderly woman in his arms and hugged her. 'Man won't
fly in steel bird again for many moons, Maria,' he teased,
his anger dispersing briefly, and the Indian woman had
chuckled goodnaturedly at his deliberate mockery.

'That's just as well for all of us,' she declared, as he
drew away from her. 'Tepee need chief to keep tribe in
order.'

Jared had sighed then, glancing round at the rest of
them as he pushed back his hair with a weary hand. 'Yes,'
he said. 'Where is he?'

'The usual place.'

Maria's reply had been laconic, but when Jared started
across the hall, Lisa had remonstrated with him. 'Jared,
don't go!' she protested. 'I—Glyn's just got home. At least
let's have dinner together, before you go looking for that
disreputable old man!'

'It's all right, Jared. You go.' Glyn's words came swiftly
on the heels of his mother's, and he left the couch where
he had been sitting to grope his way across the room. 'I'm
okay—see? I just need a bit of practice. You go find Pa.
Mom and I will look after Val.'

And after a moment's hesitation, Jared had left them,
disappearing down the passage that led to the back of the
building, leaving Lisa to stare after him with angry
sparkling eyes.

Surprisingly, it was Maria who had taken matters in
hand, directing Lisa to look after Glyn, while she showed
Rhia to her room. Glyn had objected, but to no avail,
and Rhia had found herself accompanying the Indian
woman up the curving staircase, followed by the boy
Troy, carrying her cases.

Her rooms were entered through double panelled doors,
the wood dark and heavy, and gleaming with the patina
of age. Beyond lay a sitting room and bedroom carpeted
in a soft melon-coloured pile, with drapes and bed-cover-
ings of maple-brown velvet. The sitting room contained
chairs and tables grouped together, and deliciously
scented by the logs glowing in another open hearth, while

through a wide archway, the bedroom revealed a massive four-poster bed, with a matching chest and fitted walk-in closets. The walls were plain, but hung with woven rugs and primitive paintings depicting the old West, their vivid colours adding warmth and beauty to the rooms. There was a bathroom, of course, but Rhia did not discover this until after Maria had left her with the information that supper would be served in a little over an hour.

'Don't bother dressing up, if you were planning to,' she added, pausing in the doorway. 'We don't stand on ceremony at Moose Falls. Not lessen someone's coming special.' She smiled. 'From the way Glyn behaves, I'd guess he'd say you were someone special, but you know what I mean.'

Rhia managed a weak smile in reply, but after Maria had left her, she breathed a sigh of unease. Apparently Maria hadn't been told of her real identity, and she felt the weight of the responsibility she was carrying bearing down on her.

The bathroom, predictably, was enormous, too. Tiled in toning shades of cream and yellow, it offered a deep, step-in bath and shower, as well as the usual fittings. Deciding a bath was just what she needed to remove the lingering sense of apprehension she was feeling, Rhia turned on the taps, and while the bath was filling, opened her suitcases. She took out the most crushable items, and hung them on hangers in the huge closets provided for the purpose, and then took off the navy skirt suit she had worn to travel in and wrapped her pink towelling bathrobe about her.

The bath was delightful, but in spite of her assertion that she could not be tired, she was, and after she had soaped her body thoroughly, she couldn't resist the temptation to close her eyes for a moment.

She awakened to what sounded like a thunderous knocking at the bathroom door, and her lids lifted sleepily to the awareness that the water was almost cold.

'*Rhia!* For God's sake, are you all right? Answer me, damn you!'

Rhia blinked rapidly, and scrambled up in the bath, reaching for her bathrobe. Jared! her brain registered

clumsily. What was Jared doing in her room? And what a
blessing she had locked the bathroom door.

'Rhia——'

'All right, all right, I'm coming!'

Finding her voice, Rhia wrapped the bathrobe closely
about her chilled body, and turned the handle that automatically released the lock. Then she opened the door
apprehensively, to find Jared standing outside, glaring
down at her with scarcely concealed fury.

'What the hell have you been doing?' he snarled, before
she could say anything. 'Do you realise how long you've
been up here?'

'I—I think so.' Rhia swallowed a little convulsively,
noticing almost inconsequently that he had showered and
changed, and how well his shirt of dark red silk suited his
sombre colouring. 'I—I was just taking a bath——'

'Like hell you were!' snapped Jared savagely. 'It's
nearly ten o'clock. Supper was ready soon after nine!'

'Oh—I'm sorry——' Rhia moved her head back and
forward in dismay. 'I—I must have fallen asleep——'

'Asleep! You mean—in the bath?' And at her timid
nod of assent, Jared's hard hands were suddenly biting
into her shoulders. 'Are you crazy? You could have
drowned in there!'

'But I didn't.' Rhia struggled to free herself without
much success. 'Jared, I think you've made your point,
don't you?' She was intensely aware of his nearness and of
how vulnerable she felt, naked beneath the loosely-tied
folds of her bathrobe. 'I—I'm sorry if I've inconvenienced
you, but I didn't mean to fall asleep. I—I just did.' She
looked beyond him towards the archway that led into her
sitting room. 'Ought—ought you to be in here? I mean,
if—if anyone came in——'

'And found us?' His mouth twisted. 'Is that what you
mean? Glyn, for instance,' he added, regarding her with
dark resentful eyes, and Rhia wondered what had
happened to arouse him so.

'Well—yes,' she conceded, deciding it might be safer
to remind him of his responsibilities, but Jared was not
listening to her.

'Why did you do it?' he asked unexpectedly, his hands

flexing and unflexing against her tender flesh, and when she gazed up at him with wide anxious eyes, he went on: 'Why did you change your mind? About coming back with us? I was sure nothing would persuade you.'

Rhia quivered. 'Does—does it matter? I'm here now——'

'I want you to tell me,' Jared persisted, his voice softer now, but no less insistent, his breath filling her nostrils as he bent towards her, warm and moist, and fragrant with the scent of alcohol.

Rhia's pulses raced, but common sense and reason warred within her. This was getting out of hand, she thought unsteadily, realising he would likely regret his behaviour in the morning, and twisting her head away from him, she said accusingly:

'You've been drinking—I can smell it on your breath. I—I think you'd better go——'

'Not until you tell me.' Jared's hand curved round her nape, dislodging the loose knot in which she had confined her hair while she took her bath, and allowing it to tumble down around her shoulders. It added to her feeling of vulnerability, and she felt a rising sense of panic as he threaded his fingers through it.

'Jared——'

'I'm not drunk,' he told her huskily. 'I've only swallowed a little fire-water. Not a lot, compared to the state my father was in when I found him,' he added bitterly.

'Your father?' Rhia strove to keep her head. 'Mr—Frazer?'

'My father. Mr Frazer,' he agreed harshly. 'He had—as we say over here—tied one on, if you know what I mean.'

'He—he was—drunk?'

'High as a kite,' Jared confirmed grimly, and Rhia thought she understood why her actions had proved so inflammatory. After a scene with his father, her behaviour must have been the last straw.

'I'm sorry——'

'Why should you be sorry?'

'Well, because it's—upset you,' she ventured uneasily, resisting when he would have drawn her closer.

'Why should it upset me?' he demanded, allowing his hands to slide down, over her shoulders and her upper arms until they reached her waist. 'Rhia, my father's an alcoholic—you might as well know it. You'll find out soon enough.'

'Oh, no!' Rhia gazed at him with wide sympathetic eyes, forgetting her own fears for the moment. 'I am sorry, Jared, truly. And that's why you're so—so angry.'

'Angry?' Jared's echo of her question was full of derision, though whether for himself or her she couldn't decide. 'You know why I'm angry, Rhia. God, I've been sitting downstairs for nearly an hour, swallowing scotch, and listening to Lisa and Maria mouth platitudes about how tired you must be, and that we should have supper without you, because you're obviously not going to join us.' His mouth set in a grim line. 'Angry! Of course I'm angry. But only because you've behaved so bloody recklessly!'

Rhia gasped. 'What gives you the right to say that to me?'

'This——' he muttered vehemently, and overcoming her futile resistance, he covered her mouth with his.

With her lips parted in protest, she had no chance to evade the searching intimacy of his kiss. His hand at her nape, tangled in the silken curtain of her hair, allowed no escape from the hungry exploration of ers mouth, and her overheated senses did the rest. Her mouth opened to his, permitted his urgent assault, and unknowingly invited a deeper consummation. Coherent thought ceased at the moment she stopped fighting him, at the moment her fingers uncurled and spread against the soft fabric of his shirt, feeling, even through the cloth, the taut muscles with their overlying sprinkling of coarse dark hair.

'Rhia——' His groan of protest was nevertheless accompanied by his fingers, probing the loose neckline of her robe, and finding the swollen nipple beneath. His mouth trailed fire across her cheek to the curve of her neck, while his hand cupped her breast's fullness, and stroked the roseate peak to a quivering frenzy.

Rhia had never experienced anything like this before, and innocence kept her moulded to him when experience

would have warned her to draw away. As it was, his knee
probing between her legs loosened the cord of her bathrobe, and his hands slid beneath the gown to bring her
fully against him.

'Jared——' she breathed, mindlessly seeking his mouth
with her own, then froze into horrified immobility when
another voice spoke from the sitting room.

'Val? Val, where are you?'

It was Glyn, and the youthful tenor of his tones brought
Jared abruptly to his senses. With an expression of anguish
crossing his dark face, he thrust himself away from her,
dragging the sides of her gown together, across her lissom
sensuous body. Then, he turned in the direction of Glyn's
voice, and gesturing grimly for Rhia to go back into the
bathroom, he strolled towards the archway saying:

'She's taking a bath, Glyn. I've just alerted her to the
fact that we're waiting for her. She must have fallen
asleep.'

Rhia gazed resentfully at Jared, stung by the cool indifference of his tone. She couldn't believe that only
moments before he had been caressing her body with unguarded passion, ravishing her mouth with his, and
allowing her to feel the pulsating heat of his loins. It was
as if it had never happened, as if by pushing her out of
the bedroom he could push what had happened out of his
mind.

For several seconds she just stood there, appalled by his
callous behaviour, and when he turned and saw her, a
swift spasm of emotion crossed his face.

'Go!' he mouthed, and even as he did so, Glyn's stumbling gait brought him to the open archway.

'Jared?' he exclaimed, and now his voice was sharp
with accusation. 'What are you doing in here? I thought
you were putting Pa to bed.'

'I was. I *did*!' Rhia told herself she was glad he was
being disconcerted, even while she hovered by the bathroom door, half afraid even now that Glyn could see her.
'Anyway, it was just as well I came in,' Jared went on,
dragging his gaze from Rhia and moving towards his
nephew. 'She'd fallen asleep. She might have drowned if
I hadn't disturbed her.'

'God!' Glyn turned quite pale. 'Is she all right?'

'Yes—apparently.' Jared cast another taut look in Rhia's direction, as if daring her to contradict him. 'Come on, Glyn, let's leave her to it. She says she'll be down shortly.'

Rhia's lips parted indignantly, but Jared was already guiding Glyn across the sitting room, and presently she heard the sound of the heavy doors closing.

In spite of what had happened, Rhia did sleep soundly when she finally got to bed. Weariness, and the uneasy knowledge that she should not have come here, both served to help her seek respite in oblivion, and the wide bed was so comfortable, she lost consciousness at once.

But morning brought remembrance, and not least, the remembrance of supper the previous evening. It had not been a comfortable meal. They had each seemed absorbed with their own thoughts, and Rhia hadn't been able to prevent the unwilling awareness that so far as Jared was concerned, she might not have existed.

They had eaten in a magnificent dining room, with a long oval table, and finely-polished carved chairs. Apart from the chairs and the table, there was a heavily carved sideboard, and in the window, an iron-bound chest, set with a huge copper bowl of hothouse lilies. Their cream and amber tongues blended smoothly with the lightly panelled walls, the light reflecting in the copper bowl providing a vivid flash of fire.

When the meal was over, Rhia had been eager to escape to the comparative sanctuary of her rooms, but this time Glyn had detained her, capturing her hand as she bade her goodnights, and forcing her to remain with him after the others had left the room.

'I haven't had a chance to be alone with you today,' he exclaimed, pulling her closer, and Rhia wished she had had the foresight to wear the offensive wig. 'When are we going to get together, Val? Really get together, I mean? Does my blindness offend you? Is that what it is?' he demanded bitterly. 'Or do you find Jared a more attractive combination? I should warn you, my mother would never stand for that!'

'Oh, don't be silly, Glyn.' The words had tumbled anxiously from Rhia's lips. 'I—I don't know what you're talking about. You—you've been ill. You're still far from strong, and you know it. Why you—you should really have gone straight to bed this evening, instead of draining your strength like this——'

'I'm not ill, Val,' he insisted, brushing her cheek with disturbing lips. 'I may be a little weak, but I'll get over that. What I may not get over is this accursed lack of sight!'

'Of course you will.' Rhia had to reassure him, touching his face with reluctant compassion. 'Glyn—my dear, just be a little more patient, that's all. Give yourself time.'

Glyn expelled his breath resignedly. 'And you—how much time will you give me?' he persisted, and Rhia sighed.

'Don't talk like that,' she begged him weakly. 'Come on, let's go to bed. I—I—things will look different in the morning.'

'They won't look different to me,' exclaimed Glyn harshly. 'Val, day and night—they're meaningless. So far as I'm concerned, it's permanently black—black—*black!*'

'Oh, Glyn!' Pity overcame discretion, and with a sound of protest she lifted her face and pressed her lips to his. 'Glyn,' she breathed, as his arms closed convulsively round her. 'Glyn, don't lose faith.'

Over Glyn's shoulder she saw Jared standing in the doorway, watching them, and wondered how long he had been there and what he had heard. As she endeavoured to draw back from Glyn's resisting arms, however, Jared spoke, and it was this as much as anything that forced Glyn to set her free.

'Come on, old man,' he said. 'I'll help you up to your room,' and Glyn turned on him angrily.

'I don't need your help,' he snarled, gripping Rhia's wrist. 'Val can help me. Val knows what I need. And it's not the continual reminder of my—helplessness.'

He used a word Rhia had seldom heard used before, but Jared was not offended. 'Val's too tired to run after you tonight, Glyn,' he declared expressionlessly. His eyes met and held Rhia's defensive ones. 'Aren't you, Val?'

'Well——' Rhia moistened her lips. 'Yes.'

'You don't have to say that.' Glyn turned back to her. 'Val, just because Jared's master here, it doesn't mean we can't do what we want. He knows about us, for heaven's sake! He's not a prude.' His lips twisted. 'How could he be? In the circumstances!'

'That's enough, Glyn.' For the first time there was an edge to Jared's voice as he spoke to his nephew, but conversely, Rhia knew a ridiculous desire to thwart him. What was he really doing here? she wondered. Was his offer to help Glyn a genuine one, or was he in effect preventing any intimacy between Glyn and herself? He was not jealous—she was not conceited enough to imagine that. But he might—he just might—enjoy exercising his power over them.

'I'm not—*that*—tired,' she murmured tensely. 'Perhaps I could——'

'No,' said Jared flatly and distinctly. 'Go to bed—*Val*! There'll be plenty of time for you and Glyn to renew your association. But not tonight.'

Rhia expected Glyn to argue, but perhaps understandably now, he was looking exhausted. 'Yes,' he said wearily, 'Jared's right—I am a selfish brute. Go to bed, love. We've got lots of time.'

Now, as Rhia pushed back the silk sheets and put her feet out of bed, she knew a moment's gratitude for Jared's intervention, for whatever reason. She must have been crazy to think she could thwart him in that way. Glyn had only to touch her hair to know she was not Val, and all the good her presence here was doing would be erased in the space of a few reckless seconds.

Of Jared himself she did not want to think. He had behaved abominably, and he must know that, too, or he would not have ignored her for the rest of the evening. Dear God, she thought unsteadily, she had come here determined to steer clear of Jared Frazer, but within a couple of hours of entering his house, she had betrayed everything she believed in. She was not a wanton, but he made her behave like one, and no doubt he now had as little respect for her as he had for her sister. It wasn't fair. She was not like Val. She had never felt the slightest urge to sleep with any man before. But it was terrifying to realise that such thoughts were entering her head, when hitherto her emotions had been securely under control.

Presently, however, she had other things to occupy her unruly thoughts, and as her feet encountered the deep soft pile of the carpet, a thrill of excitement swept over her. She was here, in Canada, thousands of miles from her routine existence in England, and at the start of a holiday which by any standards promised not to be dull.

In spite of the fact that her room was chilly in the early morning air, Rhia didn't stop to put on a dressing gown before padding barefoot across to the windows and flinging back the curtains. She couldn't wait to see Moose Falls in daylight, and her first view of the Frazer ranch was not disappointing.

Her rooms were situated at the side of the house, and the view from her windows was spectacular. Acres and acres of lush pastureland stretched to an horizon that was defined by the vaguely insubstantial slopes that disappeared into a shifting band of cloud. Despite their obvious existence, the mountains looked faintly unreal in that shimmering shroud, and the sun tinging the lower slopes with palest yellow gave them an ethereal beauty. She had read somewhere that a man could be enthralled by mountains, and in her first glimpse she experienced a strange sensation of exhilaration. They looked so wild and untameable, and as the cloud drifted to expose a snow-capped peak, she acknowledged their danger, too.

Below her windows, the activities closer at hand attracted her attention. Now she could see the paddocks where a handful of horses cropped the grass, and a foal on spindly legs tottered inelegantly after its mother. The buildings they had driven through the night before were partially hidden by a belt of trees, but Rhia could see two men already at work painting the picket fence that edged the drive. She guessed the men's quarters were situated sufficiently far from the house not to invade the owner's privacy, but she could hear their voices on the still morning air.

Of the cattle which Glyn had informed her his uncle bred there was no sign, and she could only assume they

had been brought in for milking. Perhaps one of the
buildings she could see was a milking shed, she decided, wondering how many head of cattle it took to
supply the ranch's needs.

At last the goose-bumps on her flesh forced her to leave
the window, and she eyed the bed longingly, wondering
whether she should get back in. But a glance at her watch
told her that it was nearly half past seven, and although
it was still early, she felt ravenous. Of course, back home
she would have had lunch by now, she reflected wryly,
and rubbing her arms to remove the chill, she went into
the bathroom.

A hot shower and a brisk towel removed the shivery
feeling, and pushing aside the memory of Jared's visit to
her room the night before, she rummaged about in her
cases for something to wear. Jeans seemed the most likely
item, and after pulling on a cotton shirt, she added a
cowl-necked purple sweater. Then, after tying on a pair
of denim track shoes, she left her room.

It wasn't difficult to find her way downstairs. She
simply remembered to turn left out of her room, and
follow the corridor to the wide landing above the hall
below. The corridor was thickly carpeted, and her feet
made no sound, but now that she was out of her room she
could hear voices from the floor below. She thought she
recognised Maria's shriller tones, and a man's voice which
could have been Jared's but wasn't.

'I've got no sympathy for you,' she heard Maria re-
marking peevishly as she descended the stairs, and the
gruff response of:

'I don't expect any from you, woman. Just get me some
coffee, will you, and stop gabbing. Jared says I've got to
ride out with him this morning.'

Rhia's steps slowed as she neared the foot of the staircase, and she saw a tall if somewhat round-shouldered
man leaning on the mantel above the fireplace. Already a
warming blaze burned in the grate, and the appetising
aroma of coffee and cooked meat scented the air. To her
dismay there was no sign of Maria now, but the man
seemed to sense her presence and turned to look at her.

She guessed this must be Jared's father, although the

resemblance between them was not immediately evident. He was tall, like Jared, but broader and less muscular, the swelling girth of his stomach indicating that he enjoyed a less active existence. His face was leathery brown, and etched with a dozen different lines, but his eyes belied the bitterness that drew down the corners of his mouth.

'Well, well,' he observed, removing his arm from the mantelshelf. 'You must be Valentina, is that right? Come along down, girl. Don't be shy. I don't bite.'

Rhia hesitated only a moment before advancing the few steps that brought her down to his level, and straightening her shoulders, came towards him with hand outstretched.

'How do you do?' she said, endeavouring to sound as confident as she looked. 'I—er—I'm Val. You must be——'

'Ben,' the man finished for her. 'Ben Frazer.' He took her hand in his gnarled one. 'Glad to meet you—Val. Glyn's told us a lot about you.'

'He has?' Rhia was surprised. When had he had the time?

'Oh, yes.' Ben Frazer patted her hand firmly before letting it go. 'He used to write, you know, before this trouble with his eyes. A bad business. Lucky you weren't hurt, too.'

'Y-yes.' Rhia caught her lower lip between her teeth.

'Sleep well?'

He switched the conversation adroitly, and she was relieved, glad to be back on surer ground. 'Very well,' she assured him warmly. 'I've never slept in such a huge bed before.'

'Haven't you?' Ben Frazer regarded her with slightly bloodshot eyes. 'Well, where's Glyn? Don't tell me he's still in bed.'

'Why not?' Maria spoke as she came into the room, carrying a tray containing a pot of coffee. 'It's where you'd be, if Jared hadn't insisted you show your face at a decent hour.' She snorted, including Rhia in her grimace of resignation. 'Do you know, that man's been out of this house since five-thirty this morning? He'll have done a day's work before he comes back for you!'

Ben pulled a face at the Indian woman. 'We can't all be saints, you old reprobate,' he grumbled, approaching the table where she had set the tray, and helping himself to some coffee. 'Want some?' he asked, raising his cup to Rhia, and she glanced at Maria, unsure of how this would be received.

'Go ahead.' The other woman gestured goodnaturedly. 'I'm just making some pancakes. You want to come and try some?'

'Could I?' Rhia's stomach reacted to this news with a decidedly hollow gurgle, and Maria laughed.

'Come along, then. After you've had your coffee. Just follow your nose.'

After she had gone, Ben handed her a mug of coffee, his hand just a little unsteady as it touched hers. 'Sorry I wasn't around to greet you yesterday evening,' he remarked. 'Not too well. Must have been something I ate.'

Rhia nodded, determined not to get into a discussion about that, and Ben gestured to one of the soft couches.

'Sit down, why don't you?' he invited. He patted his thigh. 'Easier for me to stand. Got this stiffness in my leg—shrapnel wound, during the last war. Never have gotten over it.'

'I'm sorry.' Rhia took his advice and seated herself. Then, sipping her coffee, she added: 'I suppose you find it difficult to ride.'

'He finds everything difficult,' retorted a laconic voice behind her, and she glanced round apprehensively to find Jared strolling into the hall. His eyes flickered briefly over her before settling on his father. 'Well, at least you're ready. That's something to be thankful for.'

Ben snorted. 'Don't think I've got up because of anything you said, boy!' he declared, and Rhia thought how odd it was to hear Jared addressed as 'boy'. 'No, I—er—I wanted to meet Val, here. I was just telling her, I was sorry I wasn't here to meet her last evening.'

'Were you?' Jared's tone was cynical. 'Ah, well, I see you've remedied that deficiency now.' His eyes switched disconcertingly to Rhia. 'Did you find your room comfortable?'

'Oh, yes. Yes, very comfortable.' Rhia was glad of the mug of coffee to use as a barrier between them. Even though they had exchanged those few words after supper the previous evening, she was still on her guard with him, and it wasn't easy to ignore someone who was watching you so closely.

Not that this morning Jared looked much like the man she had become used to seeing. Gone was the sleek three-piece suit, and the fine silk shirt he normally wore. Now he was dressed like the men she had seen from her window—thigh-hugging denim replacing fine wool and mohair, the black leather jerkin, that sat so well on his shoulders, worn over a coarse shirt tied with leather thongs. The cuffs of his jeans revealed heavy boots, and Rhia thought she would not have been surprised to hear spurs jingling on his heels. He even had a hat, but he was not wearing it at present, and it hung lazily from his lean brown fingers.

'Val says she's never slept in such a huge bed before,' Ben remarked, finishing his coffee with a flourish. Then, turning to her, he went on: 'Y'know, Jared's always complaining when he visits England, that the beds there aren't big enough. Seems to me, it depends whose bed you're sleeping in.'

Rhia flushed, and as if taking pity on her, Jared intervened. 'You'd be something of a connoisseur, Pa, wouldn't you?' he remarked sardonically, and as the older man started to protest, he added: 'Are you ready? I don't intend to stand around here all day.'

Ben put down his mug and grimaced at Rhia. 'I guess so. As ready as I'll ever be, anyway. You planning on being out all day?'

'I do have a lot of time to make up,' retorted Jared briefly, flicking his stetson against his knee. 'Now, do we go?'

'What about Val?' asked Ben peevishly. 'What's she going to do all day?'

'Lisa and Glyn will look after—Val,' declared Jared firmly, his eyes meeting Rhia's briefly and then moving away again. 'Stop playing for time. Horse is waiting for us.'

'Horse!' grumbled Ben, collecting his own stetson from where he had left it lying on the back of a chair. 'I don't like Horse. He don't like me.'

Rhia listened to this exchange with some amazement, and as Jared urged his father towards the door, he paused to explain: 'Horse,' he said, 'is my ranch foreman. His real name's Chief Running Horse, but he settles for the shorter handle.'

Rhia's lips parted. 'He's an Indian?'

'Maria's son,' Jared informed her flatly. 'But he stopped taking scalps *months* ago!'

The door closed behind them before Rhia could make any cutting retort, and she got up from the couch, cradling her mug between her fingers. But, with Jared's departure, and the knowledge that she was unlikely to see him until this evening the day had distinctly lost its sparkle, and despite a feeling of self-disgust she knew she had not succeeded in keeping him at bay.

CHAPTER EIGHT

RHIA had breakfast in the kitchen. She surprised herself by eating two of the enormous apple-filled pancakes Maria provided and served with maple syrup. She had not felt very hungry after Jared's abrupt departure, but talking to Maria, she found the pangs of isolation dispersing.

The kitchen, like the rest of the house, was built on the grand scale, but its atmosphere of warmth and the smell of good food made it seem smaller. Warm, brick-coloured tiles covered the floor and were matched along the walls between pinewood cupboards and copper-bottomed pans. There were all kinds of gadgets for cooking and preparing food, and Maria explained that she prepared all the meals, as well as dealing with the other members of the staff. She needed help around the house, she declared, because it was simply too big for one person to handle, but from what she told Rhia, it soon became apparent that Lisa

Frazer played little part in household affairs.

'Mrs Frazer's not strong,' remarked the Indian woman, offering Rhia more coffee. 'Ever since Angus died, leaving her to bring up that boy alone, she's come to depend more and more on Jared.'

'Angus?' Rhia shook her head to the coffee and frowned.

'Jared's brother. You've heard of him.'

'Of course—Glyn's father.' Rhia nodded. 'I'm sorry, I'm not very bright this morning.'

Maria shrugged. 'Your mind hasn't caught up with your body, I guess. It soon will. Just you take it easy for a few days.'

'I'm all right,' Rhia smiled. 'And if there's anything I can do . . .'

'To help me, you mean?' Maria chuckled. 'Bless you, no.' Then she sobered. 'You're here to help Glyn get well and strong again. Please God, he gets his sight back soon.'

'Amen,' murmured Rhia fervently.

'Not that he was ever any use around the spread,' Maria added, turning back to the stove. 'Seems like he couldn't wait to get away. But I guess you know that— even if his mother would like to think different.'

Rhia hesitated. 'The ranch is—important to her?'

Maria gave a strange look over her shoulder. 'You might say that.'

'I—I suppose it would have eventually passed to Glyn, if his father had lived.'

'No.' Maria shook her head. 'Mac left the farm to Jared.'

'Mac?'

'Jared's grandfather.'

'I see.' Rhia tried to understand this. 'You call him Mac, but what was his name?'

'Macdonald,' declared Maria with a certain amount of pride. 'Jared Macdonald!'

'Then—he wasn't Ben—I mean, Mr Frazer's father.'

'No. No.' Maria shook her head. 'He was Jared's mother's father—Miss Margaret.' She smiled reminiscently. 'Now there was a lady.'

'You knew her?'

'Heavens, yes. She brought me to Moose Falls. I was with her up until she died.'

Rhia was beginning to understand. 'And—and Mac: Mr Macdonald, that is, he must have cared for her a lot.'

'That he did.' Maria sighed regretfully. 'He used to worship her. What with his wife—Miss Margaret's mother, that was—dying soon after Miss Margaret was born, he devoted himself to his daughter.'

'And—and his grandsons.'

'Mmm.' Maria did not sound so sure now. 'He was happy enough when she married Ben Frazer, I guess, but I guess he was disappointed Ben never took more interest in the ranch. Ah well, Miss Margaret's been dead these fifteen years, and Mac himself followed her ten years later.'

Rhia absorbed what she had learned. It was obvious, though Maria was loath to admit as much, that Margaret Macdonald's marriage to Ben Frazer had not been as happy as her father would have liked. Yet, after meeting him, Rhia could quite see that he might once have been an attractive man, before age—and perhaps bitterness— had etched those lines upon his face. Life must have been harder here, forty years ago, when roads had been rougher, and aeroplanes had not yet proved themselves reliable. A man like Ben Frazer would have found it hard. He did not strike her as being the stuff of which pioneers were made. But for all that, she liked him. He was human.

'I think it's about time I took Glyn up some breakfast, don't you?' Maria remarked, breaking into her reverie, and Rhia got quickly to her feet.

'Let me,' she exclaimed, glad she had thought to wear the wig this morning. Although she did not think Maria presented much threat, she was glad Ben Frazer had not seen her without it. Somehow she had the feeling he was the kind of man who might discuss her appearance with Glyn.

'Well ...' Maria looked doubtful, but presently she smiled. 'Why not? I guess he'd be happier to see your face any day than mine.' She paused, a wry expression crossing

her lined features. 'Not that he's seeing much at all, right
now. Poor kid, my heart bleeds for him.'

Glyn's room was situated some distance from Rhia's,
for which she was grateful. Had that been Jared's doing,
or Lisa's? she wondered, as she carried the tray along the
corridor. They each had their reasons for keeping her and
Glyn apart. Her lips trembled suddenly, and she had to
bite on them to still their betraying quiver. She had
thought she understood Jared's reasoning; now she was
not so sure.

To her surprise, Glyn himself opened the door to her
knock. He was already up, though not dressed, and there
was still a night's growth of beard on his chin.

'If I'd known you were going to bring my breakfast to
me, I'd have stayed in bed,' he told her, bestowing a
warm kiss on her parted lips. 'I thought you'd still be
sleeping. It's early, isn't it?'

'It's nearly nine,' Rhia agreed, using the tray as a
reason for keeping him at bay. 'Where—where shall I put
your breakfast?'

'Oh—er—there's a table near the window, isn't there?
Put it there. You can talk to me while I eat.' He grimaced.
'So long as you can bear to watch a blind man groping
for his food!'

'You're not a blind man!' Rhia made a sound of compassion. 'Glyn, you've temporarily lost your sight.
Temporarily, that's all.'

Glyn hesitated a moment, then he closed the door.
'Okay,' he said, 'have it your way. But temporarily is
lasting a hell of a long time.'

Glyn talked while he had his breakfast, telling her about
the ranch, explaining how it was run. 'Running fifty
thousand head of cattle takes a lot of organising,' he explained, making Rhia smile ruefully at her foolish image
of a dairy herd. 'And although Jared has a ranch foreman,
he keeps pretty close to it himself when he's home.' He
shrugged. 'I should tell you, much as I enjoy visiting,
Moose Falls isn't in my blood like it's in Jared's. I guess
I'm like my father. I'm lazy.'

'But——' Rhia hesitated, 'your mother seems to like it.'

'Oh, yeah!' Glyn was sardonic. 'Mom loves being

around Jared. She always has, I guess. I don't know why she ever married Dad. They were never happy together.'

Rhia caught her breath. 'Glyn!'

'It's true.' He was laconic. 'I guess that was why he spent so much time away, fishing. He couldn't stand the arguments. Anyway, according to Mom, she and Jared are planning to get married in the fall.'

Later in the morning, Rhia was able to view that prospect with controlled equanimity. But right then she was stunned and showed it, and she was unutterably relieved that Glyn could not see her expression.

'Do you ride?'

Glyn's question gave her something else to concentrate on, and moistening her lips, she said: 'I—yes, a little. We did ride a bit when we were at school.'

'We?' Glyn frowned. 'Oh, yes. You and—Rhia, isn't it?' His sightless eyes seemed to impale her. 'What did she say when you told her you were coming to Canada?'

Rhia forced a smile he couldn't see, but she couldn't seem to get it into her head that those blue eyes really were blind. 'Oh, she was—very pleased for me,' she replied carefully.

'Was she? You surprise me.' Glyn leaned across the table to grip her chilled fingers. 'Didn't you tell me she was generally jealous of the things you did?'

Rhia's gasp was barely audible. 'I—did I say that?'

'Sure you did. You said she was always grumbling at you, forcing you to do things she wanted you to do, instead of letting you have any fun.' He shook his head. 'She sounds quite a drag. Not at all like you.'

Rhia expelled her breath unsteadily. 'No,' she agreed unevenly. 'No—no, she's not at all like me.'

'So——' Glyn raised her fingers to his lips, 'you do ride.'

'A little, as I said.'

'Okay. So how about we take a ride this morning, hmm? I can feel the sun on my face, so I know it's not raining. I'd like to show you the ranch, or at least some of it.'

Rhia hesitated. 'Oh, but—I mean—can you——'

'——find my way about?' Glyn interrupted her a little tersely. 'Yes. Blindfold, as they say. Val, I was born here.

I've ridden these ranges since I was three years old. I guess, with a little help, I shouldn't make too much of a fool of myself.' He paused. 'Besides, I want to ride down to the bunkhouse and see Foo Sung.'

'Foo Sung?'

'That's right.' Glyn grimaced. 'Taking a bath and putting on my clothes—they're not too difficult; but shaving—that's beyond me.'

'And Foo Sung——'

'He's the cook,' explained Glyn, getting to his feet and drawing her up with him. 'He also cuts hair and gives the odd shave, if and when he's asked for it. You'll like him. And I want the guys to see you, to see what a peaches and cream English rose looks like.'

'Glyn——'

Rhia put her palms against his chest, but he was infinitely stronger now, and perfectly capable of overcoming her puny efforts to keep him at bay. 'Relax,' he breathed, his lips seeking hers with increasing urgency. 'This is my room. No one's going to interrupt us here.'

'Glyn, I—your chin's rough,' she protested, seizing on the first thing that came into her head, and he heaved a deep sigh.

'Okay,' he said, lifting his head, but still continuing to hold her against him, 'I get the message. Jared's told you to lay off me, hasn't he? Him and that know-it-all doctor. What was his name—Singh? He told me not to exert myself. Hell, doesn't he know anything about the male constitution?'

'Just give yourself a little more time,' appealed Rhia tremulously. 'D-darling, I don't want you to—upset yourself.'

'Upset myself!' Glyn groaned. 'Holding you like this is upsetting me, don't you know that?' He bent his head suddenly and buried his face in the nape of her neck. 'You know, I think you've put on a little weight. And I like it—I like it very much.'

Rhia's breathing was quickening with nerves when someone tapped at Glyn's door. It was like a reprieve, and Glyn made a sound of irritation when the tap was repeated.

'Who is it?' he called, without releasing Rhia, but his answer had assured his mother that she was not disturbing him, and without further ado the door opened, and Lisa appeared on the threshold.

Rhia did not know who was the most embarrassed, herself or Glyn's mother, but Lisa quickly recovered herself. 'Oh, darling,' she exclaimed, her sharp eyes taking in Rhia's appearance and moving on to the breakfast tray behind them, 'I didn't realise you wouldn't be alone. I just came to find out how you'd slept.'

Realising Lisa was not about to leave without an assurance of his good health, Glyn was forced to release Rhia and face his mother. 'I slept pretty well,' he declared, as Rhia endeavoured to resume her composure. 'I've just had breakfast, and after I'm dressed Val and I are going riding.'

'Is that wise?' Lisa moved further into the room, her long skirts rustling against the carpet. Like her son she was not yet dressed, but her frilled silk houserobe was as feminine and attractive as an evening gown. 'Glyn dear, we all know you're taking this affair marvellously well, but there are limits.'

'I think your mother's right, Glyn.' Much as Rhia disliked supporting Lisa in this, she was forced to agree. 'Maybe tomorrow we could take that ride together. Don't you think you're being a little ambitious, for your first day?'

Glyn's face contorted briefly, then he reached for her hand. 'I'm not helpless, you know,' he muttered, 'I'm only blind!'

'Glyn!'

His mother gave Rhia a hostile look. 'I must insist that you rest today at least,' she declared, addressing her son, but still looking at the girl. 'I'm sure—Val—can control her interest in seeing the ranch.'

'Of course.' Rhia refused to let the other woman disconcert her. 'Darling,' she caught her lower lip between her teeth as the involuntary endearment fell from her lips, 'take everyone's advice, and don't try to rush things.'

Glyn sighed, but it was evident he was weakening. Perhaps he was beginning to realise how weak he still was, thought Rhia compassionately, as he released her hand and grasped the post at the end of the bed.

'Okay,' he said, moving round the bed and sinking down on to the mattress. 'I'll promise to be good today, if you'll promise to go riding with me tomorrow.'

Rhia hesitated, looking at Lisa. 'Well . . .'

'Shouldn't you wait and see how you feel tomorrow?' his mother suggested tautly. 'Speak to Jared——'

'Jared's not my keeper, Mom,' retorted Glyn shortly. 'Don't crowd me, please. I have to learn to stand on my own two feet.'

Lisa drew a deep breath and fixed Rhia with a baleful stare. 'Very well,' she said, 'I'll say no more. But if anything happens, I shall hold you personally responsible.'

Rhia knew she meant her, but Glyn's interpretation was different. 'Of course,' he agreed. 'It's my own fault, and no one else's. Calm down, Mom. Nothing's going to happen to me.'

'I sincerely hope not.' Lisa' pale eyes were malevolent, and Rhia had the greatest difficulty in sustaining that critical gaze. 'However, I must go and dress now. I'll come back later, Glyn. When you're alone. We haven't had a chance to be alone together yet. I want to hear all about college. I'm sure—Val—will permit me that small favour.'

Later in the morning, Rhia thought how good it was to get outside, into the crisp morning air. She could not have admitted it to Glyn, but the ambiguity of her position was a constant drain on her emotions, and his mother's attitude tended to sour the atmosphere around her. It was a relief to get away from the house, and from Lisa's unconcealed dislike, and she wondered why Glyn's mother resented her so much. After all, she was here for Glyn's benefit, not her own, and even if Lisa had disliked Val and what she stood for, surely she, Rhia, presented no threat.

But outside, she was able to shed her anxieties in the pure delight of feeling the sun on her face, the sweet smell of damp grass invading her nostrils. She had asked Maria if it would be all right for her to go for a walk, and the old woman had offered no objections.

'Just don't go too far,' she warned her sagely. 'I don't think Jared would want you getting lost, you hear?'

Rhia didn't see how she could. In this undulating

landscape, one could see for miles, and the distant line of the mountains provided the perfect beacon.

Even so, she took Maria's advice and remained within range of the house. For one thing, she did not wish to encounter any of the men who occupied the buildings she could see through the trees, and for another, she did not want to spoil Glyn's pleasure in showing his home to her. Besides, the horses in the paddock took her attention and she spent a happy hour talking to them before walking back to the house.

Only she and Lisa occupied the dining room at lunch-time and it was not a comfortable meal. The older woman seemed determined to find fault with everything she did, and catching Maria's eye, Rhia found an unexpected ally.

'You really shouldn't encourage Glyn to believe his life can go on as before,' Lisa declared, forking cubes of honey-roast ham into her mouth. 'I mean, it's not as if you're going to share that life with him. After you've gone, I'll have to pick up the pieces, and quite frankly, I resent your efforts to interfere with his recovery.'

Rhia gasped. 'I didn't know I was.'

'You know perfectly well that going riding is the last thing Glyn should do. In his condition! If he should fall off——'

'Glyn's ridden a horse since he was knee-high,' Maria remarked, placing a delicious quiche in the middle of the table. 'Seems like you're going to destroy his confidence, Mrs Frazer, if you don't let him prove he's still a man.'

'When I want your opinion, Maria, I'll ask for it,' Lisa retorted brusquely. 'I—I've got a headache. Do you think you could get me my tablets?'

Maria took her dismissal in good part, and Rhia applied herself to her own meal. She didn't want to get involved in an argument with Glyn's mother. She was right. It wasn't really anything to do with her. But somehow she had the feeling that Lisa's dislike went deeper than a concern for her son's well-being.

Lisa disappeared after lunch, and guessing she had gone to see her son, Rhia spent the afternoon unpacking her cases. There was plenty of room in the deep drawers of the chest and the capacious hanging area of the walk-in closet to take all her things and more, and afterwards she seated herself at the desk and wrote a letter to her father. She did not mention Valentina, she merely told him she was holidaying in Canada. And let Val make of that what she liked, she thought moodily, wondering how her sister would have handled Lisa Frazer.

Dinner was a more entertaining meal, primarily because Ben Frazer was present. Glyn, too, had joined them, pale but otherwise normal, only the growth of beard on his chin, indicating his continuing problem. He seated himself beside Rhia, asking her where she'd been all afternoon, and she realised Lisa had not been with him.

'I thought—your mother——' she began, not quite knowing how to explain herself, and suffered another killing look from Lisa as Glyn shook his head.

'Oh, Mom spent the compulsory fifteen minutes with me, didn't you, Mom?' he remarked mockingly. 'Afterwards, I listened to the television. You'd be surprised how entertaining a baseball game can be when you can't see it.'

Jared had joined them, too, but apart from asking Rhia how she had spent her day, he played little part in the conversation. He seemed withdrawn, as he had the night before, and only occasionally when Rhia's eyes encountered his did she glimpse a brooding anger in their depths and wondered what he was thinking. But mostly, she knew a tight resentment towards him for taking advantage of her as he had, and her own responses to his questions were as non-committal as his own.

His father, conversely, was quite loquacious, and it was he who kept the flow of conversation going. Drinking nothing but orange juice, Rhia noticed, he kept her amused with stories of the old West, though she guessed, from the expressions of the rest of the company, that he had told these stories many times before.

Nevertheless, she was grateful to him for his friendliness, and even Glyn commented on this when the meal was over and he had allowed his uncle to guide him into a cosy sitting room.

'I guess Pa's setting out to show he can be as sober as the next man,' he remarked, after Jared had left them.

'He knows that Jared's threatened to put him into one of those institutions to dry out if he doesn't behave, and last night he really let Jared down.'

Rhia frowned. 'Jared wouldn't really—I mean—would he?' she finished lamely, and Glyn laughed.

'Maybe not. But Pa will kill himself if he goes on at this rate. I guess Jared has to decide the lesser of two evils.'

Rhia nodded. She had not thought about that. But then her thoughts were distracted by Glyn's fingers probing the soft curls of the wig.

'Y'know, your hair feels softer than it used to,' he murmured, turning to press a kiss against the side of her neck. He gave a rueful sigh. 'Sometimes, I get the feeling I never knew you before. You know, being blind has its compensations. I mean—my sense of touch seems greater somehow, and my sense of smell. I always knew you smelled delightful, but I like it when you get nervous, like now, because your body exudes its own perfume.'

Rhia quivered. 'Glyn, you're making me nervous——'

'Why? Because I find you fascinating?' He paused. 'What if I told you, I like you better like this. More—feminine, somehow. Not so aggressive.'

Rhia expelled her breath unsteadily. 'I think it's time you went to bed, Glyn.'

'Hmm.' His lips nudged her cheek. 'Is your room comfortable? Or would you rather share mine?'

'Glyn——'

'Okay, I'll be patient.' He grimaced. 'That's another aspect of this affair I'm not enjoying.'

Rhia accompanied Glyn to the foot of the stairs, but then he insisted on going on alone. 'I'll find my way,' he said tautly, 'and without that walking stick Singh gave Jared at the hospital. I'm not going about with a white stick. Not until I have to anyway.'

Rhia watched him mount the stairs and then went slowly back to the sitting room. She was tired, too, but it was important to allow Glyn to feel independent, and she could not bear to watch him as he groped his way up the stairs.

To her surprise, Jared was just emerging from the sitting room, but he stood back to allow her to enter and then spoke as she sought the sofa where she and Glyn had been sitting earlier.

'Where's Glyn?' he asked impersonally. 'I was going to take him up to his room.'

'He's gone,' said Rhia indifferently, avoiding his eyes. 'He wanted to do it himself. I thought it was the best thing.'

There was silence for a few moments, and she thought that he had gone. But when she glanced round, he was still standing there, looking at her, and her cheeks suffused with hot colour as she intercepted his gaze.

'I suppose I should apologise,' he said, his voice low and impatient. 'I didn't get the chance to do so last night, and this morning my father would have rather complicated things. So—will you forgive me? I'm not normally so barbaric. You must put it down to lack of sleep.'

Rhia said nothing, sitting on the edge of the couch, her arms hugging her knees. She wished he would go. She didn't want his apology, and she didn't actually believe he meant it. He was simply trying to ease himself out of what could be an awkward situation.

'Well?' He spoke again, and to her consternation, he walked across the carpet to stand in front of her. She could see his leather-booted feet, and the narrow line of his suede pants, but she didn't look up, and his feeling of irritation was audible. 'Don't you have anything to say?'

Rhia shrugged her slim shoulders. 'All right,' she murmured, too nervous of his reactions to go on ignoring him. 'I accept your apology.'

'Good.' And then, palpitatingly, his hand touched her artificial curls. 'I'm sorry about this. It appears you need to wear it more than I had anticipated.'

Rhia permitted herself a quick look up at him, surprising a curiously gentle expression in his eyes. 'I—I can't imagine why you should have thought I might not need to wear it all the time,' she blurted, unwillingly disturbed by his compassion. 'You must have a curious notion of how your nephew behaves. Glyn thinks I'm Val. He wants to touch me. How could you think otherwise?'

'At least I prevented you from having to explain why you couldn't go to bed with him!' retorted Jared harshly, his dark eyes showing he was angered by her sarcasm.

'Unless that was what you wanted, of course. I didn't consider that.'

Rhia sprang to her feet, uncaring that by doing so she was erasing the space between them. 'That's a foul thing to suggest!'

'But justifiable, don't you think?' Jared countered grimly, as her heaving breasts brushed the fine silk of his shirt. 'You didn't exactly jump at my offer of escape, did you?'

'After what you'd just done, no!' Rhia stepped back from him, as the scent of his body rose from the opened collar of his shirt. 'I didn't need your help.'

Jared's mouth thinned. 'I'll remember that.'

'Thank you.'

Rhia made the retort as she strode blindly towards the door, only to fall back instinctively as Lisa appeared.

'So this is where you are, darling,' Glyn's mother exclaimed artlessly, ignoring Rhia and advancing into the room. 'I've been looking for you, Jared.' She slid her hand possessively through his sleeve. 'At last I've got you to myself.'

Rhia did not need the pointed reminder to make herself scarce. She had had quite enough of the Frazers for one day. But she was aware of Jared's eyes on her as she left the room, and of his fingers sliding smoothly over the silky curve of Lisa's head.

CHAPTER NINE

In fact it was three days before Rhia and Glyn took their ride together. Two days after their arrival, delayed exhaustion took its toll on his weakened system, and he spent most of his time in bed, just getting up in the evenings.

It meant that Rhia was often at a loose end, but she found solace in Maria's company, often joining the Indian woman in her kitchen and listening to her tales about how things used to be.

One afternoon, Ben showed Rhia over the ground floor

of the house, proving himself as knowledgeable about the family's history as anyone. The house was even bigger than Rhia had imagined from the little she had learned of it, and as well as the hall, which was used as a meeting place for all the family and their friends, there were several reception rooms, whose contents were swathed by dust-preventing sheets.

'Wasn't necessary to build all these rooms,' remarked Ben, closing the door on a ghostly-shrouded parlour. 'But Mac wanted the biggest and the best house hereabouts, and that's what he got.'

There was even a music room, elaborately decorated, and furnished with an enormous grand piano. 'Margaret used to play,' he said, running his fingers over the yellowing keys. He indicated a harp standing in a corner. 'She used to play that, too, but after the boys were born, she didn't have much time for music.'

'I suppose not.' Rhia looked about her, admiring the silk moiré curtains at the long windows, the polished wood floor strewn with creamy fur hides, that would give so much better acoustics than a carpeted floor could have done. As well as the piano and the harp, there was also an organ, inlaid with rosewood and set in a window embrasure, and several violin cases were laid reverently on a marquetry table.

'She wanted the boys to play piano, too,' Ben went on, fingering the taut string of a bow. 'But Angus never had time for such things, and although Jared learned to play, he seldom comes in here.'

Rhia thought she could guess why. From what she knew of Jared, little though that was, she doubted he would feel at home in these surroundings. She thought it was much more likely that he kept this room as it was in deference to his mother's memory.

She herself preferred the library. The tall book-lined room delighted her, smelling deliciously as it did of leather and tobacco. Although it was just as impressive in its way as the other rooms of the house, it had a comfortable lived-in atmosphere, and Rhia sank into one of the squashy leather armchairs, running her fingers over the arms.

'This is where you'll generally find Jared, if he's not in

his den,' remarked Ben, pulling out a leather-tooled volume and inspecting the flyleaf. 'Hmm. *The Compleat Angler!* I don't guess Mac bought this for Margaret.'

'Who do you think he bought it for?' Rhia asked, resting her chin on one knuckle, before catching sight of Jared advancing up the curve of the drive visible from the windows. Immediately, she got up from the chair, unwilling for him to think she was taking advantage of his absence, drawing back behind the heavy red velvet drapes.

'Oh, I guess it belonged to Angus,' shrugged Ben, pulling a wry face. 'My eldest son was a keen fisherman, Val. He was happy to go out in all weathers.' He sighed, not noticing his younger son's approach. 'He was killed, you know. The plane he was flying came down in the forest, north of here, on his way home from a fishing trip.' He grimaced. 'Poor Angus, he always was a loser.'

Rhia was interested in what he was saying, but the sound of the outer door opening and closing tightened her stomach muscles. However, although Ben's voice must have been clearly audible through the half-open door, Jared did not come to find them, and presently she realised he must have gone straight upstairs. To find Lisa, no doubt, she thought bitterly, her emotions stirred by what Ben had told her. She had learned that Lisa rested in her rooms most afternoons. But in spite of what Maria had said, she did not believe that Glyn's mother was as frail as she strove to appear.

The morning Glyn was well enough to go riding, the air was clear, the sun warm on their faces as they walked down to the stables. Rhia had taken Glyn's advice and put on long boots and a warm sheepskin jacket, though she had shunned the stetson he had suggested for her head. The wig was quite warm enough, and she always found it a relief to reach her room and pull off its confining web of nylon cord.

The stables were situated near the men's quarters, but fortunately at this hour of the morning, there were few of them about. Two men who were attending to the repair of the fence surrounding a corral called a greeting, however, and came over to shake Glyn's hand.

'We heard,' one of them, whom Glyn introduced as

Will Henley, exclaimed sympathetically. 'But you'll make it son. You've got Mac's blood in your veins, and no Macdonald ever gave up.'

'That's good to hear.' Glyn patted Will's shoulder affectionately. Then: 'Is Foo around? I want to introduce him to Val.'

'Sure. He's in the cookhouse,' agreed the other man, who Glyn had addressed as Crow. Like Maria, his features showed his Indian ancestry, but both men were obviously genuinely fond of their employer's nephew. 'What d'you want Foo for? To cut those curls of yours? Hell, Miss Val's hair is shorter than yours, ain't it?'

'Is it?' Glyn's fingers probed insistently against her scalp. 'Yes, I guess it is at that. But I want these whiskers cutting. She doesn't like me with a beard, do you, honey?'

Rhia's face suffused with becoming colour. During the last few days Glyn had developed quite a beard, but he had insisted he could wait for Foo to cut it. 'It's probably warmer,' she conceded with a little shiver and Glyn took the hint, bidding goodbye to the two men, and directing Rhia to the bunkhouse.

The Chinese, Foo Sung, was in the kitchen, and while Glyn and he exchanged greetings, Rhia looked around the room where the men took their meals. There were several long trestle tables, indicating the numbers that were accommodated, with long benches beside them. At the end of the bunkhouse were several layers of bunk beds, and after introducing her to Foo, Glyn explained that at round-up time, they were often in use.

'Jared takes on extra hands at that time,' he remarked, as Foo installed him in a chair and disappeared to collect shaving cream and a razor. 'We employ upwards of fifty men full-time, and some of them live with their families. Those who don't are accommodated in single units out back.'

Rhia nodded. 'I always thought they lived in the bunkhouse,' she confessed, grimacing. 'Shades of the old West!'

'They used to, years ago,' Glyn agreed, as Foo returned, stropping a razor on a strip of leather. 'Some still do, I guess. But Jared believes in keeping his men happy, and although Foo still cooks for them, their leisure time is as private as they want to make it.'

Rhia's lips tightened. 'I suppose Jared can afford it.'

'Jared is a fine man,' declared Foo Sung proudly. 'He is fit to be Macdonald's grandson.'

'Meaning my father wasn't,' said Glyn, without rancour. 'Foo is a faithful admirer of Jared's, aren't you, Foo? Just because he pulled him out of the lake one time.'

'Jared saved my life,' asserted Foo firmly. 'I would have drowned, or died of cold. He risked his own life to save mine. He could have frozen, too.'

Glyn grinned. 'Well, I'm glad you're still around. There's no one else I'd trust to scrape my throat with a blade as sharp as this one.'

The horses that were provided for them later did not meet with Glyn's approval, however. 'Where's Prince?' he demanded, when the stable boy, Troy Cummings, the youth who had met them at the airport, led out a bay gelding for him to ride. 'I don't want this rocking horse, Troy. I want my own mount.'

'Mr Jared said you weren't to be too ambitious first off,' Troy responded uncomfortably. 'Honest, Glyn, it wasn't my idea, but Mr Jared said if you came looking for a mount, I was to give you Breaker, and Miss Mallory Dawn Wind.'

Glyn grimaced. 'I don't care what Mr Jared said. I want Prince, and you'd better get him saddled and out here pretty damn quick.'

'I can't do that, Glyn.'

'Why can't you?'

' 'Cause he ain't here, Glyn. Horse is riding him this morning. Like as not to stop you from doing so.'

'Damn Horse!' Glyn's jaw grated mutinously, and Rhia knew he was restraining his tongue with difficulty. 'Okay, I'll ride Breaker. But you can tell Mr Jared that I'm no novice, even if I am blind!'

Rhia's mount was a docile mare, and she was not dismayed by the animal's lack of initiative. She had more than enough to do remembering all she had learned, and keeping an eye on Glyn, who was inclined to be too ambitious.

Nevertheless, leaving the yard behind them, it was invigorating to give the horses their heads and gallop across the springy turf. It was a beautiful morning, the sun just gradually creeping up the sky and turning the distant mountains to pale pink and gold.

'I'm sorry if I was bad-tempered back there,' Glyn apologised, when she came close to guide his mount with hers. 'I'm not usually so bloody-minded, but just sometimes this whole mess gets me down.'

'I understand. Don't worry about it.' Rhia reached out and touched his hand where it rested on his thigh. 'Now, you tell me where you want to go. There's so much space—I couldn't begin to decide for myself.'

Glyn nodded and grinned. 'Okay.' He reined in his mount and she did the same beside him. 'Now, let me think: can you see the range over to the left of us?'

'Yes. You mean—the mountains?'

'That's right. They look close, don't they? But they're not that close. You'd be surprised how far you'd have to ride before you reached the foothills.'

'Hmm.' Rhia nodded. 'They are beautiful though, aren't they?'

Glyn's lips twisted, and she could have bitten out her tongue for being so thoughtless. But happily he took it in good part. 'I guess they're the most beautiful mountains in the world, at least so far as I'm concerned,' he agreed. 'But dangerous. Don't forget, dangerous. The lower slopes look innocent enough, but if the mist comes down . . .'

'I can imagine.' Rhia shivered. Then: 'So—where are we going?'

'Well——' Glyn turned his head, as if striving for a mental picture, 'if I'm right, away to our right is a wooded area. The ground slopes down into a kind of ravine, and I want to show you the falls that give this place its name.'

Rhia hesitated, staring towards the trees he indicated, and realising that unlike the open plain, it would be infinitely more hazardous riding into a ravine.

'I can see it,' she conceded now, biting her lip. 'But Glyn, isn't that a little dangerous? I mean—couldn't we just ride on?'

'What? Into oblivion?' Glyn was impatient now. 'Rhia,

there's nothing ahead of us but miles and miles of grass-land and cattle, thousands of cattle.' He snorted. 'Look ahead of you—can you see how long the grass is in places? Is that really all you want to see? *Grass?*'

'No.' Rhia was honest enough to admit that it wasn't. 'But this is your first outing, Glyn, and your mother——'

'To hell with my mother,' he retorted harshly. 'Since when is my mother so all-fired keen to assure herself of my well-being? I haven't noticed any strong motherly tendencies up until now. This is all for Jared's benefit, can't you see? Jared expects her to be concerned, so she's concerned. But that's all.'

'Oh, Glyn, I'm sure——'

'What are you sure? That she's a good mother? That she cares a —— what happens to me?' He swore again, more crudely this time, and Rhia knew a helpless sense of pity for him. 'Val, she wants Jared, and she'll do anything she can to get him. Even if it means playing materfamilias to impress him!'

Rhia shook her head. 'Nevertheless, she's right to be concerned about you, and—and riding into the ravine does seem—reckless!'

Glyn's mouth tightened. 'Are you refusing to come with me?'

'Refusing to come—no! No, I'm not—refusing exactly. Glyn——'

'Then let's go, shall we?' he suggested, nudging his mount forward, and with an impending feeling of disaster Rhia was forced to go with him.

The ground became rougher as they left the open plain to enter the wooded slopes that led down into the ravine. Grassland gave way to tussocky shrubland, and the trees grew thicker as the path narrowed. Below them, Rhia could see a lake, glinting in sunlight, and closer at hand, she could hear the sound of water falling over stones. She realised it was the creek she had seen from her windows, emptying itself into the lake below, and in so doing creat-ing a waterfall, crystal-clear and icy-cold.

Because she dared not let Glyn lead the way, Rhia rode ahead of him down the sloping path turning her head frequently to assure herself that he was all right.

Fortunately, her own mount seemed surefooted, and she was able to give Glyn her undivided attention. Even so, she was tense and on edge, aware that if anything happened, both Jared and Lisa would blame her.

It was an enchanting place, she had to admit, and when they emerged on to a plateau just above the cataract, she caught her breath at its sheer beauty. Set about with moss and ferns, the steady cascade of water was not heavy, but it was constant, causing a misty spray to rise up above the undergrowth and create its own spectrum of colour.

'Moose Falls,' said Glyn, moving his mount closer, so that his leg brushed hers. 'You can guess how it got its name. In summer we can swim in the lake. Let's go down.'

'Oh, do you think we should?' Rhia glanced back up the slope behind them. 'Don't you think we've come far enough for today? You must be tired.'

'I'm okay.' Glyn was aggressive, and with a sigh, Rhia pressed her heels into Dawn Wind's sides, urging her forward.

The way became steeper as they neared the bottom of the ravine, and the mossy surface underfoot was damp and a little slippery. Rhia guessed the sun seldom penetrated the trees guarding the path, and the moist smell of rotting vegetation was all around them. She watched Glyn anxiously, alert for any unwary slip he might make, and omitting to look where she was going, was suddenly wrenched from the saddle by the bare branch of an aspen jutting across the path.

The cry she emitted was involuntary, the instinctive response to being tossed from the saddle into a clump of damp vegetation. She landed on her back, winded by the lash of the branch across her midriff, and numbed by the hard spiky earth against her spine. She lay there sickly for several seconds, too dazed to immediately answer Glyn's anxious call of concern, and not until his voice took on an angry urgency could she struggle to reassure him.

'It's all right,' she got out weakly, as he climbed down from Breaker's back, and began threshing about in the undergrowth. 'Glyn, I'm all right. Just—just winded, that's all. I'm afraid I've made an absolute fool of myself.'

'Where are you? Keep talking,' ordered Glyn impatiently, and after a few moments, his searching fingers closed over one booted foot. With impersonal thoroughness, his hand ran up her legs and thighs, and he knelt in the moss beside her, to take both her hands in his.

Rhia pulled herself up into a sitting position, wincing as the effort jarred her spine, but relieved that at least she seemed to be in one piece. 'I was so busy looking out for you, I forgot to look out for myself,' she exclaimed, trying to make light of it. 'Honestly, Glyn, you should see the state I'm in—covered in mud and goodness knows what else!'

'You're sure you're all right?' Glyn was not happy with her reassurance. 'Heavens, you could have broken your neck! It's my fault for insisting we come down here.'

'Don't be silly.' With a determined effort, Rhia got to her feet, hastily tucking a few errant strands of her own hair inside the wig. She was relieved it had stayed firm during her fall. She might have had a job finding it again among all the twigs and ferns. 'Come on,' she added, 'let's go back. I'm sorry to cut short our outing, but I really could do with a wash and change of clothes.'

The journey back up the ravine was accomplished without incident, and Rhia thought wryly how ironic it was that she should have been the one to fall off. Still, at least that should please Lisa, she reflected, hoping against hope that neither Jared nor Lisa would witness their return.

Her wish was granted. Only Troy Cummings saw them ride into the compound, and although his eyes mirrored his concern at Rhia's dishevelled appearance, he caught her warning eye and said nothing.

Glyn climbed down slowly, and Rhia realised that in her eagerness to get back, she had not given a thought to the possibility that he might have needed to rest before attempting the ride home. His determination to go down to the lake could have been a covert attempt to gain a little time to relax, but after her tumble she had thought only of herself.

Contrite, she disguised her own stiffness, and the pain that jarred her spine, and allowed him to lean on her all the way back to the house. Why had she acted so carelessly? she asked herself impatiently. After only a few days of recuperation she should have realised how quickly Glyn would tire. She should have been firm. She should not have given in to his blackmail. She felt pretty sure now that if she had refused to enter the ravine, he would have had to abandon the idea.

Happily, only Maria was about when they reached the house, and apart from pulling a face at Rhia's mud-smeared clothes, she made no comment. Instead, she suggested that Glyn might like to join her in the kitchen, while Rhia went to change.

'Yes. Yes, I'll do that,' he agreed, transferring his weight from Rhia's shoulder to the Indian woman's. 'I could surely use some coffee, and some of your home-made muffins, Maria.'

In the bathroom, Rhia undressed with some difficulty. Every bone in her body seemed to have been jarred, and her limbs ached from the effort of riding some distance in that condition. Her clothes were damp, too, chilling her flesh and clinging to her skin when she attempted to remove them.

Successful at last, she ran herself a hot bath, and plunged into its steaming depths. The water acted as a balm to her abused body, and she closed her eyes wearily, allowing the heat to seep into her bones.

The sound of voices below her windows alerted her to the fact that the men had returned, and with an effort, she pulled herself out of the bath and towelled herself dry. She was amazed to discover it was lunchtime, and she hurried into her bedroom to find something else to wear.

Fortunately she had more than one set of jeans, but she decided to wear cords instead. A slim-fitting pair of jade green corduroy accented the slender line of her long legs, and with them she wore a cream blouse and matching sweater.

She did get quite a shock when she took off the bath-robe, however. As she stepped into bikini briefs she caught a glimpse of her back in the long closet mirrors, and caught her breath at the purpling bruise that followed the curve of her spine round to her buttocks. It looked and felt very tender, and she pulled her trousers on carefully to avoid any undue abrasion.

Downstairs, the hall seemed to be filled with people, and she hesitated uncertainly, unwilling to intrude. Glyn was there, she could see him, ensconced on one of the couches and talking with an older man and a younger girl, and Lisa was holding court near the fireplace, the glass she was holding reflecting the sparks of the logs burning beside her. Of Jared there was no sign, but Rhia guessed he would be about somewhere. However, it was Ben Frazer who looked up and saw her, and it was his friendly invitation that brought her into the throng.

'Come and meet some people you should know,' he exclaimed, tucking his hand beneath her elbow. 'Just one or two folks who've called in for a drink and to welcome Glyn back home. Now, let me see, this here's Martin Palmer, our local medic, and this lovely lady is his wife, Pamela. That guy talking with Glyn is Frank Stevens, who owns the spread next to ours, and the young lady with him is his daughter, Lory.' He grinned. 'Come on, I'll introduce you.'

'No—really——' Rhia hung back, wishing someone would ask her to sit down. Her legs felt decidedly shaky, and when Ben offered her a drink, she accepted with gratitude.

Although he brought her the sherry she asked for, she noticed Ben was drinking nothing stronger than orange juice again. She wondered if Jared felt a sense of satisfaction at this transformation, but he hadn't yet made an appearance.

'Ben tells us you're training to be a nurse, Val,' Pamela Palmer remarked beside her. 'I used to be one, too. That's how I met Martin.'

Rhia cleared her throat. 'I—er—I'm just a student nurse, Mrs Palmer,' she explained. 'I only began my training six months ago.'

'Really?' Pamela's reddish brows arched. 'How old does one have to be to start one's training in England? I understood from Ben that you took up nursing after leaving school.'

'I was a late starter,' said Rhia uncomfortably, sure that the lines of strain she knew must be evident in her face were adding years to her age. The curly wig didn't help either. She had never liked short hair.

'Oh, well——' To her relief Pamela gave it up, and Glyn, hearing her voice, summoned her to join him.

Excusing herself to Ben and the Palmers, Rhia crossed the floor to Glyn's side, sighing with relief when he pulled her down on to the arm of the couch beside him. It was hard, and not particularly comfortable, but at least it was easier than relying on her legs.

'Let me introduce you to Frank Stevens and Lory,' he said, squeezing her hand reassuringly. 'Lory and I have been friends since schooldays.'

Rhia smiled at the slim dark girl seated on the couch beside her father. Lory Stevens was not beautiful, but she was attractive, and Rhia was not surprised that her attitude towards herself was hardly enthusiastic. No doubt, Lory had had some leanings in Glyn's direction, too, and Rhia wished she could tell her that she presented no threat.

The gathering broke up about half past one, still without Jared putting in an appearance. Happily, Glyn seemed to have completely recovered from his earlier exhaustion, and the four of them ate lunch together, served by Maria, and her rosy-cheeked assistant, Rebecca.

'Why hasn't Jared joined us?' Lisa demanded of Ben, as they tackled a delicious hot soup, smelling strongly of beef. 'He knew I'd asked Martin to stop by and take a look at Glyn. The least he could do was show his face!'

'Oh, Mom!' It was Glyn who answered her. 'You know Jared has no time for chit-chat in the middle of the day. And in any case, why should he come back here? He sent Pa, didn't he?' His blue eyes narrowed disconcertingly. 'Or did you just decide to come yourself?'

Ben snorted. 'Jared's not my keeper, you know.'

'You could have fooled me!'

'Glyn!'

'Glyn!'

Both Rhia and Lisa spoke simultaneously, and Glyn gave a shamefaced grimace. 'Well,' he muttered, 'I wish you wouldn't try to involve me in your schemes, Mom. I don't need any hick doctor looking me over. Dr Singh has made arrangements for me to see the specialist at the

Mackenzie Hospital in Calgary in two weeks. Until then, there's nothing anyone else can do.'

'I should have thought, after spending almost two weeks in the hospital, you would have appreciated the need to monitor your progress,' retorted Lisa shortly. 'Honestly, Glyn, I'm only thinking of you. You can't expect me to behave as if *nothing* had happened.'

Glyn ground his jaws together. 'Okay,' he conceded moodily, pushing his plate aside. 'But I'm no invalid, Mom, and I wish you'd remember that.'

During the afternoon, Ben offered to entertain Rhia while Glyn took a reluctant rest. The younger man had protested that he didn't need to rest, but after lunch it was obvious to all of them that he was having a struggle to keep awake.

'Go to bed, Glyn,' Rhia pleaded with him gently. 'You know you should. You don't want to have a relapse, do you?'

'I will if you will,' he remarked huskily, keeping her beside him, and Rhia sighed.

'Glyn——'

'Okay, okay,' he nodded, 'I'll be good. But just you remember whose girl you are.'

Rhia stiffened, apprehensive of what was coming next, but to her relief Glyn only laughed. 'Pa's been known to make it in his time,' he explained, mocking his grandfather, and Ben scowled goodnaturedly.

'Making it!' he exclaimed. 'What an expression to use! Let me tell you, there was a time when Ben Frazer was in demand.'

'What for? Robbing a bank?' Glyn ducked to avoid an imaginary punch and Ben snorted.

'Young whipper-snapper! It's just as well I've got an excuse to keep my hands off you!'

Glyn's animation faded. 'Yeah,' he said soberly. 'You could be right,' and the awkward silence that remained after he had left the room was almost tangible.

'Tactless, as usual,' observed Lisa, having no care for the old man's feelings. It was obvious that Ben regretted his impulsive words, but she was not going to let him get away with it. 'I don't know why Jared puts up with you,' she sneered. 'You're too old, and too unreliable. No wonder you drink! It's your only escape, isn't it?'

Lisa followed her son out of the room, and Rhia wished she had left, too, before Ben's humiliation. However, he seemed to recover quite quickly, and shrugging his shoulders, he said: 'She's only put out because Jared wasn't here for her party. Could have told her he wouldn't show. Not for a cocktail party. Not when there's work to be done.'

Rhia got to her feet slowly, her legs protesting at the effort. 'I—Jared seems to put in a lot of time on the ranch,' she said, glad of the diversion. 'I should have thought he could have delegated his duties.'

'Guess he could,' Ben shrugged. 'But that's not Jared's way. Wasn't Mac's way either. Me, I can take it or leave it, but Jared's got ranching in his blood. Besides,' he grimaced, 'I sometimes think he enjoys the men's company more than anyone's. Particularly Horse.'

'Horse? Oh, yes, that's Maria's son.'

'Yeah. He told you that, did he? Well, he and Horse were brought up together, and after Margaret died, Maria was the closest thing to a mother he had.'

Rhia nodded, edging herself carefully away from the table. 'I understand.'

'So,' Ben spread his hands, 'what say you and me take a ride down to the stockyards? Or have you had enough riding for one day? Seems like you're acting pretty stiff to me.'

Rhia forced a smile. 'I—I am, a little,' she admitted. 'If you don't mind, I'll spend some time in the library. I've always loved books, and I've never seen so many in one place before. Except in a public library, of course.'

'Sure. Why not?' Ben grimaced. 'I guess I can find something else to do.'

Rhia's tongue probed her upper lip in sudden anxiety. 'You don't mean—that is—do you mean you'll ride down to the stockyards on your own?'

'Happen.' Ben scratched his grey head. 'You take it easy. I'll see you later.'

Rhia spent the afternoon in the library, with one eye on the drive in case Jared should come back. Right now, the last thing she needed was a taste of his sarcasm, and she refused to admit that she was allowing her persistent, and unwelcome, attraction to him to sour her mood. No matter how she tried, she could not ignore him, and it was humiliating to realise that her real dislike of Lisa stemmed from that unwilling awareness.

However, by the time she left the library to go up to her room, the lower half of her body had become one agonising ache, and she felt like nothing so much as tumbling into bed. Even the thought of food did not appeal to her, and she wished she dared announce that she had a headache and avoid the inevitable gathering at the dinner table.

As it happened, Rebecca was in the process of turning down her bed when Rhia entered the room, but although she turned to the other girl smilingly, her cheerful features sobered when she saw Rhia's pale face.

'Is something wrong, Miss Val?' she asked, with friendly concern. 'You're not sickening for a cold, are you? You look mighty peaky to me.'

'I—I think I'm just tired,' Rhia replied evasively. After all, it was true. Tiredness did play a part in her condition.

'Well, why don't you have a rest before supper?' suggested Rebecca reasonably. 'You got more'n an hour till you need to get ready. Or if you like, I could ask Miss Maria to send you something up.'

'Oh, no. No, that won't be necessary.' The last thing Rhia wanted was to draw attention to her ailments. 'I—er—I think I will take your advice and lie down for a while. Do you think you could give me a call in an hour?'

'Sure thing,' Rebecca nodded agreeably. 'You take care now. Mr Glyn is relying on you.'

But later that evening, seated at the dinner table, Rhia was miserably aware that Glyn appeared to be bearing up rather better than she was. Unlike her, he made short work of the food he was served, and Rhia was glad he could not see the amount she was sending back to the kitchen.

Jared had joined them, as usual, bringing with him a dark-skinned man whom he introduced to her simply as Horse. Recognising the name of Maria's son, who was Jared's ranch foreman, she was not entirely surprised when he and Jared spent most of the meal talking shop.

She was more concerned with the fact that Ben was absent, and she couldn't help remembering what he had said to her that afternoon.

However, Lisa objected to being neglected, and when the conversation turned to breeding methods, she put aside her napkin with carefully controlled impatience. 'Is it necessary to bring cattle into the dining room?' she demanded, her lips curling with distaste. 'I've hardly spoken with you all day, Jared. Is it too much to ask that you show me a modicum of respect in the evening?'

'I'm sorry, Mrs Frazer. It's all my fault.' Horse's attractive drawl was low and apologetic. 'I guess with Jared being away so much recently, we've had a lot of time to make up. But you're right—over the supper table is not the place.'

'It's okay, Horse.' Jared cast a warning glance in his sister-in-law's direction. 'I guess Lisa's just feeling that way. Where's Ben? Don't tell me he hasn't been around the house all afternoon.'

'I suppose he has.' Lisa was offhand. 'I wouldn't know. I've been resting—I had a headache. Handling our guests alone wasn't easy.'

'*Your* guests, Lisa,' Jared reminded her, narrow-eyed. 'And what do you mean, you *suppose* Ben was here? Either he was, or he wasn't.'

'He went to the party, if that's what you mean,' replied Lisa unwillingly. 'He had lunch with us.'

'And afterwards?'

'Val and I went riding this morning,' put in Glyn tersely. 'When I went to rest, he took care of you, didn't he, Val?'

Rhia sighed. 'He—he offered to take me down to the stockyards,' she admitted, and Jared's brooding gaze turned on her. 'But—but I didn't go,' she added quickly. 'I—I was a bit tired, too.'

'So where did he go?' Jared's gazed flicked all of them in turn, and Rhia shook her head.

'I—I don't know.'

'What does it matter?' Lisa was growing impatient with this conversation. 'He'll be about somewhere. He probably took the station wagon into Moose Bay. You told him it needed servicing. God knows,' she gave Horse a rueful smile, 'any activity is better than none at all.'

'What my sister-in-law means is that she's bored,' Jared remarked, apparently abandoning the subject of his father for the time being. 'What she needs is a change of environment, isn't it, Lisa? I guess living on the ranch can be a lonely life for a woman. We'll have to see what we can do to change that.'

'Jared!' Lisa's eyes sparkled. 'Do you mean it? Oh, you know how much I'd love to spend a week or two in New York! Shopping, sightseeing; seeing the latest shows! Do you think we could do it? I mean—while Val's here, Glyn doesn't really need me.'

'You can go whenever you like,' declared Jared indifferently, as Rhia's lips parted in unknowing anticipation. 'We can cope. As you say, Glyn doesn't really need you right now.'

Lisa's face changed. 'What do you mean? *We* can cope? Won't—I mean—you'll be coming with me, won't you?'

'Me?' Jared relaxed in his chair, his fingers playing lazily with the handle of his dessert fork. 'Lisa, you know I can't get away right now. Besides,' he moved his shoulders dismissingly, 'I don't like New York.'

'*Jared!*' Lisa's lips curved petulantly. 'Oh, that was a rotten trick to play!'

'What trick?' Jared glanced impatiently round the table, and Rhia avoided those brilliant dark eyes. 'Lisa, I'm not stopping you from doing anything you want to do. Go to New York. Take Pam Palmer with you. You know she'd be delighted to accompany you.'

'I don't want to go with Pam Palmer,' retorted Lisa icily, and Rhia could almost touch the wave of hostility emanating from Lisa's end of the table. 'I shall stay here until you do have time to take me. Even if I have to wait all summer.'

The significance of this remark was not lost on Rhia, and her mouth felt dry as Jared shrugged his broad shoulders and returned to his conversation with Horse. It was Lisa's way of reminding him where his responsibilities lay, and Rhia was glad she would not be here in the autumn—or the fall, as Glyn had called it—to witness the coming nuptials.

When the meal was over, the two men disappeared into Jared's den to continue their discussions, and Lisa departed from the room in a storm of pique. That left only Rhia and Glyn at the table, and before he could say anything, she got to her feet.

'Would you mind awfully if I went to bed, too, Glyn?' she asked, stifling the groan that the mere effort of rising now brought to her lips. 'I—I'm very tired, and—and—well, a bit stiff, too.'

'You're all right.' Glyn's brow furrowed. 'You haven't done yourself any permanent injury?'

'Heavens, no!' Rhia managed to dismiss his fears quite convincingly. 'I'm just—tired, like I said. I'll see you in the morning.'

But in the morning, Rhia found it was virtually impossible to get out of bed. It took an actual physical effort just to go to the bathroom, and she returned to the bed sweating with the agony that even walking had become. She ached in every limb, and weakness forced a tear or two into her pillow as she contemplated the mess she had got herself into.

She didn't go down for breakfast, hoping that her absence would not be remarked upon. Jared would probably go out early again, and if Ben went with him, only Maria or Glyn was likely to come looking for her. Maria she could cope with, and Glyn—well, she could tell Glyn exactly what was wrong with her, and know that he would understand.

However, the morning was almost over before anyone came to find her, and then it was not Maria or Glyn, but Jared. His sharp tattoo rattled her door a little before twelve o'clock, and she called 'Come in!' faintly, feeling weaker than ever now that she was hungry, too.

Even so, nothing could prevent her from rising up on her elbows when Jared came into the room, pausing in the archway that led from the sitting room, gazing at her with dark brooding malevolence.

'Are you ill?' he asked shortly, little concern evident in his voice, and Rhia drew the velvet quilt closer to her chin.

'No,' she denied jerkily, shocked by his appearance. 'I—I feel a little tired, that's all. I thought I might—spend the morning in bed.'

'Did you?' Jared propped his shoulder against the arching framework. 'Or was it perhaps to avoid facing the inevitable questions we might be obliged to ask?'

'Questions?' Rhia was confused. 'What questions? I don't know what you're talking about.'

'So you know nothing about why my father should have chosen to disobey my instructions, or why Glyn should be running a temperature this morning.'

CHAPTER TEN

'YOUR father? Glyn?' Rhia was confused. 'No. Why? What happened?'

'You tell me.' Jared was abrupt. 'But you went riding with Glyn yesterday, and you were the last person to speak to my father before he swallowed the best part of two bottles of whisky!'

Rhia sank back weakly against the pillows. Right now, she did not feel capable of coping with this, and her mind ran riot with images of what two bottles of whisky could do to a man.

'Well?' Jared was waiting for her answer, and she shook her head.

'Your—your father seemed perfectly all right when he left me yesterday afternoon,' she said. 'As—as for Glyn, you knew we went riding. I thought he had your permission.'

'He did not have my permission to over-exert himself,' retorted Jared harshly. 'Haven't you any sense? You're supposed to be looking after him.'

Rhia gazed at him with tremulous indignation. 'Glyn's not a child, you know. He does have a mind of his own. And—and right now, he needs to prove himself. For his own sake.'

Jared's lips curled. 'So you chose to take him down into the ravine, where the air is damp and unhealthy at this time of year, and the track is unfit for horses.' He swore angrily. 'You must have been crazy. He could have broken his neck down there!'

Rhia forbore to mention that these had been her fears too. He would not have believed her. Instead, she said: 'I didn't want to go down. It was Glyn's idea.'

'And you couldn't stop him, I suppose,' sneered Jared. 'Rhia, if anything had happened to him——'

'I know.' Rhia drew a trembling breath. 'But it didn't. And—and you have no right to accuse me of—of carelessness. You can't blame me for something that never happened.'

Jared glanced over his shoulder and then, leaving the curving lintel, he approached the bed. 'Perhaps I find your dindifference bloody hard to swallow,' he snapped. 'I mean, you're supposed to be keeping Glyn company, and what are you doing? Lying in bed!'

Rhia moistened her lips. 'I—I didn't feel very well this morning.'

'Really?'

'Yes, really.' Bitterness made her gather the quilt even closer about her. 'But if I'm betraying *orders*, go away and I'll get up. Or,' her eyes turned resentfully up to his, 'do you intend to repeat your behaviour of the other evening? I suppose brute force would seem to offer a more satisfying outlet for your frustrations!'

Jared's mouth thinned. 'Don't taunt me, Rhia. I've apologised for my behaviour the evening we arrived, but I have to say, it was not without provocation.'

Rhia gasped. 'That's not true!'

'Isn't it? You're a provoking young woman, and you'd do well to remember you're not dealing with some callow youth like Simon Travis.'

'Why don't you go?' Rhia was weary of this conversation. 'Tell—tell Glyn I'll come to his room as soon as I'm dressed.'

Jared nodded. 'I'll tell Maria to give him that message.'

'Oh, yes.' Rhia's tone was bitter. 'Get someone else to

tell him. It wouldn't do for him—or Lisa—to learn how freely you make use of my apartments.'

Jared walked back to the archway, pausing to rest his hand against the wood. 'Let's leave Lisa out of this, shall we?' he declared tersely, and Rhia pressed her lips together defeatedly as he disappeared from her sight.

With a helpless feeling of depression she turned to thrust her leg out of bed, only to let out a sob of agony at the pain that ravaged her spine. Dear God, she thought tearfully, turning her face into the pillow. How was she going to get through the day? Her limbs were trembling with even this small effort.

The hands that turned her over were not gentle, but her consternation at discovering Jared was still here when she had thought he was gone kept her chokingly silent.

'For God's sake, there's no need to cry,' he muttered, gripping her shoulders through the quilt, and giving her a shake.

The spasm of agony that crossed her face at this mild admonishment caused his dark brows to draw scowlingly together. 'God, I'm not going to hurt you,' he snapped fiercely. 'Stop looking at me as if I was some kind of inhuman monster!'

Rhia moved her head from side to side. 'Please,' she whispered, 'go away,' and then could not deny the groan that escaped her when he thrust her back against her pillows with evident frustration.

Jared's eyes narrowed then, and watching her all the while his hands determinedly drew the covers away from her scantily-clad shoulders. Still able to see nothing amiss, he dragged the covers brutally to the foot of the bed.

She did not know what he had expected to find, but he shook his head impatiently as she made a half-hearted effort to draw the folds of her virtually transparent nightgown about her. 'For God's sake, Rhia, what is it?' he demanded, gazing down into drowned violet eyes that seemed to be reproaching him. 'What's wrong with you? What have I done? If I've hurt you in some way, then for heaven's sake tell me!'

Rhia expelled her breath weakly, her hands shaking as she attempted to reach for the covers. 'I—I had a fall

Yesterday,' she admitted reluctantly. 'I didn't want to tell you, because I knew what you would think.' She caught her breath. 'But it doesn't really matter now, does it?'

Jared's heavy lids hooded his eyes. 'How bad a fall was it?' he asked harshly. 'Where did you fall? Why on earth didn't you tell me before this? I might have been able to help you.'

Rhia shook her head. 'It—it's not important. I—I'm a bit stiff, that's all. I'll get over it.'

Jared's mouth twisted, and then, to her complete humiliation, he turned her over on to her stomach, catching his breath at the darkness he could see through the thin silk of her nightgown. Her mortification was complete when he hauled up the nightgown to expose the bruised skin at the base of her spine, and she quivered uncontrollably when his hands lightly touched her flesh.

'God, why didn't you tell me?' he demanded thickly, and she felt the depression of the mattress as he seated himself beside her. 'You could have broken your back,' he muttered, with an oath, and Rhia, though she knew she would despise herself later, knew a melting delight in just feeling his hands upon her.

'It—it probably looks worse than what it is,' she ventured, after a moment, realising the possible interpretation someone else might put on his behaviour. 'I didn't have any liniment, you see.' She forced a tremulous laugh. 'I felt such a fool!'

'Mmm.' Jared was not amused, his hands stilled now, only his thumbs lightly massaging her spine. 'I've got something that might help.' He got to his feet. 'Stay as you are. I won't be a minute.'

'Oh, but——' Rhia half turned, but the effort was too great, and she lay there, prone, until she heard the sound of someone coming.

She had wondered whether he might get Maria to bring whatever it was he thought would help her, but her heavy lids disclosed Jared's tautly-moulded thighs as he came round the bed.

'It's an old Indian medication,' he remarked, showing her the jar he was carrying. 'It doesn't smell too sweetly, but I can vouch for its efficacy.'

'Thank you.' Rhia stretched out her hand for the jar, but Jared held it out of her reach.

'I'll do it,' he stated, resuming his position on the side of the bed. 'Now, relax, if you can. I'll try not to hurt you.'

His hands massaged the abused flesh with exquisite tenderness, moving in a rhythmic motion, soothing and relieving the taut muscles. He spread the ointment smoothly over her skin, opening the pores and allowing the healing unguent to invade the aching tendons. And as his fingers gently kneaded her spine, she felt a flooding wave of well-being washing over her.

'Better?' he asked huskily, his palms lingering in the small of her back, and Rhia nodded her head vigorously against the pillow.

'Don't stop,' she breathed, nestling more comfortably into the mattress, but with a sound of aggravation Jared drew his hands away.

'I've got to,' he muttered harshly, and she turned her head confusedly to meet his smouldering eyes. 'I'm not an automaton,' he told her roughly, and getting up from the bed, he strode swiftly into the bathroom.

When he came back, Rhia had straightened the covers on the bed and was sitting anxiously, waiting for his return. He came to the bathroom door, drying his hands on one of her towels, and spoke with crisp detachment.

'I suggest you stay in bed for the rest of the day. Glyn can do without your company for once.'

'Oh, no!' Rhia shook her head in protest. 'Jared, you've made me feel so much better——'

'Even so, you need to rest,' Jared retorted shortly, dropping the towel into the laundry basket. 'I'll have Maria send your meals up.'

'All right.' Rhia moved her shoulders a little disconsolately. 'If that's what you want.'

Jared's lips twisted. 'What I want doesn't come into this,' he replied flatly. 'I'll explain the situation to Glyn. He'll understand.'

'Thank you,' Rhia nodded.

'Okay.' Jared moved towards the archway. 'Try and

get as much rest as you can. We don't want three invalids in the family.'

'Three——' Rhia broke off nervously. 'Jared—about Ben: I couldn't believe—I mean, I did think about what you said, but——'

'I know.' Jared cut her off without emotion. 'See you.'

Alone, Rhia found herself abysmally near to tears. A feeling compounded of her pity for Ben and herself weakened her already torn emotions, and when Maria came into the room carrying her lunch tray she found the patient's eyes swollen and puffy.

'Now what's happened?' she exclaimed, putting the tray to one side while she shook Rhia's pillows and made her comfortable against them. 'Jared told me you'd had a fall from your horse. He didn't tell me he'd upset you.'

'He didn't.' Rhia sniffed into her handkerchief. 'As—as a matter of fact, he was very nice. He brought me that ointment—there, and—and it's made my back feel much easier.'

'Really?' Maria viewed the jar with thoughtful eyes. 'Well, I must admit, I had misgivings when he came up here. He was pretty mad, I can tell you.' She grimaced. 'Not that he was much different when he came down.'

Rhia arched her brows. 'No?'

'No.' Maria set the tray across her legs. 'And finding you crying, I thought I'd found the cause. Seems like I was wrong.'

Rhia hesitated. 'You—you're very fond of Jared, aren't you, Maria?'

'Like my own son,' said Maria simply, folding her hands.

'And—his brother?'

'Angus?' Maria shrugged. 'Angus was so much older. Eight years, you know. Miss Margaret shouldn't have had no more children after Angus, but Mac wanted sons.' She sighed. 'It weakened her, having Jared, but she never regretted it.'

Rhia nodded. 'And now Angus is dead, too.'

'Yes.' Maria's tone became crisper. 'Have you got everything you need?'

Rhia looked down at the laden tray, at the succulent

steak nestling in its bed of salad, and the waffles cooling
in their bed of butter. 'Oh, yes,' she said, shaking her
head. 'I just hope I can do justice to it.'

Maria smiled and turned towards the door, but in the
curving aperture she paused. 'I know it's none of my
business,' she said, causing Rhia to look at her in anxious
anticipation, 'but when do you and Jared plan to tell
Glyn you're not the girl he thinks you are?'

The fork Rhia had used to take a slice of tomato to her
mouth clattered on to the plate. 'You—you know?'

'It's just as well I do,' Maria essayed dryly. 'If not, I'd
have been mighty suspicious. No one in their right mind
would hide hair like that less'n they had a reason.'

'Oh!' Rhia put up a horrified hand to her head. 'I
forgot.'

'That's okay. Jared told me the truth days ago. You're
Val's sister, and you agreed to come on doctor's advice.'

Rhia nodded. 'Something like that.'

Maria frowned. 'He also said that you already had a
boy-friend, is that right? Or was that just for Mrs Frazer's
benefit?'

'Lisa?' Rhia was confused.

'That's right.' Maria was complacent. 'Seems like a
reasonable thing to do, seeing as how he's taken with you
himself.'

'Jared?' Rhia's pulses raced. 'Don't be silly——'

Maria gave her an old-fashioned look. 'You're not that
ignorant, Rhia. You've seen the way he looks at you, same
as I have. And why not? He's a virile man. Just because
Mrs Frazer considers him her property, doesn't mean he
hasn't got eyes in his head.'

Rhia was trembling. It should not have shocked her,
but it did. Heavens, hadn't she known there was that
unwilling attraction between them? Hadn't she herself
fought that very attraction every time he came near her?
But hearing it from Maria, hearing her put into words
something which had been so nebulous, was not the sweet
fulfilment she had imagined. On the contrary, it sounded
coarse and sordid, hinting as it did at an illicit relationship, and the confirmation of Jared's involvement with
Lisa was as painful to bear as her bruises had been earlier.

'I'd better go.' Maria was suddenly all bustle, as if regretting that revealing confidence. 'I'll send Rebecca up for the tray later. You try and get some sleep.'

But although Rhia made a valiant effort with the meal, her appetite had completely disappeared, and she pretended to be asleep when Rebecca came to take the tray, to avoid any unnecessary scoldings. She did not sleep, however. She lay there wishing she had taken Simon's advice and told Jared she couldn't help him. It seemed as though every day brought some new complication, not least the growing knowledge that she was falling in love with a man she could never have.

By evening, she was feeling physically more comfortable at least. The soothing salve had done its work, and the stiffness was gradually easing out of her bones. She could actually get out of bed and go to the bathroom without groaning every inch of the way, and she thought by the morning she would be able to put this particular disaster aside.

Rebecca brought her dinner and looked surprised to find Rhia seated at her dressing table, brushing her hair. Belatedly, Rhia saw the wig residing beside the bed, and knew a feeling of frustration when the Canadian girl admired her hair. Earlier on, when Rebecca came to collect the tray, she had kept her head half under the covers, but now there was no disguising its length.

'Hey, you must be feeling better,' she exclaimed, setting the tray on the table close by. 'But my, I wouldn't wear any wig if I had hair as pretty as you.'

Rhia sighed, making an indifferent gesture. 'I—Glyn likes my hair short. I—let him think I'd had it cut.'

'Oh, I see.' Rebecca accepted her explanation without question. 'And right now, he's not seeing too good anyway.'

'That's right.'

'My, but it's pretty,' Rebecca repeated enviously. 'I think he'd change his mind if'n he could see it.'

Rhia forced a smile. 'You could be right. You—er—you won't tell him, will you? It's a secret.'

'My lips are sealed,' declared Rebecca dramatically, and exited the room still shaking her head over Rhia's transformation.

Rhia managed to drink the soup and eat a little of the chicken supreme Maria had served, but the creamy jacket potatoes were beyond her, as too was the spicy apple strudel. Instead, she helped herself to a Californian peach, peeling it carefully and enjoying its succulent flesh.

She was wiping her lips on her napkin when she became aware that someone was watching her, and she looked up from the tray to find Jared leaning against the arched entry. He looked pale himself this evening, as if he had spent the day in his den instead of out in the open air, his black silk shirt and narrow tie matching the tight-fitting moleskin that closely moulded his thighs. Every taut muscle was thrown into sharp relief by the light behind him, and Rhia averted her eyes from where they were disposed to linger.

'What are you doing out of bed?' he demanded, leaving his support to advance some way towards her. 'I thought I told you to stay in bed all day. Sitting on a hard surface is not going to relax those muscles.'

'This—this chair isn't hard,' Rhia exclaimed, edging to one side so that he could see the cushioned seat. 'And—and I don't like eating in bed. I don't like the crumbs.'

'Have you finished?'

'What? Oh——' Rhia glanced down at the soiled napkin. 'Yes. Yes, I've finished. Why? Have you come for the tray?'

Jared's lips twisted. 'Would I?' He strolled across to the bed and lifted the jar of ointment from the bedside table. 'No, I've come for this. Horse has wrenched his shoulder, hauling up some timber.'

'Oh, I'm sorry.' Rhia moistened her lips. 'Is he all right?'

'He'll live,' remarked Jared dryly. 'How about you?'

'Oh—I'm much better.' Rhia hesitated. 'How's Glyn?'

'His temperature's subsided. I guess it was just a touch of fever. And you'll be happy to learn that Pa is recovering.'

'I'm so glad.'

'Yes.' Jared paused. 'I guess it was something Lisa said that drove him off the rails. It generally is.'

Rhia opened her mouth as remembrance of what Lisa had said returned to her, but then she closed it again. It was not up to her to say anything. If Ben wanted Jared to know, he would tell him.

'So——' Jared rocked back on his booted heels. 'I'm glad you're feeling so much better. Glyn told me what happened. I won't tell you what I said.'

Rhia's lips quivered. 'I can guess.'

'Can you?' Jared came round the end of the bed, surveying her intently. 'Did Maria repeat the treatment this evening?'

'Maria?' Rhia looked up at him blankly. 'I—why, no.'

'Why not?'

'Well, because I haven't seen her since lunchtime. Rebecca brought my dinner.'

'Damn!' Jared gazed down at her impatiently. 'I asked her to take care of it.'

'Well, she didn't.' Rhia shrugged. 'It doesn't matter, I'll do it myself.' She glanced round. 'If you could leave me a little of the ointment——'

'I'll do it.' Jared snapped the words abruptly. 'Go on, lie on the bed. It won't take long.'

'It's not necessary.' Rhia got to her feet, but made no move towards the bed. 'Jared——'

'I've said I'll do it, and I will,' he declared harshly. 'It's no hardship, God knows!'

Rhia's mind reeled with the implications of that statement, but then Jared was pushing her towards the bed, and she tumbled on to it helplessly as he squatted down beside her.

Her robe and nightgown were peeled back and the chill of the ointment was accentuated by the chill of Jared's fingers. 'I'm sorry,' he muttered roughly, taking his hands away and rubbing them together. 'I'll go wash them in hot water. A frozen massage is likely to do more harm than good.'

Rhia obediently remained where she was, and presently he came back, laying his now warm hands against her waist. 'Is that better?' he asked huskily, but before she could answer him, she felt the sudden heat of his lips against her skin.

'Oh, God,' he groaned, resting his forehead against the curve of her hip. 'I'm not going to be able to do this, Rhia. Not without touching you . . .'

'But——' Rhia half turned towards him, on the point of saying that of course he had to touch her when she saw the burning darkness of his eyes. 'Oh—Jared!' she whispered, expelling her breath in a little gasp, and with a smothered oath he pulled her up into his arms.

Perhaps if his lips had begun by being violent or aggressive she might have stood some chance of resisting him. But they weren't. His mouth moved on hers with persuasive sensuality, a wine-dark possession that flowed around her and over her, drugging her senses and seducing her into a state of trembling acquiescence.

Almost instinctively, her hands moved against his chest, parting the buttons of his shirt so that the warm scent of his body rose into her nostrils. There was a bittersweet enchantment in touching him in this way, in feeling the response her timid hands were evoking. There was pleasure, too, and a thrilling sense of power in the knowledge that she could arouse him as he was arousing her.

With an exclamation of impatience he tore off his tie and jerked the remaining buttons of his shirt apart, and only as she felt the abrasive touch of his hair-roughened chest against her breasts did she realise he had pushed the nightgown off her shoulders. Looking down, she knew a trembling delight in seeing those hard peaks crushed against his brown skin, and following her gaze, Jared's eyes narrowed and darkened until they were almost black.

'You want me,' he said, winding his hands into her hair and drawing it across his lips. 'You want me—and heaven knows, I want you!'

Now, when his mouth sought hers, it was hard and demanding, pressing her lips against her teeth, hungrily devouring its sweetness. With a muffled groan, he bore her back against her pillows, half covering her body with his, and Rhia's aching spine was forgotten as his lean limbs entwined with hers.

His hands caressed her urgently, his lips following their tantalising trail to her throat and her shoulders, and the hardening curve of her breast. With his tongue inflaming one taut nipple, she offered no resistance when his fingers probed the inner curve of her thigh, stroking the sensitised skin until an unfamiliar ache began in the pit of her stomach and spread down her legs.

'Don't stop me,' he said, burying his face in the hollow between her breasts, and her instinctive response was to curl her hands into the hair at his nape and pull his parted lips to hers.

He moved on her then, and she could feel the heat of him through the taut barrier of his slacks. His body thrust against her softness, and even through the cloth she could feel his pulsating strength, his maleness. Weakness flooded her being, weakness and a mindless hunger that gave itself up to his assuagement, and blindly knew what he wanted of her.

Her hands moved over the hair that arrowed down to his navel, finding the zip that was all that was keeping them apart. Her fingers captured the clip and began to propel it downwards, and she had to tear her hands away when she heard the sound of a door closing in the adjoining room.

'Rhia——' Jared's barely audible groan was muffled against her neck, but he had felt her withdrawal and made his own interpretation of its cause. With grim determination he dragged himself away from her and up from the bed, and she gathered the quilt about her, breathlessly waiting for someone to expose them.

Nothing happened. There was no further movement, no sound at all from the sitting room, but the steady ticking of a clock. With an expression of bewilderment Rhia turned her eyes up to Jared's—and met a dark and hostile accusation.

He was rapidly restoring his clothes to order, fastening the buttons of his shirt, slotting his tie beneath his collar. But the bitterness in his face was more than she could bear, and with a helpless shake of her head she mouthed her fears.

'Someone came in,' she whispered, loath even now to

give an intruder the satisfaction of knowing she was alarmed. 'I—I heard them.'

Jared's mouth took on a downward slant. 'Did you?' he said sceptically, making no attempt to moderate his tone. 'Well, where are they?' He walked to the archway and looked into the room beyond. 'It's empty. There's no one here, Rhia. You just got cold feet, that's all. But perhaps it's just as well.' He shook his head. 'I must have been out of my mind!'

Rhia caught her breath. 'No, there was someone. Jared, you've got to believe me.' She looked up at him beseechingly. 'I—I didn't get cold feet.' Her lips parted. 'Please—don't go!'

A look of anguish crossed his face for a moment, and she thought she had got through to him. But then it was as if a mask came down and he schooled his features, adjusting the knot of his tie as he moved towards the door.

'Go to sleep, Rhia,' he said harshly, picking up the tray. 'I'll see this is delivered back to Maria. Perhaps it was she who came for the tray. I suppose it's possible.' His lips twisted. 'Except Maria's not the kind of person to enter a room uninvited.'

CHAPTER ELEVEN

RHIA slept badly, her dreams haunted by the memory of Jared's face as he pulled himself away from her. She had let him down, she didn't need any previous experience to understand that, and her own over-stimulated emotions would not allow her to relax. In her dreams, she re-lived those moments when Jared's hard body had been pressing hers down on to the bed, when his mouth had played tantalisingly with hers, and his throbbing masculinity had probed the inviting softness of her thighs. She trembled in the grip of feelings she had never felt before, her breasts hard beneath the thin silk of her nightgown, her limbs aching for a fulfilment they had not received. She thought

with incredulity of the association she had had with
Simon, and began to understand Valentina's impatience
with the chaste relationship they had shared. That was
not love, that colourless friendship, whose high spot was a
fumbled embrace in Simon's car. She had never known
what the relationship between a man and a woman could
be like. She could never have believed herself capable of
behaving so eagerly, so wantonly, wanting Jared so badly
that it created an actual physical ache inside her. She had
never felt that way with Simon, never felt the slightest
desire to find out what lay beneath the neatly-laundered
shirts and pullovers his mother provided. But with Jared
she was always aware of the man beneath the casual elegance of his clothes, his unconscious sexuality acting like
a flame to her already smouldering senses.

At least in the morning she was able to get out of bed
without too much discomfort. Despite the fact that Jared
had not repeated the treatment the night before, the
warmth and rest had worked their own miracle, and apart
from a little stiffness, she felt free from pain. However, she
was a little disturbed to find the jar of ointment lying on
the floor when she got out of bed, and she hoped that
Horse would not blame her for its absence.

She was washed and dressed by eight o'clock, and instead of waiting for Maria to bring her breakfast tray, she
went down to the kitchen. The Indian woman was relaxing for once, sitting at the scrubbed pine table drinking a
cup of coffee, and her dark eyes widened in surprise when
Rhia entered the room.

'Didn't Jared tell you to rest a while?' she exclaimed,
getting up and putting her cup aside. 'Seems a little foolish
to leave your bed at this hour of the morning, specially
since you spent the whole of yesterday in it.'

'Oh, really, I feel fine.' Rhia brushed a careless hand
over the revealing shadows beneath her eyes. 'That—er—
that ointment Jared—brought me——'

'Worked good, did it?' Maria grimaced. 'Well, I'm
pleased to hear it. I guess that recipe's been around longer
than I have, and I've never known it let me down yet.'

Rhia forced a smile. 'I—Jared said that Horse had
wrenched his shoulder. He came back last night to get the

ointment, and then went away without it.' She shrugged, a little awkwardly. 'I don't know why.'

'No problem.' Maria pulled a face. 'We got more than one bottle of the stuff.'

'You have?'

Rhia could feel her face deepening with colour. So that had only been an excuse, she was thinking unsteadily. Jared had really come back to find out how she was. Her hands were trembling, and she thrust them into the hip pockets of her purple jeans to prevent Maria from seeing them.

'You want some breakfast?'

Maria was laconic, but all of a sudden Rhia felt as if she could eat a horse. For some reason best known to himself, Jared had wanted to come back last night, and no matter how crazy it might be, she was glad of that.

She surprised the old woman by eating everything she set in front of her, including a cereal with cream, grilled ham and eggs, and even a slice of buttered toast, with home-made strawberry conserve.

'You were hungry,' Maria commented, clearing the plates. 'Just as well. As I recall, you hardly ate a thing yesterday.'

Rhia bent her head. 'Yesterday was yesterday,' she declared. 'How is Glyn? Do you know?'

'I checked on him at seven-thirty,' Maria agreed, pausing. 'His temperature was definitely down. I'd say he was okay.'

'Thank goodness.' Rhia sighed. 'And——' she looked up, 'and Ben?'

'That old soak!' Maria grimaced. 'He'll survive, though how his liver stands the pace, I don't know. He's not a young man, y'know. All of sixty-five. You'd think he'd know better at his age, wouldn't you?'

Rhia bit her lip. 'Maybe he's not happy,' she ventured, and Maria grunted.

'You could be right. Since Angus died, things have been worse.'

'Things?' Rhia blinked. 'What things?'

'Oh——' Maria turned away, 'I guess he realises there'll be changes when Jared—well, when Mrs Frazer——'

'—marries Jared,' Rhia put in succinctly, her elation fading, and Maria nodded.

'I guess so.'

Rhia rested her elbows on the table and cupped her chin in her hands. 'But——' she felt compelled to go on, 'Mrs Frazer—Lisa, that is—was married to Angus.'

'That's true.' Maria paused, resting her hands on the table. 'But Jared runs the ranch. Angus was often away. He never had much interest in farming, like his son.'

'And I suppose—Mrs Frazer went with him.'

'That's right.' Maria shrugged. 'And I guess she may want to make some changes, when she's mistress here.'

Rhia felt an overwhelming sense of compassion. 'I see.'

'So,' Maria became businesslike, 'how about you taking up Glyn's breakfast this morning? I guess he'll be pleased to hear that you're all right.'

But Glyn wasn't awake when Rhia entered his room with the tray, and she carried it to the bedside table, setting it down carefully. She knew if she intended leaving the tray, she would have to wake him, so that he didn't blindly knock it aside. But it seemed a shame to disturb him, and she stepped a little closer, looking down at him affectionately. She realised she had become fond of him over these weeks, and the effort of being Val was not as arduous as it had been at first. Nevertheless, she would be glad when it was over, even if the idea of never seeing Jared again filled her with despair.

As she turned away, her toe brushed against something lying just under the bed. Had she not come so close to stare down at him, she would never have noticed it, but now she bent and picked it up, finding it was a magazine.

At first the realisation that a magazine should be lying under Glyn's bed did not ring any warning bells. It was simply a glossy rag, the kind of publication printed to titillate the male appetite. Almost unthinkingly, its pages slipped through Rhia's fingers, exposing the female form in a variety of poses. Her lips were parting in amusement when the incongruity of her find struck her a shocking blow. This was a visual periodical, something that required to be *seen* to be enjoyed. How long had the magazine been there? And what did it mean?

The date was that of a current issue, but she had no way of knowing whether Glyn had brought the book home with him, or whether someone else had left it beneath the bed. But no—she dismissed that theory. Maria would never have allowed Glyn to use this room without first cleaning it from top to bottom, and no girlie magazine was likely to escape her notice. But did this mean that Glyn had put the magazine there to hide it from his mother, perhaps? Or, incredibly, had his sight come back, without anyone knowing anything about it?

She wanted to wake him up then. She wanted to take him and shake him, and demand that he tell her the truth. But if it was true, if he had regained his sight, he would see immediately that she was not Val, and she was afraid of the inevitable consequences.

She had to tell someone, she thought, twisting the magazine between her fingers. But who? *Who?* Jared was the most obvious person, but he was unlikely to return before lunchtime at least, and by then her identity could have been exposed.

Lisa! Her brain seized on the obvious alternative. Lisa should be told of the possibility, at least, and perhaps she would have some suggestion. After all, she had no reason to fear her son regaining his sight, and armed with the magazine, she could ask the pertinent question.

Pushing the magazine back beneath the bed, Rhia lifted the tray again and carried it to the table by the window. She dared not leave it where it was, just in case she was mistaken, and her nerves prickled with impatience as she moved the bowl of flowers which occupied the table aside, and made the tray secure.

However, as she turned back towards the door, Glyn stirred. She was still several yards from freedom when he opened his eyes, and she froze to the spot, cursing her bad luck.

'Maria?' he mumbled sleepily, shuffling up on his pillows, but Rhia stared at him mutely, unable to say a word.

Could he see her? Even with the curtains drawn, the light was filtering through and she could see him clearly.

But then his face was in the light, while hers was in the shadow, and in those first few seconds she felt rooted to the spot.

'Who is it?' he muttered, rubbing his eyes, and her breath escaped on a trembling sigh. If she didn't answer him soon, she would be unable to answer him at all, and she could imagine the ignominy of having to creep out of the room without making a sound.

'It—it's me, Glyn,' she got out, her voice several degrees higher than it normally was. 'Oh,' she cleared her throat nervously, 'have I woken you? I—I didn't mean to. I just brought your tray.'

'You're better?' To her relief, Glyn seemed more intent on straightening his covers preparatory to taking his tray than in her appearance, and a persistent throbbing began behind her temple. Could he see, or couldn't he? she exhorted silently, before resignedly picking up the tray and carrying it to the bed.

He looked up at her as she set the tray across him, and with loving tenderness, placed a kiss at the corner of her mouth. She felt numb when those blue eyes encountered the cloudy mauve of hers, and her trembling apprehension communicated itself to him.

'Is something wrong?' he asked, staying her with his hand loosely about her arm. 'Val? Why are you so nervous? Did I frighten you? I didn't mean to.'

He couldn't see. All the strength went out of her in an enervating stream, and it was all she could do to remain standing. 'I—I expect I'm still a bit weak,' she got out, giving a shaky laugh. 'That was quite a tumble I took, wasn't it?'

'You're sure you're okay?' His concern for her made her feel doubly guilty. Not only had she been poking about in things that did not concern her, she had also suspected him of keeping his improvement a secret from the people who cared about him.

'I'm—I'm fine,' she conceded huskily. 'And relieved to see that you're so much better. I—Jared told me you had had a temperature.'

'It was nothing.' Glyn released her with a grimace. 'Just over-excitement, I guess.'

'Over-excitement?'

'Going riding, having visitors,' declared Glyn, applying himself to identifying the various items on the tray. 'And the shock of you falling off, I guess. That really shook me up.'

'I made a fool of myself, didn't I?' murmured Rhia, moving away from the bed. 'Well, I'll go and let you get on with your breakfast. It's a bit of a misty morning, so I don't think we'll be going riding today.'

Glyn let her go, promising to join her downstairs after he was dressed. 'Ben's lent me an electric razor for the time being,' he said. 'It's not as efficient as a blade, but it'll do.'

Rhia smiled, realised he couldn't see her, and said: 'I'll see you downstairs, then,' and left him, closing the door behind her with an overwhelming feeling of relief.

To her surprise, Lisa was up and dressed when she went downstairs. The older woman was looking her age this morning, Rhia thought, and then reflected ruefully that she probably looked Lisa's age, too. Lisa was dressed for going out, in a slim-fitting pants suit made of dark blue wool, her make-up flawless in spite of the lines that were furrowing her brow.

'Good morning,' she greeted the younger girl, with unusual affability. 'Is Glyn awake? Maria told me you'd taken up his tray.'

'He is now,' agreed Rhia regretfully, prepared to meet her half way. 'I'm afraid I woke him.'

Lisa stilled suddenly. 'Did he say anything?'

'What about?' Rhia shrugged. 'He seems much better.'

'Ah,' Lisa seemed to relax. 'That's good. Even so,' she went on, 'I think he should take it easy for a few days.'

'Oh, so do I.' Rhia was quick to agree with her. 'Riding's definitely out, for the time being.' She paused, colouring. 'I—I suppose Jared told you I had a fall.'

'I'm afraid so.' Lisa actually smiled. 'It was what I was afraid of. I did try to warn you.'

'Yes.' Rhia acknowledged this with a faint answering smile, but she was pretty sure Lisa's fears had not been for her.

'Anyway,' Lisa moved her shoulders in a dismissing

gesture, 'you seem quite recovered this morning. And as you haven't been off the ranch since you arrived, I wondered if you'd like to drive with me into Moose Bay.'

Rhia was taken aback. Even this cordial, and entirely unexpected, conversation had not prepared her for such an invitation, and she didn't know what to say. 'I—but what about Glyn?' she ventured, glancing up the stairs. 'He's getting up later. I'd have to ask him.'

'All right.' Lisa was agreeable. 'I don't think he'll object. He's had your undivided attention since you arrived, hasn't he?'

Rhia could feel the warm colour sweeping up her face again, so she turned away. 'I'll go and tell him,' she muttered, making for the stairs, and wished she felt more enthusiastic about accepting Lisa's company.

Glyn was still lingering over his breakfast, and he seemed a little put out when she knocked at his door and entered without waiting. 'Hey, where's the fire?' he exclaimed, when she burst into the room, and it wasn't until she and Lisa were driving away from the ranch house that Rhia realised he had spoken before she had. Of course it could have meant nothing. He might even have perceived the scent of her perfume, and recognised its owner. But it was disconcerting to realise she was not completely convinced.

The morning was grey and dismal, and Rhia had put on warm woollen slacks, that tied at the ankle, and a chunky orange sweater. Overall, she was wearing the beige suede coat she had brought for special occasions, the sheepskin jacket that would have served still bearing the marks of her fall in the ravine.

Lisa had put on a pair of stout boots over her slacks, and Rhia had shown a little surprise. Surely they were not necessary for shopping in Moose Bay, but perhaps Glyn's mother knew better than she did.

It had been dark the night they drove home from the airport, so Rhia was interested to see her surroundings in daylight. But the cloying mist obscured all but their immediate surroundings, and she was glad of the warmth of the station wagon's heater to stave off the chills of the damp atmosphere.

'Why did you decide to come to Canada, Rhia?' Lisa asked abruptly, as they turned left on to a rough highway, and Rhia was startled.

'Why?' she echoed. 'You know why. To help Glyn. To help him get his sight back.'

'But Jared told me you had refused to consider it. Only the day before Glyn announced that you were coming, I was told that you wouldn't go against your fiancé's wishes.'

Rhia sighed. 'I don't have a fiancé, Mrs Frazer. Simon and I—well, we were friends, it's true. But so far as I was concerned, there was no commitment.'

'You say "were". Are you not friends any more?'

Rhia bit her lower lip. 'Simon couldn't see this my way. We—we decided to give each other a breathing space.'

'I see.' Lisa's features were intent on the road ahead, but Rhia had the distinct feeling that her thoughts were not on her driving. 'And who changed your mind?' she asked now. 'Glyn? Or Jared?'

Rhia caught her breath. 'Why, Glyn, of course.'

'Of course?' Lisa sounded sceptical. 'Somehow you don't convince me, Rhia.'

Rhia turned her head to look at her. This was more like the Lisa she was used to. The hostile adversary, who had shown her venom on more than one occasion. 'I don't think it matters, Mrs Frazer,' she responded. 'My being here has served its purpose.' She paused, and then deciding Lisa ought to be told her suspicions, she said recklessly: 'I found a magazine in Glyn's room this morning. It was under his bed. I—I think—at least, I believe that—he might be regaining his vision.'

To her astonishment, Lisa showed no surprise at this news. 'Oh, yes,' she remarked carelessly, 'he told me. He's been gradually regaining his sight over the last three days. Ever since you fell off your horse, in fact.'

'Ever since I—but why didn't he tell me?' Rhia was both delighted and disappointed. 'Oh,' she pressed her palms against her cheeks, 'thank God! I was beginning to believe it was never going to happen.'

'He didn't want you to know,' declared Lisa curtly,

and then, as Rhia looked stricken, she added: 'Oh, not because he wanted to hurt you. No. He simply wanted to be sure before he said anything.'

Rhia shook her head. 'I can hardly believe it! Oh, that's wonderful! Wonderful! I can't wait to see him.'

Lisa's lips tightened. 'Can't you? Even though you know this means your presence here is now superfluous?'

'That doesn't matter.' Rhia stared at her. 'But—but if Glyn can see, he must already know——'

'—that you're not Val?' Lisa's lips curled. 'Yes, he does. But apparently he's known that all along.'

Rhia gasped. 'But how? My hair——'

She put her hand up to touch the curly wig, but Lisa shook her head. 'Nothing so simple, I'm afraid. Your—er—friend Simon Travis—he told him.'

Rhia's lips parted. 'Simon?'

'That's right.' Lisa felt about in the locker in front of her and brought out a pack of cigarettes, placing one between her lips. 'He went to the hospital before we left England. Jared and I knew nothing about it, of course, but he was obviously determined to stop you any way he could.'

'Oh, Simon!' Rhia clasped her hands tightly together as she imagined the harm he could have done. If Jared had found out, he would have killed him, and she was amazed that Glyn could have taken the news without any evident reaction.

'Apparently Glyn had had his suspicions before that,' Lisa went on, applying the automatic lighter to the end of her cigarette. 'He knew your sister so well, you see. And I suppose there are differences only a—lover would know.'

'Then why didn't he tell me?'

'I don't know. Perhaps he felt you and your sister had made a fool of him, and this was his opportunity to make a fool of you.'

Rhia flushed. 'Perhaps. Only it wasn't like that.'

'Well . . .' Lisa's smile was not pleasant, 'now you know. What are you going to do about it?'

'What am I going to do about it?' Rhia was confused. 'I'm afraid I——'

'I mean, will you now pack up and return to England?'

'Return to England?' Rhia despised herself for blankly repeating everything Lisa said, but she felt too dazed at the moment to think coherently.

'Of course,' Lisa continued. 'There's nothing for you to stay here for now, is there?'

'I suppose not.' Rhia shook her head. 'Does—does Glyn want me to leave?'

'Glyn?' Lisa made a sound of impatience. 'What has Glyn to do with it? It's your decision.'

Rhia frowned. 'I'll have to talk to him.'

'And give him some sob-story?' demanded Lisa brittlely.

'Sob-story? No——'

'You know perfectly well, Glyn will expect you to stay on until the end of your holiday,' Lisa retorted. 'Another two weeks, at least!'

Rhia lifted her shoulders. 'If he wants me to——'

'But I don't want you to, Rhia,' Lisa told her harshly. 'And Jared doesn't want you to. You've become an—embarrassment to him. To both of us.'

Rhia's face flamed. 'I don't know what you mean.'

'Oh, I think you do.' Lisa snorted. 'Do you think I haven't noticed the way you look at him, the way you hang on his every word? It's—it's disgusting! And he's too polite to tell you what a fool you're making of yourself!'

'That's not true!'

'It is true.' Lisa slowed at the junction of two roads and turned on to the narrower track. 'My dear girl, Jared is a man, and if anything is made sufficiently easy, he's going to take what's offered. Do you get my meaning?'

Rhia felt sick. 'You're wrong——'

'No, I'm not wrong. When he came to my room last night, I could smell you on him. I wanted to throw up!'

Rhia wanted to throw up, too. That Jared could go straight from her bed to Lisa's made her feel ill, and turning her head away, she closed her eyes.

Nausea kept her silent as the station wagon began a bumpy climb, and she was scarcely aware of the twists and turns they were taking as pain and humiliation blinded her to all else. Lisa was jealous, she thought tautly, of course, she was, and with good reason. If she and Jared were going to be married, she had every right to object if he indulged in extraneous relationships. And she, Rhia, had known of his commitment to his sister-in-law, right from the beginning. She had no excuses for the way she had behaved, and it was a point in Lisa's favour that she had chosen to talk it out with her privately, instead of embarrassing her in front of the whole family.

The station wagon stopped, and Rhia took a deep breath before turning her head. 'Mrs Frazer,' she began, realising that the only honourable thing to do was offer to leave immediately, and then broke off in surprise when she found she was alone in the vehicle. In those seconds when she had been torturing herself with guilt and humiliation, Lisa had thrust open the door and got out, and Rhia's stomach plunged at the possibility that Lisa might be desperate enough to do herself some injury.

'Mrs Frazer!' A mild sense of panic gripped her, as she looked all about her, and could see no one. Where on earth were they? With the mist swirling all about the car, it was impossible to make out much at all, except that the ground all about them seemed grey, and rock-strewn. She certainly didn't remember coming this way the night they drove back from the airport, but it could be another way into the town. Unless—— Her heart skipped a beat. Unless Lisa had come this way deliberately, because she intended doing something desperate.

'Mrs Frazer!'

Rhia opened her door and got out. The air was icy, and although the wind was not strong enough to clear the mist, it cut through her clothes like a knife.

'Mrs Frazer!' she called again, staring all about her, and expelled her breath uncertainly as her own voice swept back to her in an echo.

If only it wasn't so misty, she thought frustratedly. If only she could see where she was. There was no sign of habitation at all, so Lisa couldn't have sought refuge in some lonely farmhouse, but obviously she had left the car for some reason, and Rhia could not just sit patiently waiting for her to come back. If anything happened to Lisa, she would never forgive herself, and while Jared might bear equal responsibility, she had to do something.

'Mrs Frazer! Lisa!'

Again, only the echo answered her, and thrusting her hands into the pockets of her coat she walked a short way down the track away from the car. The surface of the road was hard for walking, and she sought the scrubby verge, which at least was softer to her feet. She should have worn thicker shoes, she thought, or boots——

The thought had scarcely entered her head when she clearly heard the engine of the station wagon start up. It was difficult to see the car through the mist, but evidently someone had got inside, and relief enveloped her in a wave of weakness. Lisa was not lost or desperate. She must have left the vehicle to answer some unexpected call of nature, a contingency Rhia had not even considered in connection with Glyn's mother.

With a humorous grimace, she turned to make her way back to the car, but as she did so, she realised the sound of the engine was retreating, not getting nearer. Heavens, she thought, in consternation, Lisa must have imagined she had gone the other way. Her beige coat must have melted into the mist, and she could not see her.

Then she released her breath weakly. Of course, once she discovered her mistake, Lisa would come back. Like her, she would know her companion couldn't have strayed far from the car—*so why hadn't Lisa answered when she heard Rhia calling*?

Pushing this disquieting thought aside, Rhia paused to take a deep breath. There was no point in upsetting herself unnecessarily. Lisa would come back. She had to come back. What possible reason could she have for abandoning her out here?

The answer came back equally quickly: Lisa hated her, she was jealous of her, she wanted her to leave Moose Falls. And belatedly, Rhia remembered the sound she thought she had heard from her sitting room the night before, the sound Jared had dismissed so contemptuously. What if she had heard a door close? What if it had been Lisa? It was not difficult to imagine the effect their be-haviour would have had on Lisa's highly-strung emotions.

Rhia hunched her shoulders, and started walking again. This was all supposition, she told herself severely. Lisa might not like her, she might be jealous of her, but abandoning her out here, miles from anywhere, and in these temperatures—surely that was nothing short of criminal. She was trying to frighten her, that was all. She was playing a rather unpleasant game. But once she got tired of tormenting her, Lisa would come back and find her.

Or would she? a small voice taunted her. Yes, she told herself fiercely. Yes, she would come. Lisa might be reckless, but she was not without conscience. Leaving her here had been done in a fit of pique, a moment's rashness, that she would soon regret. And yet, as she tried to console herself with these assurances, Rhia remembered the boots Lisa had been wearing when they left Moose Falls, the heavy boots, that she had thought so unsuitable for walking in town. But entirely suitable for climbing over rocks and boulders, and hiding out of sight . . .

CHAPTER TWELVE

JARED was in the hall, when Lisa arrived back at Moose Falls. He was lounging on one of the squashy couches, scanning the morning's newspaper, and he thought she looked somewhat taken aback to see him there at this hour of the morning.

'Why, Jared!' she exclaimed. 'I thought you'd left for Calgary. Didn't you say that was where you were going yesterday evening?'

'Did I?' Jared put the newspaper aside and got to his feet. 'I said a lot of things last night, Lisa. You let me do most of the talking.'

Lisa moved her shoulders indifferently. 'Oh, well, I must have got it wrong. I'll just go up——'

'Wait a minute.' Jared stepped between her and the stairs. 'Why didn't you tell me about Glyn?'

'Glyn?' Lisa drew a deep breath. 'I don't know——'

'Why didn't you tell me his sight was coming back? He asked you to.'

'Oh, darling . . .' Lisa moved her head impatiently, 'I

didn't want to raise your hopes unnecessarily. You know how these things can be.'

'No, I don't know. Enlighten me.' Jared was brusque. 'It seems to me you kept that information to yourself deliberately to spite me.'

'Oh, Jared . . .' Lisa put up a hand to touch his cheek, but he flinched away from her touch, and her expression hardened. 'Jared, stop looking at me as if you despised me. I've told you, I did it in your best interests.'

'And not because of what I told you about my feelings for Rhia?'

Lisa's lips tightened. 'No.'

'No?'

'Why should I?' Lisa linked her slim fingers together. 'I don't remember half of what you told me last night!'

'But you do remember what I said about Rhia?'

'Oh, Jared . . .' Lisa moved her head from side to side. 'I think this whole situation has got out of hand. It was a mistake to bring the girl here—I said so at the time. And as it turns out, Glyn's known who she was all along.'

'So he told me.'

'You've spoken to him?'

'This morning, yes.' Jared paused. 'You were right, I had planned to go to Calgary today, but Horse hurt his shoulder yesterday, and I went to see him before leaving. When I got back to the house, Maria told me you and Rhia had gone out together, so I went to see Glyn, to find out if he knew where you had gone.'

'I—I see.'

'Which reminds me——' Jared's eyes narrowed, 'where is Rhia?'

Lisa shrugged. 'Somewhere about, I guess. How should I know? I'm not her keeper.'

Jared's mouth hardened. 'But she came back with you?'

Lisa pursed her lips, and then, disturbed by the glinting anger in Jared's eyes, she reluctantly shook her head. 'No.'

'What do you mean—no?' Jared caught her by the shoulders. 'Where is she?'

'I've told you, I don't know.' Lisa winced as his fingers

bit into her flesh. 'Jared, you're hurting me! Let go!'

Jared took no notice. 'Where is Rhia?' he demanded. 'You might as well tell me. I'm not going to let go of you until you do.'

'I don't know.' Lisa gazed up at him with wounded eyes. 'Jared, I really don't. If I did, I would tell you.'

Jared held her eyes with his, ignoring the inviting warmth that spread into hers. 'Where is she?' he persisted. 'Where did you leave her? She went out with you. Why didn't you fetch her back?'

Lisa sighed, her fingertips stroking the soft brown leather of his lapel. 'Darling, I know it was naughty of me, and you're probably going to be very cross, but—well, I parked the car, and—and we arranged to meet at a certain time. When I got back to the car, Rhia wasn't there. So I left.'

'You left her in Moose Bay!' Jared was incensed.

Lisa said nothing, merely continued to look up at him with a warm, melting submission, and with an exclamation of distaste he let her go.

'You—bitch, Lisa,' he said harshly. 'You selfish little bitch! I could wring your bloody neck!'

'Darling!' Lisa caught her breath in pained affront. 'How can you be so cruel! After—after all we've been to one another.'

'We've been nothing to one another, Lisa—nothing,' retorted Jared curtly, but she caught his sleeve.

'That's not true. Jared, you wanted me. Before—before Glyn was born, you wanted me——'

'And could have had you, too, if I hadn't had more respect for my brother,' replied Jared brutally. 'Stop kidding yourself, Lisa. I was eighteen—a youth! I guess I was flattered because an older woman showed me she found me attractive.'

'Not so much older,' declared Lisa resentfully. 'You're thirty-six, Jared——'

'And you're nearly forty, Lisa!' Jared was in no mood to spare her feelings. 'Now, where is Rhia? Where will I find her?'

'That's your problem.'

Lisa turned towards the stairs, and as she did so, Ben

came in from outside. He looked askance at his son's brooding features, then gave his attention to his daughter-in-law.

'Y'know you've got a flat?' he asked, and she was obliged to answer him.

'Yes, I know,' she said tersely. 'I'll get one of the men to fix it.'

'Seems like you're going to need a new tyre,' exclaimed Ben, glancing at Jared. 'Threaded it to ribbons, she has. Not surprising, I guess, on those mountain roads.'

Jared's eyes darkened. 'What mountain roads?'

Ben studied his son's angry face for a few moments, then looked up at Lisa. She, sensing Jared's sudden vigilance, made to escape upstairs, but Jared was too quick for her, his booted strides easily overtaking her before she reached the landing.

'What mountain roads?' he demanded of her savagely, and Lisa's face crumpled beneath his savage glare.

'I—I don't know, do I?' she sobbed. 'I don't know what he's talking about, drunken old fool. If—if I had my way, he'd be in a home, where he belongs. He—he's not fit to live with decent people—*oh*!'

She broke off abruptly as Jared's fingers stung across her cheek, and then went with him sullenly when he hustled her back downstairs. In the hall again, he turned to his father, and keeping a firm hold on Lisa he demanded harshly: 'What do you know?'

Ben shifted a little uncomfortably now. 'Look here,' he muttered, looking unwillingly at Lisa, 'a tyre's easily replaced. It's nothing to do with me, really——'

'No, it's not,' spat Lisa coldly, but Jared's warning look silenced her.

'Go on,' he said to his father. 'What did you see? I guess you saw Lisa, on your way back from town.'

'Town?' echoed Lisa, frowning, and Jared nodded his head.

'You didn't know Pa had gone to town, did you? He went to see Doc Palmer. I guess you wouldn't see him, if you went—oh, my God!' His face paled visibly. 'Rhia! My God, Rhia! What have you done to her?'

He shook Lisa violently, and her teeth were chattering

as she tried to answer him. 'D-done?' she stammered. 'I've done nothing. Stop shaking me, Jared, you're making me feel ill.'

'I'll do more than that, if I have to,' snapped Jared savagely. 'She took Rhia—*Val*—out with her, and didn't bring her back,' he explained briefly to his father. 'Where did you see the station wagon? What direction did it come from? For God's sake, if Rhia's out there, we've got to find her!'

'Calm down, son, calm down!' For once, Ben took control, turning on the sobbing Lisa without hesitation now. 'I saw her on the road from Grifter's Pass,' he declared steadily. 'She didn't see me. She was having some difficulty keeping the wagon on the road with that flat tyre. I followed her in.'

'So——' Jared turned to Lisa, 'are you going to tell me where she is, or do I beat it out of you?'

'You wouldn't——'

'Don't try me.' Jared was grim. 'You crazy little fool! If you've harmed her——'

'I haven't.' Lisa was sulky. 'I haven't done anything. I—I only wanted to frighten her, that's all. I intended going back for her.'

'Did you?' Jared was sceptical. 'You expected me to be away today, remember? If I hadn't been here when you got back, who would have guessed where Rhia was?'

'That's right.' Ben looked anxious. 'Gee, Jared——'

'What's going on?' They all stiffened at the sound of Glyn's voice as he slowly descended the stairs. He was bathed and dressed, his hair neatly combed, and a pair of dark glasses resided on his nose. 'Do you know I can hear your voices right across the house?' he exclaimed humorously. 'What is it? Some kind of private party, or can anybody join?'

'Your mother's taken your young lady out into the mountains and marooned her,' declared Ben, before either Jared or Lisa could say anything.

'My young lady—you mean, Rhia?' Glyn blanched.

'Rhia?' Ben looked confused now, but Jared had no time to enlighten him.

'I'll explain later,' he said, pulling Lisa after him to the door. 'Are you coming? I'll get Horse to join us. The more eyes that are looking out for her, the better.'

'I'll come, too,' said Glyn eagerly, but now Jared held up his hand.

'Glyn——'

'I know, I know. She's not interested in me,' Glyn exclaimed tautly. 'You don't have to paint a picture. I'm not blind any more. I guessed how it was between you two, the night we arrived here.'

Jared stared at him, wanting to say something by way of mitigation, but Glyn only shook his head. 'Get Horse,' he said. 'I'll get my coat. Like you said, the more eyes looking for her, the better.'

Rhia was frozen. Even though she was wearing gloves, and her hands were pushed deep into the pockets of the suede coat, her fingers were numb, and her feet had long since lost the ability to feel pain.

How long was it since Lisa had driven away and left her? One hour? Two? She was afraid to look at her watch, afraid to discover that it was later than she thought, and that soon the darkness of evening would begin to shroud these rocky passes. She had guessed where she was. Through the drifting shrouds of mist, it was occasionally possible to glimpse the rocky crags around her, and she had come to the conclusion that she was no small distance above sea level.

The mountains, she thought bitterly, those innocent-looking foothills she had seen from her bedroom window; they were not half so appealing as they had been from that safe distance, and although she tried to still her fears, deep inside she was terrified.

It wasn't just the fact that she was cold and hungry, and likely to die of exposure. There was also the horrible suspicion that she was not alone on the path, that something or someone was stalking her, and she wondered with a feeling of panic whether bears had been known to attack unwary travellers. There were bears in these mountains, and goats, and caribou. She had read about them in guide books before leaving England. But what had had a primitive charm in the civilised surroundings of her flat had a

distinctly alarming aspect when one was alone and helpless, and although she still clung to the belief that Lisa
would come back for her, she was rapidly losing faith.

She only hoped she had not lost her way. The track
over which Lisa had driven had been clear to start with,
but the intermittent rain had made the ground soggy,
and she could no longer be sure she was on the right
path. She seemed to be going down, but in what direction?
What if she had somehow turned back on herself, and
was now going deeper into the mountains, instead of
coming out?

With thoughts like these for company, she had no difficulty in staying alert, even though she had the distinct
apprehension that sooner or later exhaustion was going to
take its toll on her. It wasn't as if she was completely fit.
Her back still ached from the fall she had taken in the
ravine, and the longer she trudged over these rocky trails,
the more certain she became that she did not have the
strength to walk back, even if she could find her way.

Her first awareness that she was no longer alone with
her fears came with the blaring of a car horn. It was still
some distance from her, but the sound was distinct, even
to her frozen ears, and she almost collapsed from the relief
of knowing that Lisa had come to her senses.

Stumbling as she went, she hurried down the shingly slope
in the direction of the sound, opening her mouth and calling,
but unable to make much noise. Her throat was raw from the
biting air, and humiliatingly unsteady. The sounds that
emerged were a mixture of words and broken sobs, the
most coherent being: 'Lisa!' and 'Here I am. I'm here!'

The car's headlight swept her only a few minutes later,
and the relief at realising she was rescued robbed her legs
of all strength. With a helpless sob, she sank to the ground
and ignominiously wept for the hours she had spent in
frightened isolation. She didn't care any longer what Lisa
thought of her, whether it gave her some vicious kind of
satisfaction to see her humbled like this. She no longer
cared about anything but escaping from this awful place.

'*Rhia!*'

At first she thought she was hallucinating, that somehow she had imagined the car's horn and the headlights,

and the certainty of rescue. When Jared spoke her name
in that rough unguarded way, she felt sure she must be
imagining it, and she bowed her head still lower, brough
to complete submission.

'Rhia—God, if she's hurt you, I'll kill her!' Jared's voice
spoke again, harsh and emotive, and when strong hand.
lifted her and possessive arms closed about her, she decided
that if this was a dream, she much preferred it to reality

But it was no dream, she realised incredulously, looking
over Jared's shoulder and seeing Ben and Horse getting
out of the car. And then she became aware that Jared
was shaking almost as much as she was, and unable to
think of anything but comforting him, she closed her arms
about him.

He lifted his head then, from the chilly hollow of her
shoulder, and tearing the wig from her head he allowed her
hair to spill down through his fingers. 'God, Rhia, I've been
half out of my mind,' he muttered thickly, and her husky
response was stifled by the searching pressure of his mouth

It was crazy really, she thought, as one half of her mind
stood back from herself and surveyed the spectacle they
were making. It was cold and wet, and she was chilled to
the bone, but with Jared's arms about her, she would not
have changed a thing.

'If she'd hurt you——' he choked, unfastening his coat
and drawing her inside it, close against the warm hardness of
his body. 'I really think I would have killed her, you know.

'But she didn't,' whispered Rhia softly, snuggling against
him. 'And she must have told you where I was, mustn't she?'
she added. 'Or how else did you find me so quickly?'

'Quickly!' groaned Jared harshly, as Ben put a hand on
his shoulder. 'Do you realise how long we've been searching these trails? The better part of four hours! God, I was
beginning to lose hope!'

'Jared, get in the car,' said Ben quietly, patting Rhia's
arm. 'The girl's frozen, can't you see? Explanations can
wait until we get her back to the house, can't they? You're
not helping her by keeping her out here.'

'Yes, get in the car, Jared,' Horse agreed behind them,
smiling diffidently at Rhia. 'Get in the back. I'll drive.'

'Okay.' Jared allowed Rhia to move away from him

with reluctance, and when they got to the car, he made her get inside first, and then got in beside her, drawing her possessively against him.

Lisa was in the back of the car, Rhia saw with some misgivings, and the older woman viewed her appearance with narrow-eyed sullenness. 'You see, Jared,' she declared coldly, 'she's perfectly all right. All this stupid panic was totally unnecessary.'

'Shut up, Lisa,' said Jared tersely, pulling Rhia into the circle of his arms, and Rhia allowed him to do so, too bemused to care how she might feel when the euphoria of being safe again subsided.

Glyn was up front, Rhia realised, as she allowed her head to rest against Jared's shoulder, and her eyes widened anxiously at his appraising look. 'It's okay,' he said, reaching over to pat her hand. 'I guess we all had something to hide, didn't we? Will you forgive me for fooling you for so long?'

Rhia moved her head helplessly. 'I'm sorry Simon——'

'Forget it. I'd already realised you couldn't be Val. You don't know your sister very well, Rhia, if you think she would have stuck with me the way you did.'

'But——'

'It hurt,' he admitted honestly, as Horse got behind the wheel and began reversing back down the ravine. 'But Jared's told me about her clearing off to South Africa.' He sighed. 'I guess my main reason for bringing you out here was to get back at both her and your boy-friend. I didn't realise then that Jared's interest was of a more personal nature.'

Rhia lifted her eyes to Jared's face, but in the halflight she could read nothing from his expression. His arms didn't hold her any closer, his concern for her was no less real. But Glyn's words had left him unmoved, and she felt the first faint twinges of apprehension. Moments before, she had almost been prepared to believe his concern for her was that of someone who cared, cared very deeply. Now, with Lisa watching them with glowering eyes, and Jared staring broodingly out of the window, she wondered if all of them had not overreacted to a traumatic situation.

It didn't seem to take long to get back to the house, but

Horse drove fast, and the huge limousine fairly leapt along the track. Even so, it was a relief when the car drew to a halt in front of the house, and Maria's gaunt face appeared, pale and anxious.

Jared got out first, addressing the Indian woman with a curtness Rhia had never heard him use to her before. 'Run a hot bath,' he directed, helping Rhia to alight. 'We've found her, but she's chilled to the bone. And then fetch up some hot soup. She's probably starving as well.'

'Yes, sir.' Maria's response was eager, showing none of the resentment Rhia might have expected. With a quick smile for the girl, she turned back into the house, and by the time Jared had carried Rhia upstairs, the sound of running water was coming from her bathroom.

Rhia had objected to him carrying her, but Ben had taken his part. 'You let him, my girl,' he declared firmly. 'It will give him something to do. The amount of adrenalin he's released into his veins during the past few hours, it's time he allowed it some outlet.'

In her room, Maria came bustling out of the bathroom, clucking her tongue when she saw Rhia's wet clothes. 'Off with the lot of them,' she declared, as Rhia shed her coat, and: 'Don't lock the bathroom door!' said Jared, before he, too, left her.

The bath was deliciously soft and warm and scented with rose water. Rhia could feel the chilliness of her flesh melting away, and she sank down into the fluffy bubbles, content just to relax.

'Are you going to stay in there all evening?' a harsh voice demanded, and looking up she saw Jared, standing at the side of the bath. He, too, had shed his outdoor clothes, and in brown corded pants and matching waistcoat, he looked dark and disturbing, and devastatingly attractive.

'I—why——' Rhia was glad of the concealing bubbles to hide her blushes. 'Has Maria brought the soup yet? I'm sorry, I was just letting the water relax me.'

'And has it?' He squatted down beside her, his eyes narrowed and intent, but she had the distinct impression he was keeping himself aloof from her.

'Very much,' she agreed huskily, wondering if she dared ask him what had happened when Lisa came back without her. But shyness, and an unwillingness to become involved in their personal relationships, kept her silent, until Jared suddenly put his hand down and touched the water.

'Tell me,' he said, without looking at her, 'are you really going to marry Travis? I mean—is that really what you want, or do I have any chance of dissuading you?'

'You?' Rhia's eyes widened as she gazed at him, but still he didn't look directly at her.

'Yes, me,' he agreed, lifting a cluster of bubbles on his fingers, and then blowing them lightly back into the bath. 'Last night—well, last night I was prepared to give you more time. Today I find I can't.'

Rhia captured his fingers and carried them to her lips, kissing each one in turn before turning his palm against her cheek. 'Oh, Jared,' she breathed, 'I thought—I thought you wanted to marry Lisa. It—it's what I've heard—ever since I came to Moose Falls——'

'Not from me,' he interrupted her harshly, 'never from me!' and with a groan of impatience, he slipped his hands beneath her arms and lifted her bodily out of the bath, uncaring that her hair was soaking or that he was soon as wet as she was. 'I love you,' he said allowing her lissom form to slide down against him, moulding her yielding limbs to his powerful frame. 'I love you,' he said again, probing the parted provocation of her lips, and then he covered her mouth with his, and hungrily took his fill from the moist sweetness within.

'You're wet,' she breathed, when he allowed her to take a breath, and he shook his head indifferently.

'So what?' he demanded. 'I can soon get changed. Just tell me that you want me, as much as I want you.'

'You know I do,' she whispered adoringly, cupping his face in her hands, standing on tiptoe so that she could touch his mouth with hers. 'I think I fell in love with you the first time you kissed me. From then on, my relationship with Simon never stood a chance.'

'Excuse me!'

Maria cleared her throat behind them, and Rhia spun round in alarm, which quickly turned to hot embarrassment when she realised she was naked. 'Oh!' she exclaimed, almost inaudibly, pressing her hand to her lips, but Jared merely reached for the towel, and wrapped it lovingly about her.

'Maria's not the type to be shocked by two people making love to one another,' he told her huskily. 'And I think she's guessed how I feel about you.'

'He's right,' agreed Maria dryly. 'Been like an old bear, he has, ever since he found you were missing. Even Horse got out of patience with him, and they're the best of friends.'

'Maria's right,' murmured Jared softly, securing the towel closely about her, but evidently loath to let go of her. 'It's just as well you're going to marry me, or Maria might—she just might—consider handing in her notice.'

Rhia's breath escaped on a little gasp. 'Did—did I agree to do that?' she breathed, and for a moment Jared's eyes darkened.

'Is it in doubt?' he demanded, his hands stilled for a moment, and Rhia found she couldn't bear to tease him about something so important to both of them.

'No—no doubt,' she whispered, tilting her face up to his, and Jared's hands pulled her to him, uncaring of Maria's indulgent eye.

But presently she spoke again, and with reluctance he let Rhia go. 'I suggest you go and change,' she declared, indicating his wet clothes. 'I'll dry the girl's hair, and settle her with this hot soup. You can come back when you've had some supper.'

But, in fact, Jared was back much sooner than that, his brown corded outfit replaced by cream suede pants and a cream silk shirt. 'I'm not hungry,' he said, seating himself on the side of the bed, to watch Rhia spoon her soup into her mouth. 'How do you feel now? Are you fully recovered?'

'Hmm, much better,' Rhia agreed, finishing the soup and putting the tray aside. Then she reached for his hands. 'How about you? Are you sure you meant what you said earlier? I mean, in the heat of the moment, the mind can—can play tricks.'

'It's no trick,' Jared told her warmly, raising her palm to his lips. 'There have been times when I've wished it were. Particularly when you told me you couldn't possibly accompany us to Canada.'

Rhia smiled. 'I thought you were only thinking of Glyn.

'I told myself I was, too, but it wasn't true. I knew if you didn't come with us, I would have to come back and see you, on some pretext or another. But I thought you and Travis—well, let's just say I was as jealous as hell.'

Rhia shook her head. 'But Lisa——'

'Forget Lisa,' he advised her roughly. 'I'm trying to. At least, I'm trying to stop myself from hating her for what she did to you.'

'She was jealous, too, I suppose——'

'Like hell she was.' Jared nodded. 'But that didn't give her the right to—well, she must have been out of her mind!'

Rhia sighed. 'She must have known you'd come looking for me.'

Jared's jaw hardened. 'What she knew—or thought she knew—was that I was supposed to have gone to Calgary today.'

'To Calgary?'

'Yes.' Jared's nostrils flared. 'God, when I think what might have happened if Horse hadn't injured his shoulder!'

Rhia frowned. 'Horse?'

'I went to see him, before leaving for Calgary. When I got back to the house, you and Lisa had already left, and as nobody seemed to know where you had gone, I went to see Glyn. That was when I found out about his recovering his sight.'

Rhia stared at him. 'You didn't know?'

'How could I?'

'Oh, but——' Rhia was caught in a trap of her own making, and was reluctant to go on. 'I mean—I thought you did.'

'Why did you think that?' Jared watched her intently. 'Is that what Lisa told you? Did she pretend I wanted you to leave Moose Falls?'

'Something like that,' mumbled Rhia unhappily, remembering exactly what Lisa had said, and Jared frowned.

'Come on,' he said, 'tell me exactly what she said. Did she imply we had some kind of relationship?'

Rhia moistened her lips. 'Didn't you?'

'*No!*' Jared was grim. 'Believe me, Rhia, no matter what you might think, what Lisa might have said, my relationship with my sister-in-law never progressed beyond—well, beyond that. Beyond a family association.

Oh——' he sighed, 'I suppose once I was infatuated by her. But that was years ago, just after she married Angus. I was eighteen, and impressionable, and she let me know she wouldn't be averse to—well, you know what I mean.'

'And—and did you?'

'Would you hate me if I had?'

'Oh, no.' Rhia's lips were tremulous. 'Darling, I don't care what kind of relationship you and Lisa had in the past. So long as it's me you want now.'

Jared's tongue stroked her palm. 'Well, I didn't,' he said huskily. 'I had too much respect for Angus to cuckold my own brother. Besides, it was only a passing fancy. It didn't last. But after Angus was killed I did feel—well, I suppose, a sense of responsibility for her. And it was this Lisa played on.'

'I think she loves you,' murmured Rhia softly, but Jared shook his head.

'She wanted the ranch for Glyn,' he said gently. 'That was all. It was a source of great annoyance to her that I should have inherited Moose Falls. She always thought Angus should. And she knew, so long as I didn't marry anyone else, Glyn was most likely to get it.'

'But Glyn doesn't——'

'I know. Glyn doesn't want the ranch—he never did. He's like his father, I guess. He wants to leave Canada, get a job in England. That was why he went to London.'

'Poor Lisa!' Rhia could afford to be generous.

'Poor Lisa be damned,' he muttered harshly. 'She could have killed you. And no one might ever have known what happened.'

'What do you mean?'

Jared hesitated. 'Love, there are predators in those mountains, bears and mountain lions. Do you honestly think your body would have lain there untouched if we hadn't found you?'

'Oh, Jared!' Rhia shivered, and with a sound of impatience Jared bent over her, opening her mouth with his.

'It's over now,' he said, his breath warm and intoxicating in her throat. 'Lisa realises she's lost. I've suggested she takes a prolonged trip away from Moose Falls, and if she hasn't found someone else to take her on by the time she comes back, I'll buy her a house in Calgary. That way, she'll have too many preoccupations to bother us.'

'Jared . . .' Rhia slipped her bare arms around his neck. 'What about—Ben? You—you won't send him away, will you? I know he annoys you sometimes, but I think he's always felt—I don't know—less of a man, somehow. Your grandfather started the process, and—and——'

'——Lisa finished it,' Jared completed the sentence for her. 'I know. He told me what she had said. I think the reason he's been so much worse lately is Lisa. I guess he thought if she ever became mistress here, I'd be forced to throw him out.'

'But you won't?' Rhia was anxious.

'He's my father,' said Jared gently. 'No matter what Lisa may have said, I'd never do that.'

'Oh, good.' Rhia relaxed, and Jared chuckled softly in his throat.

'Hey, you're making me jealous,' he murmured. 'Just because you're going to have two adoring males around you . . .'

Rhia smiled, pulling him down to her. 'I only need one,' she breathed. 'Surely you know that.'

Jared propped himself on one elbow beside her. 'Last night I wondered.' His eyes darkened. 'I frightened you, didn't I? I don't know. I guess I thought you and Travis must have——' He broke off. 'I'm sorry.'

'I wasn't frightened,' Rhia protested, her fingers probing the fastening of his shirt, parting the pearl buttons. 'Jared, I did hear someone last night. It—it was Lisa.'

Jared stared at her for fully thirty seconds, then he rolled incredulously on to his back. 'So that was why——'

'Yes.' Rhia watched him uncertainly. 'I—I know you thought I was making it up——'

'I didn't know what to think,' he muttered, rolling on to his side again, his expression melting her bones. 'Oh, Rhia, I thought I was going too fast for you. I thought you needed more time to get used to the idea. And when you froze up on me——'

'I wanted you,' said Rhia huskily. 'I want you now. Is that awfully forward?'

'Awfully,' agreed Jared thickly, but his mouth moving over hers showed no disapproval.

'Do you think this bed is big enough for two?' she whispered, when he released her mouth to probe the warm hollow between her breasts.

'If not, mine is,' he answered her huskily, and feeling the hard weight of his body crushing hers, Rhia knew there was no more drawing back.

It was early the next morning when she awakened to find Jared's lips teasing her shoulder. She had fallen asleep after midnight, satiated by Jared's lovemaking, and content just to curl her body close to his. But now she awakened sleepily to meet his lazy eyes, and shyness brought a wave of colour sweeping up her cheeks.

'Love me?' he asked, his hand sliding possessively over her thigh, and she gazed at him with adoring eyes.

'You know I do,' she said, and forgetting her embarrassment, she nestled closer to him. 'Was—was it all right?'

'Oh, God!' Jared's words were choked in the back of his throat, and tender amusement entered his eyes now. 'Honey, you know how it was.' He sobered. 'I've never felt like this before.'

'Oh, good.' Rhia stretched with cat-like grace.

'So—when are you going to marry me?' Jared demanded, the sinuous curves of her warm body stirring his to irresistible desire. He leant over her, imprisoning her with one hand on either side. 'I want to make sure you don't disappear like your sister.'

Rhia sighed contentedly. 'I won't. But that reminds me, I suppose I should write to Daddy and Val. They're going to be so surprised.'

Jared grimaced. 'I could say it's an ill wind, but I won't.'

'Hmm.' Rhia touched his cheek. 'Just think, if Val hadn't driven Glyn's car, if Glyn hadn't had his accident——'

'——we might never have met,' Jared agreed. 'Only I can't believe that. I'm sure that sooner or later, our paths were bound to have crossed. I've been waiting all my life for you.'

'Oh, Jared!' Rhia's fingers curled into the hair at his nape, pulling him down to her. 'I want to believe that, too, because I can't imagine life now without you!'

Harlequin® *Plus*
A GREAT INVENTOR

Can you imagine flying from country to country in your own private jet? Perhaps not, but today more and more executives for major international corporations do so, and not just for luxury. For many top executives earn six-figure salaries, and they can't afford to waste time!

The preferred corporation jet is none other than the famous Lear jet, named after the remarkable man who designed it—William Powell "Bill" Lear. But we owe much more to him than private corporate jets. Born in Missouri in 1902, Bill Lear is also the inventor of the car radio, the eight-track stereo cartridge, the automatic jet pilot for aircraft—for which he received the Collier Trophy from President Truman in 1950—and more than 150 other inventions in the fields of radio, electronics, aviation technology and auto engineering.

In 1967 Bill Lear considered retirement, but soon realized it was impossible for him to be anything but active. He poured his energies into further inventions until his death in 1978. An energetic, exuberant man full of creative ideas, he never stopped working a twelve-to eighteen-hour day. In fact, his last words to his colleagues were, "Finish it!" He was referring to the Lear Fan 2100, a new airplane that would travel as fast as other Lear jets, but use only a fifth of the fuel. Were he still alive, this great inventor would be gratified indeed to know that the Lear Fan went into production in 1981.

FREE!

A hardcover Romance Treasury volume
containing 3 treasured works of romance
by 3 outstanding Harlequin authors...

..as your introduction to Harlequin's
Romance Treasury subscription plan!

..almost 600 pages of exciting romance reading
every month at the low cost of $6.97 a volume!

A wonderful way to collect many of Harlequin's most beautiful love
stories, all originally published in the late '60s and early '70s.
Each value-packed volume, bound in a distinctive gold-embossed
leatherette case and wrapped in a colorfully illustrated dust jacket,
contains...
  3 full-length novels by 3 world-famous authors of romance fiction
  a unique illustration for every novel
  the elegant touch of a delicate bound-in ribbon bookmark...
  and much, much more!

Romance Treasury

...for a library of romance you'll treasure forever!

Complete and mail today the FREE gift certificate and subscription
reservation on the following page.

Romance Treasury

An exciting opportunity to collect treasured works of romance! Almost 600 pages of exciting romance reading in each beautifully bound hardcover volume!

You may cancel your subscription whenever you wish! You don't have to buy any minimum number of volumes. Whenever you decide to stop your subscription just drop us a line and we'll cancel all further shipments.